WHAT'S MINE IS YOURS

BOOKS BY LEAH MERCER

A Mother's Lie
Why She Left
A Secret in the Family
The Mother Next Door
The Playgroup
The Summer Reunion

Who We Were Before
The Man I Thought You Were
The Puzzle of You
Ten Little Words

LEAH MERCER

WHAT'S MINE IS YOURS

bookouture

Published by Bookouture in 2025

An imprint of Storyfire Ltd.
Carmelite House
50 Victoria Embankment
London EC4Y 0DZ

www.bookouture.com

The authorised representative in the EEA is Hachette Ireland
8 Castlecourt Centre
Dublin 15 D15 XTP3
Ireland
(email: info@hbgi.ie)

Copyright © Leah Mercer, 2025

Leah Mercer has asserted her right to be identified as the author of this work.

All rights reserved. No part of this publication may be reproduced, stored in any retrieval system, or transmitted, in any form or by any means, electronic, mechanical, photocopying, recording or otherwise, without the prior written permission of the publishers.

ISBN: 978-1-83525-978-8
eBook ISBN: 978-1-83525-977-1

This book is a work of fiction. Names, characters, businesses, organizations, places and events other than those clearly in the public domain, are either the product of the author's imagination or are used fictitiously. Any resemblance to actual persons, living or dead, events or locales is entirely coincidental.

To JK, the best friend anyone could ever have.

ONE

AVA

The shrill cry cut into her, twisting through the gauzy fabric of her sleep. Ava sat up and rubbed her eyes in the dark room. For a second, she thought it was a baby crying – *her* baby crying, although that was impossible. Sirens screamed through the night, and she blinked, wondering if she was still in a dream... a nightmare from so long ago; a nightmare she had lived. And, despite everything she'd done since, was living still.

But no, she thought, spotting the empty place beside her in bed as the sirens neared. She wasn't trapped in a horrific reoccurrence of the past. If she was, then her husband Dan would still be sleeping next to her, not off on one of his many work trips. Sometimes, she wondered if he needed to go or if he only wanted to get away.

She glanced at the clock, surprised to see it was only 10 p.m. These days, she went to sleep after putting her eleven-year-old daughter Lexi to bed. What else was there to stay up for? She pulled on her robe and looked out the window, eyes widening as a police car slowed in front of the next-door neighbour's house, closely followed by an ambulance. She squinted, but she couldn't see any movement inside, although the lights were blazing. At this time of night, Mr Bhandari was usually watching the news, the volume blaring so loudly she could hear it if her bedroom window was open. Something had happened, and by the looks of things, it wasn't good.

'Mum?' Lexi appeared at the bedroom door, her face pale. 'What's going on?'

Ava put an arm around her daughter's wiry frame. She'd inherited her mother's slim figure. Ava had been in her mid-thirties when she'd had Lexi, but even now she could eat like a horse without gaining weight. At first, she'd put it down to not having time to eat as a busy GP in a time-strapped practice, but she'd stopped working years ago in order to make a home for Lexi, and she'd stayed as thin. Granted, every second seemed to be filled with *something*. Lexi was her life. She'd do everything she could to make her daughter happy.

'It's all right,' she said, drawing Lexi close. 'It's just the Bhandaris next door. You know how Mrs Bhandari is always worrying about Mr Bhandari's health. He might have some mild chest pains or something, and she probably called an ambulance to be on the safe side.' She had no idea if that was the case and it didn't explain the police, but she didn't want to worry Lexi. On this quiet street in Richmond, an affluent London suburb, usually the most threatening thing was a bee buzzing around the tidy front gardens.

Sighing, Ava remembered the first time she and Dan had come to look at the house. They'd loved the huge airy open-plan kitchen, flowing seamlessly into the lounge. Foldable glass doors opened into the garden beyond, the greenery and flowers feeling like part of the house decor. The asking price had been miles above their budget, but they'd known instantly that this was the place they wanted to raise their family. With five bedrooms, there was plenty of room to grow. Both sets of parents had chipped in to help, and the dream home had become theirs.

Little had they known that they'd never need those rooms, and as much as Ava would fill the house with plants, pillows and the world's most expensive candles, it would seem emptier with every year that passed. Whenever Ava thought of leaving, though, she knew she never could. This place was all Lexi had ever known, and she loved it. After what had happened, she owed her daughter everything.

Besides, this house was where she'd locked away everything: memories that could never be unleashed; knowledge that could never be revealed. She was their guardian, and she would never leave her post. The house might seem empty when Lexi was at school, but she knew how to keep her family safe here from any more hurt and pain.

A knock on the front door jolted her from her thoughts, and Lexi turned towards her with terrified eyes.

'You stay upstairs,' Ava said, tightening her robe. 'It's probably Mrs Bhandari apologising for waking us up and letting us know all is OK.' She smiled at her daughter to show it was nothing to worry about, but her heart was pumping as she padded down the stairs and crossed the lounge, snapping on every light as she went. The house was alarmed to the hilt now, from the doorbell camera to the facial recognition door lock and the motion-sensitive lights outside, but echoes of past panic and fear rang inside.

'Police!' The shout made her hurry, and she unlocked the door and opened it. Two officers were there, a man and woman, gazing at her with tired faces. 'Sorry to disturb,' the woman said. 'We need to have a word with you, if that's all right.'

Ava nodded, her voice stuck in her throat as she stared at them, trying so hard not to let herself fall backwards to the time when officers had stood in that same place, under the same glowing light, the same summery scent of plants and leaves in the air, and—

'Ma'am?' The male officer was looking at her quizzically. 'Are you OK? Can we have your name, please?'

'Yes, yes, of course.' Ava forced the muscles in her face to smile, using every bit of strength to jerk herself firmly into the present. 'I'm Ava MacDonald. Please, come in.' She almost didn't want to hear why they were here, but they were already pushing past her into the house. 'Can I get you some coffee?'

Thankfully, they shook their heads. 'No, no. This won't take long.'

'Is everything OK?' Maybe one of the Bhandaris *had* had a medical emergency – a serious one, by the looks of things. They were both eighty if they were a day. The couple had been here when Ava and Dan had bought their house and settled in. They were stalwarts of the street, casting a beady eye as the older residents moved into care homes and younger couples swept into the street, extending and upgrading the houses until the original was hardly recognisable. Ava and Dan had been one of those couples, and the Bhandaris had welcomed them with open arms.

When Mrs Bhandari learned that Ava was pregnant, she made daily trips over to drop off food, muslins and baby clothes she'd knitted. Ava sensed she was lonely, and with her own mother miles away in Cornwall, she'd treasured the older woman's expertise and advice. She and her close friend Emily, who was also expecting, would sit for hours as they learned how to care for their babies. Even Mr Bhandari got in on the act when the babies were born, holding the infants for ages until they fell asleep.

But then... then, Ava had shut everyone out, retreating inside her house. She didn't want to speak to them; to speak to anyone. She couldn't bear the looks of pity and sympathy: the kind hand on the arm and the quiet enquiry of how she was doing. How did they *think* she was doing?

'Your neighbours reported a burglary. Did you hear

anything, about thirty minutes ago?' the woman officer was asking, and Ava blinked. A burglary? In all the years they'd lived here, the only thing that had been stolen was the roses growing by the road. That had caused a major scandal, with the neighbourhood WhatsApp group exploding.

'No, nothing. My daughter and I were sleeping.' She took in the officers' serious expressions. 'What happened?'

'We're still working on finding out the exact details, but it looks like an intruder managed to gain access to the house, and Mr Bhandari confronted him. The stress caused a medical event, and the intruder managed to flee the scene.'

'Oh my God.' Ava put a hand to her mouth. 'Will Mr Bhandari be OK?' Poor Mrs Bhandari, she thought. She doted on her husband. She must be so worried. 'Are they on their own over there? I think they have a daughter I can call, if she hasn't been rung already.'

'They've taken him to hospital,' the officer said. 'And yes, she has someone with her.'

'Mum?' Lexi's voice came from behind, and she turned. 'It's all right, honey,' she said. 'Go back to bed.'

'I think we're done here,' the woman said, smiling at Lexi. 'But if you do remember seeing anything unusual – strange cars, people who seemed out of place in the street – please get in touch. Oh, and if you have the footage from your doorbell camera, we'd love to have it. Just to see if your camera caught anything.'

'Of course.' Ava bit her lip, thinking she had no idea how to retrieve the footage. Dan had set it up. It must be filtered through to his computer. 'I'll check in the morning, if that's OK. Do you have an email I can send it through to?'

The man got out a pen and notebook, then scribbled something and ripped it off. 'My email. Thank you. And if you do think of anything, please let me know.'

Ava nodded and tucked the paper into the pocket of her

dressing gown. 'Good night.' She closed the door and turned to face Lexi, standing there like she was frozen.

'I heard what they said.' Lexi's voice trembled. 'There was a burglar?' Her eyes were wild, and Ava could feel the tension radiating from her. 'And Mr Bhandari... He's going to be fine, right? I mean... he's not going to *die*?' Her voice rose and the word echoed around the lofty space, growing larger and larger, dimming the room despite the bright lights she'd turned on.

'Of course not,' Ava answered, injecting certainty into her voice. She knew she shouldn't be saying that, but Lexi was already scared enough. She couldn't upset her more.

'Promise?'

Ava nodded. 'Promise. Now come on, let's go back to bed. Everything will be better in the morning.' It struck her how she'd been waiting for years for that to be true, and it never had. It never would be, unless she could turn back time to that morning when her world had split into two.

'Can I sleep with you?' Lexi wouldn't let go of her arm. 'I'm scared.'

Ava nodded again, thinking having someone beside her in bed would help calm her too. 'Of course.' She smoothed her daughter's hair back from her high forehead, leaving on the lights although she knew she shouldn't, and together they climbed the stairs. 'But you don't need to be afraid. I'm here. I won't let anyone hurt you.' She bit her lip, thinking her daughter had already been hurt in the worst way possible, even if she didn't know it. She'd *never* know it. Ava would make all the promises in the world if it would protect Lexi from any heartache and pain.

Heartache and pain she'd caused.

Lexi crawled into bed and Ava slid in beside her, listening to the sound of her daughter's breathing as she lay, eyes wide open, waiting for morning to come. She put an arm around Lexi and whispered an apology, knowing her daughter would never hear her. Which was just as well, because she'd never be able to forgive her, anyway.

Red and blue flashes from the police cars cut through the bedroom blinds, and Ava pulled Lexi closer, shielding her from the light. Whoever had done this terrible thing, no danger from the outside world would ever touch her daughter again.

She'd make sure of it.

TWO
LEXI

My heart pounds as I lie in bed. Despite Mum's arm clutching me, the fear is lodged inside so tightly I can barely breathe. The words I heard earlier circle around my mind, swirling faster and faster until my head feels like it's about to explode. Burglary. Mr Bhandari. Doorbell camera. *Die.*

He didn't get hurt because of me, did he? I didn't have anything to do with what happened... did I?

Mum mumbles something in her sleep. I press my freezing toes against her legs, hoping to get warm, but she's colder than me. Dad jokes that Mum would be cold on the Equator, and I think that's true. She's always throwing on extra jumpers and thick socks, like nothing can warm her up. No matter how many cheery smiles she gives me or how much she hugs me, there's this cold place inside of her for a reason I don't understand. And the tighter she holds me, the more I feel it seeping in.

I feel it when she creeps into my room before she thinks I've woken up, then leaves again to make my breakfast: pancakes and fresh fruit every morning, when I would kill for a bowl of Frosties. I feel it when she drops me off at school – in the Lexus, of course, even though St Mary's lets Year Sixes walk to school on their own, and it's only five minutes away.

And I feel it when I unwrap one gift after another: toys at first, when I was little, and now trendy T-shirts from brands I should know but are so far from the ones I want that they might as well be from another planet. Jewellery that's real gold, the latest iPhone to track my every movement, new stuff for my room. I can say 'thanks' and 'I love you' a million times over, but the warmth I send her way doesn't get through. I can't make her happy, no matter how hard I try. That's why I spend so much time in my room.

That's why I'm selling all the stuff Mum gives me. I don't want it around me, and getting rid of it without Mum's permission gives me a rush. I have a secret, something she knows nothing about in a life where she wants to know everything. I'm not even sure what I'll use the money for right now. Mum buys me all I need, and it's not like I go anywhere without her. Maybe when I finally have friends, I can take them out places. And maybe when I'm older, I can use it to get away.

Because I need to get away, like Dad does. I'd love for him to stay more, because when he's around, I feel like I *can* make someone happy. But he's always travelling for work, and I understand. He must find it hard to breathe here, as well. The cold space Mum glides through makes us shudder and gasp.

My heart starts racing again as I remember Mr Bhandari and the burglary, because maybe it is my fault. If only I could have kept selling my stuff at school. If only Miss Malik hadn't caught me. If only I hadn't started using Facebook Marketplace, pretending I'm old enough, on an ancient mobile I bought off eBay when Dad let me use his phone to check something. He got sidetracked by work, as usual, and let me have it for almost the whole night. It's surprisingly easy: people transfer me money, I put the parcels at the end of the drive by the recycling bin, and the buyers collect them. I don't have to see anyone.

Then whenever I'm out with Mum, I nip to the cashpoint and withdraw the cash in case she ever checks my balance. I hide it in my room, and she has no idea. It was working so well until Mr Bhandari got involved.

I rub my eyes, remembering the day last week when I'd heard voices in the front garden. I'd been upstairs watching YouTube, and, at first, I'd thought it was something on the video. But when I looked out the window, I saw Mr Bhandari in front of our bins, trying to wrestle a package – my package, an iPad that was due for collection – from a skinny man with a white jacket and greasy hair. I was about to run down and tell Mr Bhandari it was OK, but before I could do anything, the man gave him a shove and tore the package away from him. He ducked into a waiting car, shouting ugly words and saying he'd be back to deal with him.

Had he come back for Mr Bhandari?

It must have been him, I think, my heart pumping hard now. Who else would break into an old man's home? It's not like the Bhandaris have an expensive car out front or lots of high-end tech stuff. Their TV is from the 1960s or something.

I swallow, fear shooting through me as the rest of that night plays out in my head. I remember how the man called my mobile, saying the iPad was cracked and I owe him. How I tried to give him his money back, my fingers shaking so much I could barely do the transfer, but the bank kept saying it couldn't go through. I kept trying. I wanted him to go away. I thought he had, but now...

Will he come for me too? He knows where I live. If he did that to an old man, what will he do to a kid? My body shakes and my mouth is dry as I picture his face, twisted with rage. If he finds me, I could be in real danger.

If he doesn't come back – if, on the slim chance it wasn't him – my life will be over if Mum gives that video from the doorbell to the police. To be honest, I'd forgotten the doorbell does have video streaming to Dad's computer; I know he doesn't ever check it.

How far can it film? Did it catch me putting packages by the bins out front? Did it pick up Mr Bhandari and the man fighting, or any action from tonight? Is there anything on there that can help catch whoever did this?

I bite my lip as my mind swirls. I want to help, but Mum can't discover what I've been doing. I shouldn't be on Facebook, let alone selling things. I can forget ever getting out of here if Mum finds out. I can forget having a *life*... a life where I don't need to stare sadness in the face every day. A life where I can be happy.

I need to see what's on there, but there's no way I can check tonight. Not while Mum's holding me so tightly, like she'll drown if she lets go. I'll do it tomorrow, before school.

I close my eyes and I lie here, still as a statue, pretending everything's fine, as usual.

Even if it couldn't be further from the truth.

THREE
AVA

Grey light filtered through the blinds, and the sound of Lexi's music drifted into her consciousness. Ava opened her eyes. God, what time was it? Every muscle ached, and her head throbbed. Yawning, she raised herself on one elbow and stared at the clock: 7.30 a.m. Thank goodness Lexi had got up already – Ava hadn't noticed her stirring. The thought that she was supposed to be protecting her daughter and hadn't heard her leave the room made guilt and fear creep into her. At least the house was super secure. Lexi had been so scared last night that every bit of Ava had longed to wrap around her, to physically encompass her body.

She eyed her mobile, thinking that she should tell Dan about the burglary. But Lexi probably would. They texted every day when he travelled. Anyway, Dan hardly ever answered her calls when he was away. He was always in meetings, and as the years had gone on, the need to talk to him about anything had got less as his role at home diminished.

She slid from the bed and went into the en-suite. Standing under the steam of the shower made her feel human again, although when she glanced in the mirror, she felt like she'd aged ten years in one night. Sometimes, she found it hard to believe she was the mother of a child in primary school.

It wouldn't be for long, though. In fact, this was the last week of primary, and Ava was throwing a huge class party in a few days to celebrate moving on. What would she do when Lexi didn't need her anymore? Panic shot through her at the thought of an empty dark house, and she shoved it aside. That was miles in the future. First, Ava had to cope with her daughter starting 'big school', and, luckily, Lexi had got into the private one down the street. With money her parents had given her, savings from her job and Dan's solid salary in pharmaceutical sales, they would have enough to cover Lexi's time there.

She bit her lip as she thought of the break-in last night. She couldn't imagine someone terrorising poor Mr Bhandari. Mrs Bhandari must be beside herself – she and Mr Bhandari had always been inseparable. A memory filtered into Ava's head of her and Emily, two young mothers, eyes sagging with exhaustion, watching as the older couple waltzed around the lounge holding the babies. They'd stared at each other, smiles on their faces, their love evident.

'God, look at them,' Emily had murmured as they swayed back and forth. 'All this time, and they're still in love. I don't know how that's possible.'

Ava had nodded, thinking she never could imagine anything changing her love for Dan. He was the one person she could talk to about anything – the one person with whom, after a long day dealing with patients relying on her for answers, she could relax and be herself. He knew her inside out, with a radar that often surprised her. She'd been certain she'd always love Dan with the same intensity, but she hadn't wanted to say it. Emily was a single mum, raising her daughter all alone, and the last thing Ava wanted was to rub her face in it.

She sighed now, thinking of how much things had changed since that moment. She *did* love him. She always would, but it was buried beneath the heavy weight of all she owed her daughter. She couldn't reach to the feeling any longer.

And Emily... well, Ava knew she'd found it difficult to be suddenly shut out when she'd had no one else, but seeing her wasn't an option. Emily had tried and tried to maintain the close friendship, but Ava couldn't face the memory of those early golden days together before it all went dark. Now, the only time they saw each other was at the school gate in the morning, and there was never more than a rushed 'hello'.

Hopefully, Mr Bhandari would be OK, and they'd catch the person who'd broken in. Which reminded her, she needed to dig out the doorbell camera footage before she forgot. She padded into Dan's office, sinking onto the chair as she surveyed the dusty desktop. While she favoured tidiness and order, he was the exact opposite and – she grimaced, taking in the mess in front of her – that definitely hadn't changed. Papers were piled on chairs, books were scattered across the desktop, and there was an old tennis racket resting in the corner. She smiled, shaking her head. When was the last time he'd played tennis? When had she, for that matter?

When they'd first started dating after they'd been introduced at a mutual friend's party, they'd played every Saturday. She'd beat him thoroughly, then he'd treat her to brunch at the restaurant around the corner, listening with fascination while she told him stories about her patients, then laughing when she asked him about his job in sales for a pharma company.

'It's nothing compared to what you do, but I do know how to get doctors on board.' He'd raised his eyebrows suggestively, and she'd had to laugh. She'd been the one to invite him back to hers, and after a few months of dating, he'd moved in. She'd offered him the spare bedroom then as his office, and he'd joked it was the one room where he could live under his own rules. She'd made a face, but he'd told her he loved her strong character and how she charged through life – exactly as she played on the tennis court. They'd been perfectly matched on the court and off, with him happy to provide backup to her lead, stepping up to take over when she needed it.

Now, though, their roles had changed. He was the one who went out into the world, while she turned inwards. The person she used to be seemed a distant memory, and in this new place, Dan was a mere spectator in the stands rather than a backup. He'd wanted to be an equal partner in family life, she thought, remembering how he'd kept telling her to give him Lexi so she could have time to herself, and then, when that didn't work, organising outings for them all together. She didn't *want* time to herself now, though – not anymore; not after what had happened. And she didn't want to go out and play happy families. How could she, after what she'd done? All she'd needed was her daughter.

Dan hadn't been happy to be pushed aside, but she could see he understood: understood that she owed it to Lexi, and that she had no other choice. That radar he'd always had about her somehow remained. He'd backed off and let her pour everything into her child, carving out his own relationship with their daughter away from her. The distance between them had grown every year, but she prayed his radar could detect the love she still had, even if she couldn't show it – even if she couldn't let herself feel it. Right now, she couldn't be a wife. She could only be a mother, and that was everything. Hopefully, it was enough for him.

But was it? She bit her lip, remembering his face when he'd left on his trip yesterday morning. Usually, he crept out before she and Lexi woke up, but this time he'd still been there when they'd gone downstairs. He'd hugged their daughter tightly, then turned to her with such a look of longing that she almost moved towards him. Almost, but not quite.

Could she ever?

She shoved some papers off the chair and sat down at the

laptop he kept at home for personal use, though she had no idea how much he really used it. Dust coated the cover, but there were fingerprints on it... so he must use it sometimes. She opened it up and signed in with the same password he always used – he was as careless with his passwords as he was with everything else. Now, where should she look? She clicked aimlessly through the folders on the desktop, blinking when she spotted one simple word.

Alfie.

She froze, her eyes tracing the letters of his name, although they were already engraved on her heart. Why was this here, on Dan's computer? What was inside? Pain pushed down on her as her cursor hovered over the file, images and memories demanding entry to her mind. She squeezed her eyes closed against them. She couldn't look; couldn't let herself remember. If she did, she'd fall apart, and she had to keep everything intact – keep the wall intact. But Dan... she tilted her head, wondering how long the folder had been on the computer. Did he look at it often? Did he think about Alfie? Did he blame her, despite saying it wasn't her fault?

'Mum?'

She jerked at Lexi's voice and quickly clicked off the folder. Lexi couldn't see this. She could never know what had happened; what she had done.

'Mum? Where are you?'

'One sec!' She scanned the list of folders and applications, she did a search, but there was nothing resembling a video from a doorbell camera.

She leaned back, the chair squeaking. That was strange. She was sure he'd told her he'd set it up. True, he hadn't been super keen, asking why they needed this when the house already had an alarm. But when she'd thrown back how much he was travelling and how she'd feel safer with it, he'd given in and bought it the very next day.

Anger flashed through her. He must never have set it up. He'd simply told her he had, and let her live with the belief they'd done everything possible to protect their family. Did he even care? She breathed in, trying to calm the whirling thoughts. She knew he did. He loved Lexi as much as her, but while she'd grown ever more vigilant, he'd become the opposite, saying hadn't they seen that bad things would happen regardless of how much they'd tried? She'd snapped back that she should have tried harder, then spun away. At least they'd agreed to keep the past from Lexi. Out of everything, she had to be protected from that at all costs. That was Ava's one salvation: that she could shield her daughter from the pain and loss she and Dan suffered.

Sighing, she got to her feet and went to Lexi's bedroom.

'Morning, sweetheart,' she said, pushing a lock of her daughter's hair from her forehead. With her hair curling around her face, she reminded Ava of the smiley, happy toddler who'd loved everything about her mother. Lexi might not toddle after her any longer, but they still had the same close relationship as ever. She knew her daughter inside out.

'Have you heard anything about Mr Bhandari?' Lexi's eyes were worried. 'Did they catch the man?'

'I haven't heard anything yet,' Ava said. 'I was hoping there'd be something on the doorbell cam, but it doesn't seem like it's working. But look, I'm sure the police are on it. Burglaries here are so rare that they'll probably have their man by tonight.' She patted her daughter's shoulder.

'I'll get your pancakes ready,' she said, though the thought of mixing the batter from scratch made every bit of her wilt in exhaustion. Just once, she wished she could pour Lexi a bowl of Rice Krispies and be done with it. But then Lexi would be hungry half an hour later, and the thought of her daughter sitting in class with her stomach rumbling was unbearable.

'Mum, can you ask Dad to come home?' Lexi asked, and her

gut squeezed at the thought that she wasn't enough to make her daughter feel safe. The folder on the computer flashed into her mind's eye, and she clenched her jaw. There was no way Lexi could remember what had happened, but... 'He's only in Brighton, right?' Lexi was saying. 'It's not too far. I texted him, telling him about the burglary and asking him to come, but he was about to start work. He said he'd ring me later.'

'I'll give him a call today,' Ava responded, hoping he picked up. 'Now come have your vitamins while I get your breakfast ready.'

'Do I have to go to school today?' Lexi's eyes were wide, and Ava put a hand on her shoulder.

'This is your last full week at St Mary's! You don't want to miss out on any fun,' she said, smiling. 'Besides, you'll feel better when you're there. Sometimes, when you're scared and upset, it's better to focus on something else... to use that to get you through the day,' she said, thinking how very true that was. Thank goodness she had Lexi. She'd no idea what she'd do without her.

'I knew you'd say that,' Lexi mumbled, then got to her feet and pushed past her mother without a glance. Ava watched her go, thinking she'd pop out and get the ingredients to make Lexi her favourite meal tonight. Maybe she'd get her a pair of those trainers she'd seen her ogling on YouTube Shorts. She'd try to get through to Dan and ask him to return home too. Perhaps he'd be so surprised she was asking him to be here that he'd come in a heartbeat.

She'd do whatever it took to make her daughter happy.

It was the only thing she *could* do now.

FOUR
EMILY

Emily Dawes gulped down her coffee, the hot liquid scalding her throat. She didn't care, though. She needed something to wake her up. Last night had gone on forever, despite her attempts to get home to bed – and to see Sophie, of course. After working so many late shifts at the hotel, though, her daughter was used to her returning in the early hours. Even when she was younger, she'd let herself in from school and get her tea, then settle down in front of the telly until she fell asleep.

Sophie didn't mind. She knew she was loved, and she understood why Emily worked so hard: to have a better life. The life she'd been striving for since she'd left her family's cramped terrace at sixteen, and the life that would finally make her a person worth noticing.

An image of Ava's spacious, modern house flooded into her mind as she flopped onto the worn, threadbare sofa that also served as her bed. This small one-bedroom flat couldn't be further from the paradise where Ava lived. She wrinkled her nose as she stared at the scuffed walls she hadn't bothered to paint, the falling-apart furniture she'd bought from charity shops, and the faded, stained cushions. Sure, she could put more effort into decorating her space, but that would be acknowledging this was their home. And it wasn't. It never had been. It was only a temporary stopgap until she and Sophie found something more suitable... something more like Ava's. However long – and whatever – it took.

'Come on, Soph. We're going to be late.'

Sophie pulled a face, and Emily thought for the millionth time how she would have loved if her mum had tried this hard to get her to school before the bell. Sophie had never been a great student, but Emily had been desperate to get her into the same private secondary school as Ava's daughter. Sophie had managed to pass the test, but finding the money, well... that hadn't exactly gone to plan.

She had to, though. Right now, her sole connection to Ava was through their children, and if she lost that, she lost the only real friend she'd ever had – the only person now who actually *saw* her. She'd had that once with her mother, when the two of them had formed a tight unit after her father had taken off. But then her mum had remarried and started having babies, one after the other, and she'd been pushed to the background. Sometimes, she'd lie in bed, missing her mother so much it was a physical ache. A huge space inside her echoed with emptiness, and without the concentrated beam of her mum's love to anchor her, she feared she'd float off into the dark abyss. The thought would scare her so much that she wouldn't sleep all night, but she knew better than to call out. Her mother wouldn't hear – she never did. After struggling all day to meet the demands of her new family, she slept like the dead, and Emily couldn't bear the resounding silence after shouting out.

She hurried from the block of flats and down the street for the walk to school, making sure Sophie was following behind. It was only five minutes, but with Sophie dragging her feet, it felt like forever. Emily would have been happy to let Sophie go on her own, but dropping Sophie at the gate was her one chance to see Ava, if they timed it right. Ava would give a tight smile that never reached her eyes, as if they were strangers, and that same physical ache of longing would grip her again.

This wasn't the same, though. She wouldn't let it be – she couldn't bear to lose someone who'd promised to be there like her mother had done... like Ava had done, she'd think, recalling how Ava had squeezed her hand and said those words. She'd be back in Ava's life one day. Ava had no reason to be upset with her. She was simply going through a hard time. A *long* hard time, but still. After all that had happened, Emily could hardly blame her. She'd come out of it and open up once more.

She bit her lip, panic rattling inside that the time to reconnect was getting shorter and shorter as the end of primary school neared. She had to find that money.

'Shit!' A sleek black car splashed water from a puddle as it flashed by them, slowing in front of the school. Emily hurried over, about to confront the driver, when she noticed it was Ava and Lexi. She took in their pale, wan faces. God, they both looked awful.

'I'm so sorry,' Ava called through the open car window. Her hair was twisted into an un-chic messy topknot, and her face was make-up free. Emily blinked, thinking back to when they'd first met at an antenatal clinic. The contrast between the young woman who'd glowed with happiness and this tense, tired one couldn't be starker. But then, the difference in their relationship couldn't be starker now either.

That day at the clinic was still fresh in her head. Emily had been there alone, as usual. Ava had been on her own, too, and she'd smiled at Emily and started chatting. That was a new thing for Emily: people wanting to talk. She'd only just moved to Richmond and hadn't known a soul, but pregnancy was the ultimate icebreaker, garnering her smiles from even the street cleaner. After being invisible behind a hotel reception desk for so long – being invisible *generally* – the feeling that people were interested was a balm to the wound inside.

Ava had said her husband was away on business, and Emily had forced a smile and said she was on her own too: permanently. She'd seen the sympathy in Ava's eyes, and she'd forced away the longing for someone by her side and gone back to staring at the magazine. She didn't need anyone to feel sorry for her.

Ava hadn't turned away, though. Instead, she'd scribbled her number on a scrap of paper and handed it over. Surprise had shot through her as she met Ava's gaze, taking in the wavy blonde hair, blue eyes and that effortless yet chic style Emily longed to master. Her shiny wedding rings looked expensive, and Emily knew her watch had cost an absolute fortune. She was the kind of woman whose gaze usually slid over her, and Emily felt warmth rush into her that she wanted to connect. Maybe this pregnancy really was a blessing in disguise, she'd thought.

She straightened her spine now and met Ava's eyes. 'Oh, don't worry about it! We could do with a little cold water to wake us up. Right, Soph?' She looked at her daughter to agree, but instead she rolled her eyes.

'Are you two OK?' Emily put a hand on Ava's arm, trying not to notice how she shrank from her touch. 'You don't look like you've had much sleep.' As soon as the words came from her mouth, she knew they hadn't been the best thing to say. Sometimes, as much as she tried, the wrong words still emerged. It was probably why she'd never been able to make friends, apart from Ava. The chat that seemed to come so easily to most women eluded her, even if they did try to talk to her. Nothing she thought of to say ever seemed interesting enough to utter aloud.

'There was a break-in next door, at the Bhandaris',' Ava replied. 'Remember them?'

As their eyes met, hope flooded into Emily that Ava was recalling that precious time they'd had together. As first-time mothers, they'd both been in foreign territory, leaning on each other and learning as they went. It had bonded them forever, in a way nothing else ever could.

'Unfortunately, Mr Bhandari had a heart attack and was taken to hospital. We *were* up all night.'

'Oh my God.' Emily swallowed, picturing the old man clutching at his chest. 'That's so sad. Is he going to be all right?'

Ava darted a look at Lexi. 'Of course he will,' she said, patting Lexi's hand. 'And I'm sure the police will find whoever did this.'

Emily rolled her eyes. 'Useless sods. I wouldn't count on them to do anything. They can barely manage to arrest anyone if they do something right in front of them.' Once more, she clocked Ava staring at her, and she wanted to slap herself. What she had said was true – the police were clueless – but it was obvious Lexi needed some reassurance.

'The burglar won't come back, will he, Mum?' Lexi was looking up at Ava with big dark eyes. 'Please, can we stay somewhere else? Please. I really don't want to go back home unless Dad's there. Did you call? Can he come?'

'I did call, but he didn't answer. He's probably in meetings.' Ava sighed, and Emily bit her lip at Lexi's distress. Oh God. She'd made things worse. She had to do something to make it better – and fast. This was the longest conversation she and Ava had had in ages. She had to think of some way to keep it going.

'I'd comp you both at the hotel, but we're full up with wedding guests,' she said slowly, her mind whirring. Then she blinked as an idea hit. 'Why don't Sophie and I come stay with you? If Dan's not there, maybe some extra company will make you feel better so you're not alone.' Excitement grew inside. She'd love to stay with them in that big house. It would be like old times, when they'd spread blankets on the floor in the lounge and sit for hours, munching snacks and chatting about how tired they were.

But Lexi was shaking her head. 'I really don't want to be at home.' She swallowed. 'Maybe we can stay with you?'

Emily's heart sank. Her place wasn't exactly guest-ready and barely fit two people. But how could she pass this up? She could make it fun... it would be like a giant sleepover. It was only for a few nights, and it would be a great way to reconnect.

This could be exactly what she and Ava needed.

'That's a fantastic idea, Lexi. You two are more than welcome. It will be so much fun.'

'Oh, no,' Ava said. 'I couldn't ask you to do that. Really. Anyway, it's only one bedroom, right? There's not enough room for us all.'

'Mum, I'm not going back home.' Lexi's face was drawn and white, and Emily could see she was spiralling. She had always been on the more anxious side. No wonder, given what had happened, even if she couldn't remember. 'I'm not. Please don't make me. Please can we stay at Emily's? *Please.*'

Emily held her breath. By the look on Ava's face, she could tell she was considering it. Emily knew she didn't want to, but she would do anything for Lexi.

'I've got an idea,' Ava was saying slowly. 'It's a lot to ask, but, well, why don't you and Sophie stay at ours, and we'll bunk at yours? A house swap for a couple of nights until Dan gets home.'

Sophie was clapping her hands. 'That's a great idea! Lexi, you're going to love my bedroom. I've painted it such cool colours. Mum, is it OK?'

Emily listened to her daughter's excited babble, her mind racing. It wasn't the four of them bunked up together, like she'd wanted. It was a start, though – a step towards getting back in Ava's life. She'd be doing Ava a favour, and that could only be a good thing. Besides, how could she pass up the opportunity to stay in Ava's house? That place was like a dream, and she couldn't think of anywhere else she'd rather be than in the airy, open space. 'Sure,' she said, smiling as both girls cheered.

'Thank you so much.' Ava smiled, and she felt a glimmer of that warmth she'd missed so much. 'Let's exchange keys at school pick-up this afternoon. I need a chance to get the place ready.'

Emily nodded, thinking that Ava's place was probably perfection right now. It was hers that needed work. She said goodbye to Sophie, watching as her daughter went into the school without a backward glance. Happiness churned inside as she hurried towards her flat. Finally! Finally, after so long, she'd found a way to reconnect with Ava. To start to reconnect, anyway. She knew if she hung in there, it would happen eventually. Ava *had* meant the promise she'd made that day. Friendship and the bond they'd formed – how Ava had accepted her into her world so completely, unlike anyone ever had – wasn't something that disappeared, no matter the past. The desperate longing to feel that again was growing stronger and stronger now, rolling over her and engulfing her body in a swell of desire.

She grabbed her mobile phone from her handbag and dialled the hotel where she worked as front of house manager, telling them she had an emergency and couldn't be in today. Her boss wasn't pleased, but she hardly ever called in sick or took time off. She couldn't afford to. But this... this was the opportunity she'd been waiting for.

She couldn't wait any longer. She had to make sure to get back in Ava's life again.

No matter what she had to do. No matter *who* she had to push aside.

It wouldn't be the first time, that was for sure.

FIVE
AVA

Ava's mind spun as she drove the short distance home. Had she really agreed to stay in Emily's flat, and to let Emily stay here? Bloody hell. It would be so much easier if Dan came back, but despite trying to reach him several times, they hadn't managed to speak. Where had he said he was going this time? Brighton? Something about a conference for the week, but he'd be home on Friday in time for the party. He'd put the details in the shared family calendar, but she hadn't really looked at it. He travelled so much these days that one trip blurred into the other.

She sighed, remembering the first work trip he'd taken when Lexi was still so young. He hadn't wanted to leave them, but he couldn't avoid travelling any longer. She could see the worry in his eyes as he closed the door behind him, but if she was being brutally honest, she hadn't been able to wait for him to go. Even if he had let her take over with Lexi, he was still always *there*, his grief a reminder of the past. It was easier when he was gone: she didn't have to look at him and think of what she'd done – to think of what the future could have been. That was why she'd blocked Emily out too.

Unbidden, a memory of when she'd first met Emily popped

into her head. She'd been so excited, bursting with anticipation at being a mother. As a busy GP, she'd waited as long as she could to get pregnant, and she'd been thrilled that it had happened so quickly. She loved everything about it, from the way her belly was stretching to the knowing smiles people gave her as they passed. The world around her seemed bathed in a golden glow, and despite her age, everything had gone perfectly.

The only dark spot had been the disappearance of her wedding rings when she'd taken them off after her fingers had swollen. They'd been passed down through Dan's family, and she'd loved the notion that they held within them the long history of loving marriages. He'd been so upset when the rings went missing, helping her search everywhere and calling the police to report them stolen, but they'd never been found. He'd taken her out shopping one afternoon, and together, they'd chosen replacements, but Ava had to admit it wasn't the same. Still, that couldn't taint this wonderful time.

Visits to the antenatal clinic had been the highlight of her pregnancy. She loved talking about all things babies, staring at the ultrasound screen and listening to the heartbeat. She'd been dying to join one of the many antenatal groups to share the experience with women going through the same thing – as wonderful as Dan was, his body wasn't stretching to accommodate another life. Everyone always raved about the lifelong friends they made in those groups, and Ava had to admit that her friendship circle wasn't exactly bursting. The few friends she'd had from university had had babies long ago and moved away, and work had been so busy that she hadn't had time to invest in new ones. With Dan by her side, she hadn't felt the need to. But now... now, she felt the urge to chat to women facing the magnitude of motherhood; to reach out and connect with those who understood how crazy and magical this whole time was.

But the months had flown by, and as her belly had grown,

work at the surgery had become even busier. She'd missed the dates to register for the classes, but even if she hadn't, she'd never have been able to find the time. Dan's job had ramped up too, with meetings almost every hour, and the day she'd met Emily, she'd been on her own. Dan had felt awful, but he hadn't been able to get away. She'd promised to tell him every little detail when they met for a meal that night down by the river.

Amidst the other couples in their own bubbles, she and Emily had been the only ones alone. Emily had looked so nervous, so young, the jet-black hair making her cheeks seem paler. Her leg had been jiggling and her knuckles were white as she clutched her maternity notes, and Ava's heart went out to her. Her mother always said Ava could never resist taking strays under her wing, and something about Emily reminded her of a scared animal, desperate for kindness. They'd started chatting, and Ava had given Emily her number to meet up for a coffee. Emily had called the very next day, and their friendship had gone from there.

Emily never spoke about her family or the father of her baby, but Ava had sensed some trauma, so she hadn't asked. She admired Emily's scrappy spirit, vowing to do whatever she could to help the younger woman. Although they couldn't have been in two more different places in their lives, Emily gave Ava exactly what she'd been craving: someone who understood this strange period like no one else could. They spent hours together in the hinterland between starting maternity leave and waiting for labour to kick in, with Emily helping Ava put the finishing touches on the nursery as they tried to envision their future.

Ava had offered to help Emily set up space for her baby, but Emily had shaken her head as her cheeks flushed. Ava hadn't pushed it, thinking Emily might be embarrassed to show her where she lived. In the short time they'd known each other, Emily had blossomed, losing the jittery paleness she'd had when they'd met. Ava loved seeing how her face transformed when she smiled, and she didn't want to make her feel uncomfortable.

And when they had their babies, Emily was there when Dan had to return to work, each of them navigating those long first days of motherhood when everything was a blur and nothing made sense; when just leaving the house seemed a task too big to accomplish alone. Ava had had grand plans of hitting up all the mother and baby classes, but she could barely brush her own hair. Anyway, Emily wouldn't have been able to afford them, and after all the time they'd spent together, it seemed wrong to abandon her now. They were on this journey together, and that was invaluable, despite Dan not being Emily's biggest fan.

'She gives me weird vibes,' he'd said, when Ava asked why he didn't like her. 'I feel like I've seen her before, but I can't think where.'

'She works at the hotel down by the river,' Ava had responded. 'You've probably seen her in reception.' Dan often had meetings there. He'd nodded, and that had been that. He hadn't been too upset when Ava had blocked her from their lives, the same way she'd blocked everyone else. He probably hadn't even noticed.

Unlike Dan, who'd understood her need to turn inwards to focus on Lexi, Emily hadn't been able to let her go. She'd tried for months to maintain their friendship, dropping by at all hours with food and wine, naked desperation on her face. But Ava couldn't reconnect. She didn't want to – didn't want to remember the time before she'd ruined it all. Emily's calls and texts went unanswered, the doorbell ringing for hours. Ava knew she had no one else, but she hadn't any room left to feel badly about it. She could only think about one thing: her daughter. Emily had popped in and out of her life over the years, suggesting playdates with the girls and once crashing Lexi's birthday party. Eventually, though, she'd faded into the background. Ava didn't want that to change now.

And she didn't want to leave the house. This was the space she knew, where she could keep her daughter safe not only from the outside world, but also from the past. And with the end-of-year party coming up, she had a long list of things she had to get ready. When Dan had seen the entry in their calendar, he'd been surprised that she'd volunteered to have the festivities at their place – especially after what had happened at the last party they'd had here. Maybe he thought it might be a step forward into the world again. The reality was that this was a way for the world to come to them, without her having to venture elsewhere.

Perhaps she'd jumped the gun, agreeing to swap places. Lexi had been so upset that she would have agreed to anything in the moment to calm her. Maybe now she could get through to Dan and convince him to come home. She grabbed the mobile and punched in his number, but once more it went through to voicemail. Ava hung up. She'd call again in a few minutes.

She pulled into the drive, noticing Mrs Bhandari getting out of a car next door with her daughter. She parked and went over, praying that, as she'd told Lexi, everything would be OK.

'Hi,' she said, thinking how the older woman, who'd always seemed so strong and capable, had shrunk now, like life had leached out of her. 'How is he doing?'

Mrs Bhandari looked up with a vacant expression as if she didn't recognise Ava, and her daughter touched her arm.

'I'm afraid he passed away this morning,' the daughter said, her eyes full of grief.

Ava gasped and put her hands to her mouth. Oh my God. 'I'm so, so sorry,' she said, knowing how futile those words were but unable to think of anything else.

'He suffered another heart attack in hospital, and they couldn't resuscitate him.' The daughter shook her head. 'The police are still trying to figure out what happened. They say there's no sign of forced entry, but then Dad always did leave the door unlocked. Mum was forever reminding him.'

'That's awful. Please let me know if there's anything I can do to help.' Ava paused, thinking that she was doing the right thing, getting Lexi away from here. Being next door would keep the horrific events top of mind, and she'd be asking questions right, left and centre. If Lexi found out Mr Bhandari had died, it would be awful. Ava would tell her, of course, but not until after she'd got over the shock of what had happened. Besides, the chances of reaching Dan were practically nil. She could cope. She'd have to.

'Mum's going to stay with me for a while. Oh, I'm Jude, by the way. I'm not sure we've ever actually met.'

'Ava.' It felt too formal to shake hands, so Ava reached out to touch Jude's arm.

'We're here to get a few things for her.' Jude paused. 'Actually, I'm glad I ran into you. Do you think you could feed the cat for a little bit? Just until we get Mum home again, whenever she feels ready.'

'Of course.' Ava took the key Jude gave her and put it on her keyring. She could always pop back over from Emily's, or maybe Emily or Sophie wouldn't mind doing it until she came back.

'Great. Thanks.' Ava watched as Jude helped her mum towards the house, then went inside her own place, switching off the alarm inside the entryway. She knew their home was safe. But the thought that next door, one of her neighbours had been as good as murdered made a chill go through her, as if no matter how much they tried to fortify against tragedy, it was always lingering; always near.

Always reminding her how vigilant she had to be.

She drew in a breath to come back to the present, attempting to right herself. First things first, she'd make up the guest bedroom for Emily. As she got out the crisp linen, she tried to remember when they'd last had a guest. Both sets of parents stayed in hotels when they visited, respecting their space by unspoken agreement. The thought of anyone besides the three of them inside this house made her stomach clench.

It was all for Lexi, she reminded herself, and it wouldn't be for long. The police would find whoever had hurt Mr Bhandari. She'd do all she could to help cushion her daughter from the blow of his death, and life would go on. That much she knew for sure.

She made up the guest bed and changed the sheets in Lexi's room, wheeling out a case from under the bed to pack a few things for her daughter. Hmm, that was funny, she thought, glancing around. Her daughter seemed to be missing the brand-new Hollister shirt she'd bought her, along with the iPad she'd purchased as a backup in case hers stopped working. Well, she didn't have time to search for them now. The room was an absolute disaster zone, no matter how much Ava tried to tidy it each day. Electronics and clothes were piled high on every surface, headphones under socks and a wireless mouse poking out from a jumper. She knew she should stop buying her daughter things, but Lexi's grin when she opened each package made her feel something, even if it wasn't exactly happiness – more like atonement.

Ava shoved a few more things in the case, then went to her own room to pack, throwing in her standard uniform of jeans and jumpers. She sat down on the bed, remembering how Dan used to joke about having to wear sunglasses when he looked into her wardrobe to protect himself from the bright colours and patterns. Now, everything was muted as if someone had turned the dial down. Sometimes, she felt like someone had turned the dial down on her too.

Ava went into the corridor, closing the bedroom door behind her. Emily wouldn't need to go inside. She didn't *want* her inside. It was enough that she'd be in her home. Then she heaved the suitcases down the stairs and stood in the kitchen, every inch of her rejecting the thought of leaving. This was for Lexi, though, and she'd be back in a few days, she reminded herself. She'd be back, and nothing would be changed.

Nothing could ever be changed now. It was too late for that.

SIX
EMILY

For the first time ever, Emily was early for school pick-up. She was rarely there to begin with these days – since the start of Year Five, Sophie had made her own way home, telling teachers her mum was waiting across the street. The school must have realised she wasn't, but thankfully they let it go. They knew that Sophie was mature for her age. Now, though, Emily wouldn't miss this for the world. She was itching to get her hands on the keys to Ava's place and take this first step towards rekindling their close friendship. That feeling of warmth and acceptance; of knowing someone valued her... She'd do anything to make sure it wasn't lost. Hell, she already had.

She pushed the thought from her mind and smiled as Ava pulled up in the Lexus, then got out of the car.

'Hi! Everything's all set for you back at mine.' Her place would never measure up to Ava's, but she'd done what she could by chucking unmentionables under the bed and sofa and splurging from her hotel earnings by scattering around a few plants. The small space looked better, but it was still a far cry from what she wanted. 'Here are the keys. The big one is for the building's front door, and there's a smaller one for the flat.'

'Wonderful. I've got the guest room ready for you too. Sophie can stay in Lexi's.' Ava took the battered fob from her hands, almost as if she was afraid to touch it. 'Thank you again for this. Lexi... well, what happened last night really hit hard.'

'I could see that,' Emily said. 'She was so upset. She's really anxious, isn't she?'

'She's fine.' Ava smiled tightly, and once again she could see she'd said the wrong thing.

'Have you heard anything about Mr Bhandari?' she asked carefully, trying to restore the calm. Perhaps the police had given Ava an update.

Ava's face dropped. 'It's so sad. I spoke to his daughter, and he passed away. Mrs Bhandari is going to stay with her for a bit. Please don't tell Lexi,' she added quickly. 'I don't want to make her more upset.'

'Oh, of course.' He'd passed away? Poor Mr Bhandari. He was such a nice man, but going now was a blessing. He was so old and getting weaker every day. And life had no room for the weak. She knew that for a fact.

'Right, there's no key for our house, if you remember.' Ava's voice cut into her thoughts. 'It's all by facial recognition. I checked the system before I came, and it looks like you're still on there. I had to reauthorise you.'

'Great.' Emily's mind flashed back to the day Ava had added her. They'd both been almost bursting with babies, and Ava had needed to go to her final appointment at the clinic. She'd been expecting a delivery for the nursery, and Emily had offered to stay at her house and wait for it. She'd never forget how wonderful it had been to glide around the roomy space, running her hand over the smooth surfaces and breathing in the cool scented air. And the nursery... it was like something from a dream, all dove greys and creams. She'd loved it so much that she'd taken advantage of the access more times than she should. But then, friends always shared what they had, right?

She held Ava's gaze, wondering if she remembered exactly why they'd terminated her access. It had been Lexi's fifth birthday party – the first birthday party Lexi had had with friends, and she'd invited her whole class. Emily had overheard parents talking about it at the school gate, and the hurt had nearly floored her. Was Ava really going to leave her out of this? She of all people knew what Ava – and Lexi – had been through to get to this point. She should be there to support her. Maybe Ava had simply forgotten to invite her. It happened sometimes. She'd show Ava that, no matter what, she was still there for her like Ava had said she'd always be for her... like she would be again one day when all of this was behind them.

So she'd dipped into her savings and bought Lexi a posh present, then dressed Sophie up and taken her over, using the facial recognition access to get inside. The house had been full of face painters, magicians and kids running around. The mums had gathered in the conservatory, drinking Prosecco and refusing a cupcake before gobbling down two. Ava had been standing in the corner, holding a glass of bubbly with her eyes a million miles away. She barely clocked that Emily was there, let alone smile and thank her for the gift which meant they'd be eating noodles for the rest of the week. Emily's heart had sunk, and she'd leaned against the wall, trying to stop the panicky feeling that she was invisible once more.

She had to do something. She had to remind Ava she was here. She did matter, like Ava had shown her. And when she'd seen a gaggle of girls clustered in the corner of the kitchen, laughing as they waved a box of matches and candles in the air, she knew what she could do to show her friend that she was here – that she *should* be here.

Slowly, she took a match from the counter and held it to the paper tablecloth. In an instant, flames were racing up the table towards the kids in the corner. Fear flashed over her at the speed and ferocity of the fire. Then, quick as a flash, she grabbed the pitchers of water on the counter, waiting to be served, and threw them over the flames. The girls screamed and parents came running as the smoke alarm blared.

'What happened?' Ava raced around the corner and into the room, her face pale. 'Emily? What happened?'

Silently, Emily had pointed to the kids holding the candles and matches. 'The girls were here alone. I threw water on the fire before it spread too far,' she said quietly. 'Thank goodness.' She met Ava's eyes. 'I'd hate to think what could have happened if I hadn't.'

'What the—' Dan's voice halted as he rounded the corner and came into the kitchen. 'Is everyone all right?'

Ava turned to him with icy eyes. 'They're fine, thanks to Emily,' she'd said, and Emily had tried her hardest to stop her face from showing the happiness that was gushing through her. 'You were supposed to be making sure no one got in here,' she continued. 'Where the hell were you?' She leaned closer. 'Have you been drinking?'

The room went silent as all the mums gleefully anticipated watching another couple fight.

Dan dropped his head. 'Sorry,' he mumbled. 'Only a bit. It's just—'

But Ava had already turned to go, pushing through the crowd and into the garden. Emily followed, hoping this would finally be her chance for a breakthrough. She put a hand on Ava's arm.

'It's fine now, Ava. Everyone's OK. The fire is out.' She lowered her voice. 'I know this day is hard. But everything is all right now.'

But Ava spun around with a face full of fury and pain. 'Everything is *not* all right.' She paused, and the sounds of the party drifted towards them. 'Why are you here?' she asked, staring at Emily.

Emily held her gaze, her gut twisting that she'd only made

things worse. 'I thought... I thought you'd want me to come,' she said. 'But I'll go now.' She'd grabbed Sophie and the two of them had hurried home, voices inside berating her with every step. What an idiot she was. What had she been thinking with the fire? She'd only been trying to make Ava *see* her again, and now she'd messed it all up. No wonder Ava was so angry. She could have burned down the whole house.

'Oh, here come the girls!' Emily forced a smile, pushing away the memory. The past was the past. The important thing was the future. That was all that mattered. And this time, she wouldn't mess it up.

Sophie burst out of the school with two girls flanking each side, chattering as they traded stories. Then she turned to say something to Lexi, who was following behind with her head down, hunched over as if she was afraid to take up space. It was great to see them talking. She'd tried for ages to foster a friendship between the girls in hopes it would help her with Ava, but until now it hadn't happened. Maybe this house swap would help on that front too. The more connections between their families, the better.

'Hey, Soph. Ready to go? I got all your things here.' She lifted the heaving bag.

'Cool. Thanks.'

Emily sighed, thinking how sometimes Sophie spoke to her more like a kindly adult friend helping her out than a mother. But then they'd never had the affectionate relationship some kids had with their parents. Like Lexi, she thought, watching as Ava ringed her arms around her daughter's neck and pulled her close. Emily found herself reaching for her own daughter before Sophie shot her a strange look and moved away.

'We're off,' she said to Ava, excitement flooding through her. 'Give me a call if you need anything!'

She ushered Sophie in the opposite direction from their usual route, away from the low-rise brick buildings baking in the summer sun and onto a tree-lined street where the shade made the temperature seem ten degrees cooler and the air felt fresher. Lawnmowers buzzed, and though it was only three in the afternoon, she could already smell BBQs and hear laughter from back gardens. It was like stepping into a different world, and by Sophie's admiring eyes, Emily could see she felt the same.

'Here we are.' Emily stopped at a large white-fronted building with two bay windows either side of the deep-green door. The wide drive was paved with terracotta blocks, leading up to a two-car garage. Trees framed either side like bookends, and the front garden was like a green carpet, so soft that Emily could imagine how wonderful it would feel under bare feet. 'Do you remember being here? You came once for Lexi's birthday.' She winced, hoping Sophie wouldn't recall their quick exit. 'You spent loads of time here as an infant, but you'd have been too young to remember.'

Sophie shook her head, and Emily stared at the lock until it beeped. Then she swung open the door, ushering her daughter inside.

'This place is amazing!' Sophie said, and Emily glanced around, thinking she was right. Every inch of the space was imprinted on her mind. Despite not having been here for years, she still dreamed about it at night sometimes. And now she was back in the spacious lounge where she and Ava had traded pregnancy complaints and woes; where they'd spoken of their excitement at starting new lives as mothers. Emily hadn't exactly been *excited*, but the camaraderie between them was worth anything – even a baby. She'd believed they had years of trading tales ahead of them, and she couldn't wait.

As Sophie streaked through the house, Emily carried her case up the solid pine stairs towards the guest room. Upstairs was every bit as roomy as below, with lofty ceilings and huge sash windows letting in the light. She winced as she thought of the low, dingy ceilings and cramped windows of her own place.

She pushed open a door she remembered used to be the nursery, now transformed into Lexi's bedroom. The pinks and gold couldn't be further from the former creamy palette. Privately she'd thought Ava had been crazy to decorate that way, but Ava had laughed and told her it was a blank slate, like the lives their kids had ahead of them.

Emily forced away the thought. She wasn't going to let anything ruin this experience. She peered into the guest room, admiring the wash of blues, then turned and walked to Ava's bedroom. The door was resolutely closed, but she pulled it open, drinking in the huge king bed, the bay window with a window seat she'd always coveted, and the cream rug covering the polished wooden floorboards. *This* was where she'd stay, she thought as she dropped her case.

She tipped the picture of Dan onto its back – she didn't need him watching her. Then she lay down on the bed, relishing the soft goose-feather duvet. She closed her eyes and let peace wash over her. *Paradise*.

Finally, she was here. Back inside Ava's home, if not quite her life, once again.

She never wanted to leave.

SEVEN
LEXI

At last, the school day is over. I've been thinking about Mr Bhandari every second, hoping he's OK. *Why* did he have to argue with that horrible man who bought my iPad? If he'd left him alone, he would have been fine. Guilt sweeps over me that not only could I have been the reason for the burglary, I could also be the reason no one is ever found. At breaktime, when I couldn't stand feeling so bad any longer, I grabbed my phone from where I'd hidden it in my bag and checked the man's profile on Facebook, but it's been deleted now. I never should have erased the doorbell footage.

I never should have sold those things in the first place.

Then again, if Mum could actually be happy and get a life, I wouldn't *have* to sell my things to get them away from me. I wouldn't need to have secrets, just to feel like I have something of my own. Anger bursts through me, growing bigger when I see her waiting for me at the school gate. She has so much. *We* have so much. Why is she so sad? Does she think that I can't see it?

Is it because of me? Is there something I don't know?

I bite my lip, thinking about the folder I saw on Dad's computer when I went to erase the video. I woke up early this morning and crept into his office, sinking into his chair and inhaling his scent: leather and spice. Whenever I smell it, I feel warm and cosy, like nothing bad could ever happen when he's around. I wish he was here more.

I clicked on the computer and punched in the password he always uses. Then I found the doorbell camera videos and deleted them, then deleted them again. It would take an age to check through them, and I thought it would be less suspicious if I got rid of the lot of them. I was about to log off and hurry back to bed when something caught my eye. It was a folder with the name 'Alfie' on it, and while normally I wouldn't bother, for some reason I clicked. But I couldn't open it without a password, and I heard Mum stirring, so I ran back to my room, thoughts scurrying through my mind. Dad's usually an open book – or at least I thought he was. So, what is that? Who's Alfie? Why does it need a password when none of the other folders do?

Could that have something to do with why Mum's always so sad?

My brain is too busy to think much about it, though. All I can feel is relief that we don't have to go home. I'm safe for now. Sophie told me all about the cool stuff in her room that I can use too. It's really nice of her – she talked to me for ages at breaktime. I wasn't sitting on my own for once, watching everyone else have fun.

'Hey, honey.' Despite my anger, I can't help relaxing into Mum's arms. I breathe in the fresh flowery scent of her perfume, remembering all of those times she'd sit beside me when I couldn't sleep or let me crawl into bed with her when I was scared, like I did last night.

'Have you heard anything about Mr Bhandari?' My voice trembles.

Mum strokes my hair and pulls me closer. 'No, nothing yet,' she says. 'But I'm sure he's fine.' There's something funny in her voice, and for a second, I'm not sure if I believe her. But Mum wouldn't lie to me, would she? Not about something as important as this – not about something that's literally life or death.

'Come on.' Mum holds up the keys. 'Let's go check out our new pad.' She smiles, but it doesn't reach her eyes. I know she doesn't want to go. She never wants to go anywhere, despite me begging her every year to take me to Disneyland Paris. She says those theme parks are too big and too expensive, but I know she read that story in the news of how a child got lost there and she'll never let me go. She's even having the stupid party here. Still, at least she's letting us go to Emily's. I don't want to be anywhere near our house.

We start driving in the opposite direction we usually go in, away from the trees and wide roads and down a busy road. Mum turns into a cement forecourt and makes a face at the residents' parking only sign before swinging back out to the road and finding a place to park there, but it's only allowed for a couple of hours.

'We can walk to school,' I say. 'We'll only be here for a few days until Dad gets back. I texted him to say that we were staying at Emily's, by the way, so he doesn't need to worry about coming home.'

She nods, and I think for the millionth time how weird it is that I'm the one who's the go-between. They're my mum and dad. They're supposed to be talking to each other, not just to me.

'We can take the car back over to ours tonight and put it in the garage,' Mum says. 'Come, let's get our things and settle in.' She unclips her seatbelt, and I follow her out into the glaring sun. The air here smells like melted asphalt and diesel, rap music floats through the air, and there's the smell of smoke and something else. I can see Mum's lip curling, and my cheeks flush. I hope she's not going to be a snob about this. My teacher always says that people come from different places, but that doesn't make them any less worthy. I think she might have been talking about refugees, but still.

I keep my head down as we cross the forecourt and Mum fits the key in the lock. Then we go inside a dingy dark entry and over to a smelly lift, then up to the fourth floor. Mum opens the front door of the flat, and we take our things inside.

Wow. I stand for a minute, sweeping my gaze around the lounge and kitchen. It's open-plan, like ours, but this whole space could fit in my *bedroom*. There's not a lot of stuff and the furniture looks kind of beat up, but it's not too bad. There's no big dining table, but there's a modern-looking breakfast bar with two metal stools. There's not even a TV, actually, but there are a few random plants scattered around. They don't look like they belong here.

It couldn't be more different from our house, but somehow, I feel comfortable here. It's real. Sometimes at home, I feel as if I'm living in a magazine shoot. Everything is too perfect; like it can't deviate an inch from its place. That's another reason why I stay in my room so much. At least I can mess it up, although – no matter how much I ask her not to – Mum goes in and tidies it.

'I'm going to check out Sophie's bedroom,' I say, pushing open a door. My mouth drops open again as I take it in. The walls are painted in a dark blue, like the night sky, with thick curtains blocking out the sun. There's something that sparkles on the walls, but I can't tell if it's an effect from the paint or something else. It's amazing. It couldn't be more different from my bedroom, all creams and golds and pinks, and I love it. I wish I could have something like this. I wish I could be more like Sophie, full stop. She has a million friends, and she's always laughing and chatting with them like she did with me today. Her mum lets her do what she wants too: she even walks home from school on her own every day. I would kill for that kind of freedom.

'It's so cool!' I say, and my mum smiles, but I can see she doesn't think so. I glance around. 'Wait, where's your room?'

'Oh, there's only one bedroom,' Mum says, and my heart sinks. Will I have to share with her? One night was fine, but we're safe here, and I really want to kick back and enjoy Sophie's room. She gestures to the sofa. 'It's a pull-out, and Emily has pillows and blankets in the closet. I'll sleep here. You need to get a good night's sleep for school. Me, I can take a nap if I need to!' She smiles again, and I wonder what she does all day. I can understand quitting her job to care for me when I was a baby. But she could go back now, couldn't she? I don't get why she doesn't. She must be lonely too, especially with Dad away so much. I push away the image of her standing, all alone, in the middle of the lounge. It's not my fault she made her life about me.

It's not my fault I can't make her happy.

Is it? A little voice echoes in my head, and my stomach twists.

'Mum, who's Alfie?' The words pop out of me, despite everything else clogging my brain. It's as if they've been sitting there, on top of everything, waiting for a second to spring free.

Mum's face goes pale, and she jerks back. 'Alfie?' The word barely comes out of her mouth. It looks like she's seen a ghost. 'Where did you hear that name?'

My heart drops. Oh shit. I can hardly say that I saw it on Dad's computer while deleting the doorbell camera footage.

'Lexi?' Mum's voice interrupts my thoughts.

My stomach clenches, and I feel sick. 'I don't know. Around.'

'What do you mean, around?' She looks as sick as me, and instantly I know that whoever Alfie is, he's not just a random folder on Dad's laptop.

'Um, I dunno, maybe at school,' I mumble. 'It doesn't matter.'

Mum holds my gaze for a second, like she's trying to read my mind. Then she forces a smile. 'OK,' she says, but I can tell it's anything but. I wait for her to explain who he is, but she doesn't say anything. She turns away, but not before I see her tense, white face.

EIGHT
AVA

Ava's head pounded, and panic surged through her body. What the *hell*? How could Lexi have heard that name? It obviously wasn't 'around', like she'd claimed. That was way too much of a coincidence. Someone must have said it to her, but who? And why?

She should have asked Lexi more, but she'd been too shocked to form words. The one thing that had pushed her through the guilt was the fact that her daughter knew nothing of the past. Hearing Lexi speak Alfie's name had nearly knocked her to her knees. It was OK, she told herself, trying to contain the emotion. Everything was locked away, and at least Lexi didn't seem to know who he was. She could still keep her safe.

How could Lexi have heard it? The logical person was Dan, of course, but she knew he wouldn't do that – to her, or to Lexi. They never talked about Alfie to each other, let alone to their daughter. Dan had that folder on his computer, yes, but Lexi wouldn't know that. She never went in his office. She had no reason to use the laptop.

Ava gnawed her lower lip as her mind spun. Who else could it be? Her mum lived in Cornwall, and Dan's parents barely said boo to anyone, let alone defy their wishes to speak to Lexi of Alfie. It wasn't like there were many people in her life from that time. She hadn't let them stay.

There was one person, though. One person who'd stayed in her orbit, despite attempts to block her out. One person who'd come closer now than she had for years: Emily. She knew the horrific events of so long ago – well, most of them, anyway. Could she have spoken to Sophie about it, maybe, and Sophie had asked Lexi at school? Or... Ava tilted her head. Emily was desperate to make a connection again. Perhaps she'd thought mentioning Alfie to Lexi was a way to somehow do that.

Ava couldn't imagine why, but then Emily had always made plenty of social missteps. It was as if she'd never quite learned the same rules as the rest of them, which made sense when she'd told Ava early on that she'd never had a close friend. Never had a friend, *period*. Ava had grabbed her hand and squeezed it. She looked so lonely, and the image of the scared shaking stray in the doctor's office when they first met came to her mind. She'd told Emily that she'd always be there for her, and that she deserved someone she could count on. She winced as she remembered those words. She'd meant them at the time, but...

What exactly had Emily said to Lexi? Well, she was going to find out, Ava thought, grabbing the keys to the car. She had to go back and drop it off at the house, anyway. She would talk to Emily then. She sighed, thinking about Lexi, and glanced at the closed door. Back home, Lexi rarely shut her door – the house was so large they never felt crammed in. But now, for the first time, it felt as if there was something between them despite the closeness of the flat.

She'd have to leave Lexi here, Ava thought. She didn't want to, but she could hardly talk to Emily with Lexi by her side, and no way could she wait until morning to find out how much her daughter had discovered and make sure nothing more was said. Lexi would be fine here, Ava reassured herself, trying to quell the rising worry. After all, she was almost twelve, and it was a block of flats – it wasn't as if someone could walk in off the street here – not like at their house. Ava could keep Lexi on FaceTime until she reached Emily and then call her again once they were done.

'Lex?' It felt weird to be talking to her daughter through a closed door, and she knocked lightly. 'Are you all right to stay here on your own for about half an hour?' she said when Lexi answered. 'I'm running the car back home.'

'I'll be fine, Mum.' Lexi rolled her eyes. 'I know it's safe here. Sophie says she stays alone all the time when her mum's at work.'

Ava raised her eyebrows at the thought of Sophie here, night after night, on her own. But then, what choice did Emily have? She worked hard, and there was no one else she could call. Once again, Ava wondered how Emily had come to be here and what had happened in her life to leave her all by herself.

'OK,' she said. 'Don't answer the door if anyone knocks. I'll call to check in, and I'll be back as soon as I can.'

'Fine!' Lexi closed the door and the sound of terrible rap music that Ava had never heard her daughter play before blared from the room.

Ava grabbed her keys and mobile, then left the flat and locked the door. She shuddered, picturing the terrible bedroom Sophie had decorated like a dungeon. She'd seen her daughter's eyes light up when she'd gone inside. It couldn't be more different than Lexi's light and airy bedroom at home, and yet... Ava bit her lip. And yet she'd seemed so comfortable as she lounged on the dark blue duvet and stared up at the glittery ceiling. More comfortable and content than she seemed in her own space back home.

That was only because of the burglary, Ava told herself as she hurried through the darkened corridors, down the lift and over to where she'd parked the car. God knows *she* didn't feel any better here. The flat was smaller than she'd imagined, and although she knew Emily had been here for well over a decade, it looked like a temporary stop-off. Obviously, the hotel had given her cast-offs, since their logoed items were everywhere: the toiletries in the bathroom, the plates in the kitchen, the vase on the bookcase. Even the plants dotted everywhere to hide dingy corners and marked walls looked slightly menacing.

She pulled into the drive, opened the garage door with her fob, parked, then went in through the side door. 'Hello!' she called out, flicking on lights as she went into the kitchen, thinking how strange the quiet was. Two ready meals were sitting by the microwave, about to go in, but the kitchen was empty. 'Emily?' she called. God, it felt so weird to creep around her own space like this. Where on earth were they?

'Oh!' Emily jumped as she came down the stairs and spotted Ava. 'You gave me a scare.' Something about her voice tweaked irritation inside of Ava as if she shouldn't be here. It was her house, for goodness' sake.

'Sorry to startle you,' she said, trying to smile. 'Just came to drop off the car, since there's nowhere to park it at yours.'

'Oh, yes. Sorry, I should have warned you. I never thought.'

'No worries.' Ava paused. Now, in this place, she didn't want to mention Alfie, as if by speaking his name, she'd make the protective walls tremble. But she had to. 'Look, I need to talk to you. Did you mention...' She swallowed. 'Did you mention Alfie to Lexi? Say his name, or anything at all? Maybe to Sophie?'

Emily drew back like she'd been slapped. 'Alfie?' Her lips twisted around the name as if it was a foreign word, and she shook her head. 'No, of course not. I haven't said a word about him to anyone. I'd never do that to you – or her. You have to know that.' She reached out and clutched Ava's arm. 'Besides, when would I? We haven't got together since...' She looked quickly away. Then she took a breath and met Ava's eyes again. 'I've missed you,' she said in a low voice, almost so quiet that Ava couldn't hear her. 'I'm so glad that I can be there for you now. I'm so glad that you're letting me.'

Ava nodded, barely hearing the words as she stared at Emily. Her reaction when she'd heard Alfie's name: that couldn't be faked. It was as if she'd heard an echo of the past, an echo that had been locked away for years, only wending its way through time towards them now. It hadn't been her. Lexi must have heard the name from someone else. *Could* it have been Dan? But why wouldn't Lexi have told her that, if so?

'Oh, hi, Sophie.' Ava smiled as Sophie came down the stairs, hoping she hadn't heard anything. That was the last thing she needed. 'Lexi is loving your bedroom, by the way.'

'It's great, isn't it? I did it all myself.' Sophie grinned proudly. 'But I'm loving hers too. She has so much *stuff*! No wonder she wants to get rid of some of it.'

What? Ava raised her eyebrows. What was Sophie on about? 'Get rid of it? What do you mean?' Her mind flashed back to when she noticed the trainers and iPad missing from Lexi's room. What was going on?

Sophie's face slammed closed, the same way Lexi had slammed the bedroom door. 'Oh, nothing. She... mentioned to the class she might have some things for a fundraiser.'

'Oh.' Ava forced a smile once more. Well, that made sense, although she couldn't understand why Lexi hadn't mentioned it to her. Lexi told her everything. There were no secrets between them. Were there? An odd feeling was circulating around her, uncertainty tinged with fear. First Alfie, now this. What else was going on with her daughter? It was probably nothing, she told herself. Maybe Lexi hadn't liked some of the things she'd bought her, and she hadn't wanted to hurt her feelings. That sounded like her considerate daughter. She'd talk to her tonight about it – or maybe she wouldn't, she decided. She didn't want to embarrass her, and it sounded like the items were going to a good cause.

'I'll see you tomorrow, at drop-off maybe,' she said to Emily, who she could tell still wanted to protest she'd never told Lexi. Ava wanted to get back to her daughter now. Perhaps they could cuddle up on the sofa and watch something on Lexi's iPad. 'Give me a call if you need anything.'

'For sure! You too.'

Closing her own front door behind her felt so strange that she paused on the doorstep in the falling light. The bushes rustled beside her, and she froze as thoughts of what the police had said came into her mind. Could this be the burglar? She turned towards the dark hulk of the house, tempted to go back inside, but Emily had shut the blinds and she didn't want to show how scared she was. The house was a fortress, and she was on the outside now.

A cat streaked from the bush, and Ava laughed at herself. Just a cat! This whole thing had unnerved her too. Then her heart dropped. Oh *shit*. With all that had been going on, she'd forgotten to ask Emily to feed the Bhandaris' cat. She was about to go inside when her phone bleeped, and she glanced down to see that Dan was trying to call her – finally. Perfect timing: after her conversation with Emily, she really needed to talk to him. It was hard to believe he could be the one who'd mentioned Alfie, but she needed to hear him say that. She needed him to confirm he would never do that to their daughter; that he would keep everything where it should be. She jabbed at the screen.

'Hey,' she said, staring into the darkness as she waited for him to respond. 'Hello?' She blinked, but there was nothing but silence. 'Dan? Are you there?'

The phone disconnected and she stared at it, waiting for him to call again, but it stayed resolutely silent. She tried to ring back, but it went straight to voicemail. She sighed, thinking how that encapsulated their relationship now: so much distance between them, they couldn't connect even when she needed him. Somewhere along the way, that radar he'd had seemed to have disappeared. A memory popped into her mind of when he'd asked her to marry him and how he'd held her so tightly, it felt like they were one person. Pain darted through her at the realisation that although she'd forced that distance between them, she missed him. She missed *them*.

She blinked, pushing away the thought. The people they'd been – the couple they'd been – didn't exist any longer... thanks to her. Honestly, it was a miracle he still stayed, although it was probably more for Lexi than for her.

Ava slid the phone back into her pocket. She'd try to reach him again later. And who knew, maybe Lexi hearing the name Alfie had been a coincidence, after all. God, she hoped so. She'd wait to talk to Dan before trying to get more from her daughter. There was no reason to make it seem like a big deal if it wasn't.

She glanced up at the camera and the door clicked open.

'Emily?' No response. 'Emily!' she called louder. Right now, all she wanted was to get back to Lexi and make sure she was OK. Finally, Emily came down the stairs and crossed into the kitchen.

Ava's eyes bulged. Was she wearing her *pyjamas*?

'Hope you don't mind,' Emily was saying, her face flushing 'I forgot mine.'

'No, no, of course not.' Ava forced a smile as her mind whirred. Those pyjamas had been in a drawer in the bedroom. How had Emily found them? Had she gone through her things? What else had she seen?

There was nothing else there, she reminded herself. Anything important was stored in a locked room in the basement, the key on a ring inside a drawer in Dan's office. She wished now that she'd taken the keyring with her, but there was no need. Emily wouldn't have to go downstairs, and anyway, she wouldn't be able to get inside the room.

'Did you forget something?' Emily was looking at her with a quizzical expression, and Ava jerked herself back to the present.

'Oh, yes. Mrs Bhandari has gone to stay with her daughter, and she asked me to feed the cat until she's back again.'

'That bloody cat.' Emily was shaking her head. 'I mean, I saw it digging in your garden earlier. It's going to ruin your flowers if you let it keep doing that.'

Ava let out a breath. Right now, that was the least of her worries. 'Anyway, I wondered if you wouldn't mind feeding it until I'm back here again.' She put the key on the table in the doorway.

'Oh, of course. Happy to.' Emily smiled. 'Good night.'

'Night.' Ava went out into the night once more and hurried through the dark towards her daughter. Emily's place might not be home, but at least she and Lexi would be together.

She'd make sure nothing ever changed that.

NINE
EMILY

As she carefully steered Ava's Lexus down the street towards school the next morning, Emily caught herself with a huge smile on her face. One night in Ava's house, and she felt *transformed*. It was amazing the difference having your very own king-sized bed to stretch out in could make. Standing under the rain shower as she sluiced Ava's expensive products over her skin and hair was better than a trip to the spa. Was this why rich people looked so fresh all the time?

Not that Ava would consider herself rich, of course. She'd laugh and say they weren't even close. But with a house worth well over two million, an expensive car and more than enough extra cash to put Lexi in private school next year, that was definitely rich on Emily's scale.

She sighed, remembering the first time she'd realised that not everyone lived the same way she did. Her primary school class had taken a rare trip into the centre of Norwich to check out some museum or other. Until then, her world had consisted of going to school and home again, and she'd thought everyone lived stuffed into terraces like her. But as the school bus wended its way towards the centre of the city, her eyes filled with beautiful buildings and groomed gardens. The whole coachload of kids had plastered themselves against the windows, oohing and aahing over the expensive cars and massive houses. When an immaculately dressed woman emerged from one of the houses and got into a shiny sportscar, even the teachers couldn't take their eyes off her.

She didn't need her mother in order to feel special, she'd realised in a flash. All she needed was money. That would automatically make her someone important, someone respected. Over the next few years, as she lay alone at night listening to her siblings cry, she'd tell herself that one day, she'd be the woman everyone had stared at. People would see her. People would *want* to talk to her.

She'd held onto that as she left school at sixteen and got a job at a bed and breakfast, cleaning rooms, working her way up to reception and then to the posh hotel in the city centre. She learned not to scrape her hair back, and not to slather on make-up. She studied every guest that came in, from how they tucked in their shirts to how they greeted her. She wanted to do all she could to become that glossy, elegant woman as quickly as possible and have the life people envied. Maybe that would stop the ache inside.

Moving to Richmond had been a huge leap forward. And while she'd still been working on becoming the person she'd wanted with the life to die for, once Ava started chatting to her, it had been a massive step towards being seen; towards filling the empty place in a way she hadn't thought possible with anyone else. For the first time, she'd been able to sleep at night, knowing someone was there. After Ava had shut her out, she'd only been able to stay calm by telling herself this was temporary. She would keep pushing ahead, and sooner or later, things with Ava would go back to how they used to be.

Now, that day was here. That was, if she hadn't blown it. She bit her lip, thinking of Ava's face last night when she'd accused Emily of mentioning Alfie... and her expression when she'd seen her in her pyjamas. Her gut clenched when she remembered how she'd told Ava that she'd missed her, and Ava hadn't responded. She must have missed her. They'd been so close. But Ava had been upset over Lexi hearing about Alfie, of course. She'd been tense and angry.

Hopefully, today would calm her down. Emily slowly turned the corner to the school, a smile on her face. She'd booked Ava into the spa at her hotel, then taken the day off work again – a day she could ill afford, but she knew would be worth it in the end – and had come up with a brilliant idea to surprise her. Ava wouldn't be able to believe what she'd done when she returned home.

She pulled up to the kerb and let out Sophie, loving the looks of respect on others' faces as they clocked her in the Lexus. God, she loved this car. Eventually, she'd get one of her own, like the woman she'd seen when she was young. Using Ava's car – although she hadn't technically said it was theirs to use, she wouldn't be needing it – had meant not only could she get to school without rushing, but she could stay as fresh and unruffled as she'd left the house, without having to battle the elements.

'Emily?' Ava was hurrying over to her, looking more tired than she had yesterday. Emily knew how uncomfortable that pull-out sofa was. It had been knackered when she'd first got it, and that had been years ago.

'Ava! Just the person I wanted to see.' Emily smiled brightly. 'Hope you don't mind me using the car? Sophie was worried about being late – she was practically in tears about it.' That wasn't exactly true, but she had to come up with something, because by the expression on Ava's face, she could see that she did mind. A brief bit of irritation flitted through her. Ava had so much, and she had done her a huge favour. *Why* couldn't she open up a bit, like she had in the old days? A memory flashed through her mind of them both lounging in the back garden on a blanket, gorging on ripe raspberries and tossing back elderflower cordial while rubbing their tight and swollen bellies. Emily had never tasted cordial before, and Ava had given her the rest of the bottle to take home.

'What's mine is yours,' she'd said, smiling. 'In fact, why don't you take the other bottle in the fridge too? Dan's not a fan.'

Emily had savoured the sparkly drink, each sip a reminder of Ava's generosity – not only with cordial, but with the 'extras' she always ordered by mistake: the packet of nappies, the onesies, the soft blankets. Emily knew she shouldn't take them, but she always did. Not just because she needed them, but because of what they represented. Friendship. Someone who cared.

'It's fine,' Ava said now, pushing back her hair.

'Look, I know it's been a tough couple of days for you and Lexi,' Emily said quickly, before Ava could take off. 'So I've got a surprise for you. I've booked you into the hotel spa for a day session. They'll take good care of you, and you'll come out feeling like a new person!'

Ava blinked. 'Wow. That's really nice of you. But... well, I don't think I can. Sorry.'

Emily felt hurt judder inside. 'Oh, come on. What else are you doing today? Do you want to hang around my flat all day?' She could see her words had hit the mark with that one. 'Besides, it's already paid for.' Not to mention she'd had to promise the spa manager free drinks at the hotel bar for the month to clear their schedule to get Ava in.

Ava smiled. 'Well, I guess I could. It's been ages since I've been to the spa.'

'Perfect.' Emily opened the door. 'Come on, hop in. I'll take you and you can park the car there.' It felt so good to have Ava beside her in the passenger seat as she steered towards the hotel.

She knew the route so well; it would be a doddle to get them there. Confidently, she swung into the road.

'Watch out!' Ava's cry made her slam on the brakes, and the car rocked as a white van sped by them.

'Sorry.' Emily gulped. Oh God. Maybe this driving thing wasn't as easy as it had seemed so far. She'd never learned. She'd never had the chance. Carefully, she manoeuvred onto the road and gingerly drove them down the street to the hotel, conscious of Ava watching her. 'Sorry, it's been a while,' she said. 'But it's like riding a bike, right?'

Ava nodded. 'I guess so.' Silence fell, then Ava turned towards her. 'Thank you so much for organising this. And I'm sorry if I jumped on you last night with the whole...' Her voice trailed off, and Emily could see that she didn't want to say the name. 'It's, well, I don't know where else Lexi could have heard it from.'

'I understand,' Emily said quickly, eager to show Ava she did, although she never had. After all, she'd done nothing wrong. 'Do you think maybe Dan said something?' Emily wanted to turn to see Ava's face, but she had to keep her eyes on the road.

'He must have. That's the only explanation.' Emily could hear the upset in her voice. Still, it was better that Ava was upset with Dan than with her.

'This spa is really nice,' Emily said, keen to keep the conversation going. 'Super therapists.' She made a face. 'Not that I've ever had a chance to test them out. But clients have raved about it.' She'd overheard them in the locker rooms. And the spa *was* beautiful. The whole hotel was, actually – a real step up from the last one. Leaving Norwich had been the best thing for her.

'Here we are!' she said as she pulled up to the hotel. 'Why don't I get out and you can park the car where you like?' She didn't want to try to navigate the underground car park. That thing scared her on foot, let alone in a car. 'I've booked you in under your name. You don't need to pay a thing.'

'That's great,' Ava said, her smile seeming genuine for the first time since Emily had spoken to her that day. 'Thank you.'

'Enjoy!' Emily got out of the car and lifted a hand as Ava went into the car park. Now she had to get back to the house and prepare the best surprise ever.

Ava was going to be thrilled when she saw what she'd done.

TEN
AVA

God, she really needed this, Ava thought, as the therapist stroked fragrant creams across her face. A night of tossing and turning on Emily's sofa had left her a broken woman. Although she'd gone to bed convinced Lexi hearing Alfie's name must be a strange coincidence, when she'd lain in the dark, the doubts and fears had seeped back in. *Could* Lexi have somehow seen the folder on Dan's computer? What was inside there? What had she learned?

Was she waiting for Ava to come talk to her, or did she still know nothing at all?

She had to speak to Dan. After they'd failed to connect yesterday, he'd texted her late at night, saying he was at a work event and he'd call her today. Of course, he hadn't yet. Well, she'd try him again now. Hopefully, he'd tell her it was a coincidence, after all. She could put aside these thoughts for good.

'Can I have a minute?' she asked the therapist, who nodded and stepped away. Ava dug out her mobile and dialled her husband, hoping a miracle would happen and he'd actually answer.

'Hey.' The buzz and clink of glasses in the background

made her smile, and memories flooded through her mind of how she and Dan used to love hanging out down by the river. They'd sit for hours in a pub on a summer day like this one – on a weekend, of course, since they'd both be busy working – and talk for hours. Once more the feeling of longing swept over her, coupled with sadness that they could never be that way again.

'Hi,' she said. 'Where are you? Sounds like you're in the middle of a party!'

'It's a drinks reception.'

Ava raised her eyebrows, thinking it was rather early for a drinks reception. But the pharmaceutical industry was like that, always using whatever means they could to seduce doctors to prescribe their medications. 'OK, well.' She paused, thinking she'd get the difficult bit out of the way first before filling him in on the rest. 'Did you say anything to Lexi about...' She swallowed. This would be the first time they'd spoken his name since that day so long ago. 'About Alfie?'

'Alfie?' There was a silence. 'Why?'

Panic flashed through her at how he dodged the question. So there *was* a chance he'd said something. Oh God. Oh *God*. 'Lexi asked who he was. She said she'd heard his name somewhere. Was it you?' She took a deep breath. 'Look, I understand that maybe the name slipped out. I... I saw the folder on your laptop. But you could have warned me. You could have told me. You *should* have told me.' Anger was building inside. 'I am the one who did this, Dan. To Alfie, to her, to us. It was me. And I can't bear if she finds out. I *can't*.' She gripped the phone, barely seeing in front of her now.

'You're not to blame, Ava. I told you that a million times. And I did want to talk to you, but...' He sighed. 'I do think it's time we open up and tell Lexi. I agreed to stay quiet because I could see how much you were hurting, but it's been so long now. She should know, Ava. It isn't right to keep this from her.'

Panic mixed with the anger now. 'I'm still hurting, Dan. Do you think it's ever stopped? Do you think it ever will?'

'I know, Ava. I know, because I feel the same. We don't have to tell her everything, obviously. But she's growing up, and the longer we stay quiet, the harder it will be. Not just for her. For us too. For me.' He paused as she listened incredulously. How could he want to do this?

'Do you know why I travel so much?' he continued. 'It's because I can't bear to be in the house without even *acknowledging* Alfie – the space he held in our hearts; in our home. I thought that as time went on, it might get...' His voice trailed off. 'Not easier, exactly, but that the gap he left would gradually fill in. But it's not. It's getting bigger. The emptiness is getting bigger, and we need to talk about him before it swallows us all.' There was an urgency in his voice that Ava hadn't heard before, but she stayed silent. How could she begin to respond? She could barely believe he was saying this. She'd thought they were on the same page. She'd thought he understood.

'I can't keep going on like this, Ava. I don't want our home to feel so empty and cold. I want to be able to laugh again. And...' He swallowed. 'I miss you. I want to share life with you again. So let's take this first step, all right? Let's start to fill in that empty place. We can show Lexi the pictures on my laptop. When I'm back, we can sit down with her, and—'

She hung up. She had to. She couldn't keep talking about this. Because she would never be ready to tell Lexi what had happened. *Never.* And how could Dan say he felt the same? It wasn't his fault. Not like it was hers. She felt awful that he was struggling with their decision to not talk about Alfie, but his pain would be nothing compared to their daughter's if she found out what could have been.

And their home wasn't empty and cold. She'd done all she could to make it anything but. Lexi loved their place. She'd never known sadness or upset there, and Ava would make sure it stayed that way. If Dan really couldn't cope with how things were, then maybe... she closed her eyes, her heart wrenching despite her anger. Maybe it was best he didn't live there. Best if he kept quiet and kept away. He'd already said too much.

Every bit of her was trembling, and the therapist raised her eyebrows as she came back into the room. 'OK, hun?'

Ave shook her head. 'No. No, I'll never be OK.' She grabbed her bag, ignoring the look of surprise from the therapist. 'I have to leave. Thank you.'

'But I haven't finished! At least let me put the moisturiser on.'

'That's all right. I really do have to go.' She couldn't stay here, lying with her eyes closed in the darkened room as Dan's words stomped through her mind. She shook her head, thinking of the laptop sitting on Dan's desk, Alfie's name looming large in her mind. Dan had said there were photos on there. He'd wanted to show them to Lexi. At least he hadn't done that yet, but what exactly *had* he said? She drew in a breath at the thought that he could tell Lexi at any moment where to find those pictures.

She'd go home now. She'd take the laptop and put it somewhere safe, away from the threat of Lexi finding it – at least until she had the chance to convince Dan to stay quiet, whatever it took. She'd stash it in the storage room, she decided, wondering if Dan remembered what else was in there: a box, taped tightly shut, unmoved since the day she'd locked it inside.

She grabbed her purse and mobile, then checked out at the spa reception.

'Everything all right?' The spa manager glanced at her anxiously. 'You're in a bit of a hurry.'

'Oh, yes, it was lovely, thanks,' she mumbled as she signed out. 'Sorry, I'm late for something.'

'Oh good.' The manager looked relieved. 'I mean, it's not good that you're late,' she said, smiling. 'It's just that we've had a lot of complaints recently about things going missing from lockers and such. I was worried it had happened again.'

Ava barely heard her words as she rushed to the car park. She had to get home. Once the laptop was safely contained in the storage room, she'd feel much better. She drove to her house in a daze, heaving a huge sigh of relief when she pulled into the driveway.

She got out of the car and went inside, savouring the silence as a calm numbness descended over her once more. It was fine. Everything would be all right. She'd get the laptop, and—

A scraping and banging noise came from the basement, and she froze. What was that? For a split second, she thought of the burglar once more before dismissing the thought. There was no way anyone could get in here – the place was like Fort Knox. She walked to the stairs and peered down the dark staircase as the scraping and thudding continued. Then she heard Emily swear as something crashed to the ground. What the hell? Why was Emily here and not at work? And what was she doing in the *basement*?

'Emily? What are you doing?' She hurried down the stairs, her footsteps thudding. 'Is everything OK?'

Her eyes popped as she took in the scene in front of her. The basement had always been an extra storage area, with boxes of unused items and old furniture lining the perimeter of the large, unfinished space. When they'd bought the house, she and Dan had talked about one day converting it into a media room – or a playroom, for when they had kids. But Ava had never been able to face the work involved, and it had remained largely a dumping ground.

But now... she shook her head as she surveyed the space. Emily had cleared all the boxes and moved the furniture to one side of the room. The storage-room door was open, and—

Oh my God.

The storage room. Her pulse picked up, and her heart thudded. Inside was a box of items that hadn't been moved since she'd finally managed to pack them away so long ago. What if Emily had found it? What if, for some reason, she'd opened it? It had to stay closed. It had to.

She lunged through the open door, frantically scanning the room to see if it was still where she'd put it in the corner. But with all the other boxes Emily had moved from the main space and stacked against the wall in here, she couldn't spot it.

'Where is it?' The words flew from her mouth.

Emily shook her head. 'What do you mean?'

'The box. The box of...' She couldn't say it as she searched through the stack. It was here somewhere. It wouldn't disappear. It might have been moved, but Emily would have no reason to open it. And yet knowing the box wasn't where she'd put it – the threat of it being disturbed – made everything inside go haywire.

Finally, she saw it, and relief flooded through her. She slumped back against the wall, trying to right her world again. Everything was fine. The box had been moved, but it hadn't been opened. Thank God. Thank *God*.

She glanced up to meet Emily's eyes, anger replacing the relief. 'What the hell were you doing moving everything around like that?'

Emily jerked back as if her words were a slap in the face. 'I had a great idea. You're having the class party here on Friday, right? I thought I would make a disco area for the kids in the basement. We could play music, get a disco ball, they'd love it. After all, you can never trust the British weather, can you?'

Ava stared, incredulous. How did Emily know about the class party? Sophie wasn't in Lexi's class. And how could Emily begin to think she could come down here and start shifting around everything without asking?

'I really hope you don't mind,' Emily was saying, although it was obvious she did. 'I wanted to do something to surprise you. I guess I should have asked.'

Ava got to her feet. 'Yes, you should have.' She breathed in, telling herself to calm down. Emily didn't know the box was here and that Ava hadn't wanted it moved. She'd only been trying to do something nice, however ill-considered it was. But imagine if Emily had put the box somewhere visible? Imagine if somehow Lexi had come across it? In light of her conversation with Dan, the threat seemed more real than ever. 'How did you get the storage room open?' There was no way she could have found the keyring on her own.

Emily blinked. 'Remember when you were organising the nursery? You wanted to move a few of Dan's boxes downstairs. You said they had some important documents and you wanted to keep them safe, so I helped you put them in there. I remembered where you told me to get the key from.' She paused, her gaze lasering into Ava. 'I remember everything.'

'Right.' Ava took another breath, trying to rid herself of the panic. But still that uneasy feeling lingered. 'Look, it's all right,' she said, although it couldn't be further from the truth. 'But I think Lexi and I should come home now. You made me realise how little time we have before the party. I need to come back here and start getting ready.' She had to come back, but not for the party. She had to protect this space, and she had to protect her daughter. 'Lexi's calmed down, and I think she'll be fine. I appreciate all you've done, though.'

'But...' Emily shook her head. 'But I thought you'd want to stay until Dan gets home? It's only another two nights, and if Lexi's really scared, perhaps it's better. I mean, they still haven't caught whoever broke into the Bhandaris'. I promise not to touch anything else without checking first, and I can do whatever you need for the party. Really. I know my place isn't the most comfortable, but if it's better for Lexi...'

Her voice trailed off, and Ava stared. Was Emily trying to

guilt her into staying at her place? Her, of all people? As if she didn't spend her whole life thinking about what was best for her daughter?

What was best for her daughter was being back home, where she belonged.

'She'll be fine,' Ava said through gritted teeth. 'We'll get our things from your place after school today, and then come back.' She summoned a smile. 'Thank you so much for letting us stay at your place. It was very kind.'

Emily didn't respond; just held her gaze, but Ava could see by her face she was upset. 'Look, I do appreciate what you were trying to do down here,' she said, although it wasn't true. 'It was... a surprise.'

'I understand. I shouldn't have done it.' Emily lowered her head, then looked up to meet Ava's gaze again. 'But, well, Sophie and I had planned to have a movie night here tonight, you know? We don't have a TV at home, and I'm always working. She was so looking forward to it. I know she's going to be so disappointed.' She sighed, her eyes sad. 'But don't worry. I know you want to be back in here. I understand.' She blinked. 'Maybe... maybe we could do it together? It would be great for the girls to spend some time with each other. Soph and I will go home afterwards.'

Ava tilted her head, a tiny bit of guilt needling her. By the sounds of things, Sophie had so little time with her mum, just the two of them. This was a rare chance for them to do something together. Could Ava take that away from her? Emily had done her a huge favour, after all. It was only another few hours. They'd be back by bedtime.

And as for joining them... She swallowed, Emily's words about how she remembered everything drifting into her head. Did she remember how Ava had said she'd always be there for her? Was that why she seemed so fixated on reconnecting? Ava didn't want to rekindle a friendship with Emily. And the last thing she needed was Lexi becoming friends with Sophie. Emily would latch onto that like a dog with a bone. Right now, all she wanted was to get through the day and come back home, close the walls around her, and focus on her daughter.

'You two enjoy that,' she said, as disappointment flashed across Emily's face. 'We'll come back at eight. That will give you both enough time, won't it? It's a school day tomorrow, anyway.' She forced a smile. 'Now, would you mind helping me put all of this where it was before? We should have enough time before we go to pick up the girls.'

Emily nodded, but she didn't look happy at all. Ava sighed. She'd have to tell Emily that, as much as she appreciated everything, she simply wasn't ready to be friends again... to have friends again. They had been close, but Emily must see she was different now. The carefree woman who'd laughed and chatted over babies cooing on blankets was gone, and the bond that had drawn them together had been broken in the most brutal way possible. Emily *must* know the promise of friendship could never withstand such events. Didn't she? Well, she would after Ava spoke to her. She didn't want to hurt her again, but Emily needed to understand.

It'll be all right, she told herself again as she heaved the boxes back to where they'd been. A few more hours, and then everything would return to how it was before.

ELEVEN
EMILY

Emily was shaking as she helped Ava move boxes from the storage room back to the main space. It had looked so much better without all the rubbish, even if Ava didn't want the kids down here. Emily had thought it was such a good idea there was no way Ava could be against it. Clearly, once more, she had been wrong.

What did she have to do to get Ava to let her back in? she wondered, frustration flashing through her as she heaved a box against the wall. She'd traded places, booked a spa session, reorganised her basement, and yet Ava didn't want to spend one night together eating pizza and watching films. They used to spend hours together, almost every day.

Don't give up, she told herself, wiping the sweat from her brow. They were talking again, right? The girls were talking too. And Ava did appreciate swapping houses with her. This was a big step forward. All her friend needed was a little more time. She had promised they'd always be friends. Emily had to believe she meant that, because she couldn't take more of the coldness. She *couldn't*.

Ava carefully placed the last box on top of the others in the corner, then Emily locked the door and they went upstairs. Ava gulped down a glass of water, and Emily hurried to the toilet, taking the opportunity to slather on yet more of Ava's products. God, she was going to miss this place.

'Could I have the key for the storage room?' Ava asked, when Emily came back into the lounge.

Hurt flared inside Emily. Did Ava not trust her that much now? She needed the key to ensure nothing else was moved, despite Emily's promise?

'Sure.' Emily made a show out of looking in her pocket, trying to buy time. She knew it was stupid, but she didn't want to give it back. Holding onto it meant she'd have a reason to talk to Ava again if she needed to – a kind of insurance. Besides, how often would Ava need it, anyway? She probably wouldn't discover it was missing until weeks later. 'Oh, I'm so silly,' she said, hitting her head. 'I forgot, I put the keyring back in the drawer when I was up there just now. I was thinking about tonight with Sophie and wasn't paying attention.'

'I'll run up and make sure it's in the right place. I'll never find it again in Dan's office if not. I need to change, anyway,' Ava said. 'This shirt is filthy.'

'Of course.' Emily smiled, but her heart was beating fast. Oh God. If Ava went upstairs now, not only would she see that Emily had been lying, but she'd spot that Emily had been sleeping in her room and not the guest room, like she'd set up.

'Oh, wait! What's the time?' She made her eyes wide. 'I think Sophie's teacher said they would get out early today – I can't remember why. They were doing one of those end-of-year activities; there's so much to keep track of. Do you mind if we go now?'

Ava shrugged. 'I guess not. Not if you don't mind sitting in the car with me all sweaty like this! Come on, then. We don't want Sophie to be waiting. Lexi gets so anxious if I'm not there.'

Emily nodded and followed Ava outside, exhaling in relief.

They went into the bright sun and got into the car, and Ava expertly drove the short distance to the school. Ava's phone buzzed, and Emily glanced at it in the holder between the seats. 'It's Dan,' she said. 'Do you want me to answer?'

Ava clamped her lips together. 'No, let it ring. It's fine. I'll call him later.'

Emily looked at Ava, noticing her jaw clenched with tension. Had they fought about Dan mentioning Alfie to Lexi? But then, things hadn't been right between them for years – at least from what she had seen from a distance, mainly at school concerts and events. They hardly ever looked at each other as they sat and watched Lexi, each turning and chatting to the parent beside them rather than each other. A memory of how they were when she'd first met them – the loving glances, the quick touches on the hand, the smiles – filled her head. It was such a contrast from the couple they used to be that sometimes it was hard to believe they were the same people.

Well, maybe they weren't the same people, she thought. She certainly wasn't the same girl who'd left Norwich. The one who could make almost as much money in one night as she made here in a week.

Sometimes, she missed how easy that had been. It had been risky, sure, but the rewards were more than worth it, and the men... well, they deserved what they got for thinking she was easy pickings. Of course she had to be careful, but she got better and better throughout the years, choosing only men she knew for sure were married, usually by googling them when they came in on work trips. There were signs, too, apart from the evidence online: the sidelong glances they gave women as they passed; the drinks and flirtatious behaviour increasing the longer they were away from their wives. Behind the reception desk, she was an invisible observer.

It was almost too easy. She'd gaze into the bar until her shift was over. Then she'd change from her uniform, let down her hair, and saunter over under the guise of waiting for her taxi home. No men ever recognised her as the receptionist, which went to show how invisible she really was. Barely anyone who worked there recognised her, either, which was just as well. She'd smile and start chatting, and they'd always take her bait.

When the men were drunk, she'd go with them to their room where they'd drink some more. She didn't even need to sleep with them; simply slipped something in their drink that knocked them out. They were pretty much comatose with alcohol anyway by that point. That was when she'd start filming, taking pictures and recording, whatever she could. She'd undress them, drape herself over them, then ease out of the room. A few days later, she'd send the photos with a threatening note to tell all if they didn't pay up. These men had everything, and they were throwing it away on tawdry one-night stands. They didn't deserve what they had. She didn't feel guilty at all.

It had worked like a dream until she'd got pregnant.

They pulled up to the school, and Ava turned towards Emily in surprise. 'No other parents are here. I thought you said Sophie was getting out early.'

'I thought so too.' Emily feigned confusion. 'That email...' She picked up her phone as if she was looking for the message. 'I can't find it now, but I'm certain that's what it said.' She shook her head. 'I must be wrong, though. I'm sorry. There's been so much going on.'

'I'm sure staying in another house didn't help, either,' Ava said, and Emily swung towards her. 'Look, I want to talk to you.' Her tone was almost warm, like she used to sound years ago. Emily felt a glow light up inside as she met Ava's eyes: that familiar feeling of being seen. God, she'd missed that.

'Fire away.' She basked in the warmth that engulfed them.

'I appreciate you doing this for me and Lexi,' Ava said. 'I really do.'

'It's my pleasure. You know that.' Emily reached out to

touch her arm, eager to grow that sense of connection. 'I'm so glad we're talking again. I really did miss you.' That warmth got bigger. 'I was thinking that we should get the girls together this summer. Maybe we can all take a trip to the beach or something. They'd love that.'

But Ava was biting her lip as she moved away from Emily, and Emily felt that glow dim. What was Ava going to say? They were connecting again, right? Maybe she was coming on too strong, too quickly. Or maybe Ava was still upset about the basement. Had she scared her off now?

Just in time, the school bell rang and the teachers opened the doors.

'Oh, here's Lexi.' Emily forced a bright smile to cover her emotions as Lexi hugged her mum, her brain churning. She couldn't let Ava walk back out of her life after she'd got this close again. But what could she do?

She had a solid foothold right now, she thought. She had the storage-room key as insurance, of course. But she had more: she had the *house*. What if she came up with something to stay behind this evening? If she and Lexi were there, Ava would have to interact with her. She couldn't shut her out – literally. She tilted her head, an idea jigging in her brain. Ava wouldn't be happy, but she'd understand it was a simple slip-up. And it would be worth it in the end, if it got her more time. More time to make up for today, and to solidify the tentative strand between them.

'Hi, Lexi,' Emily said, getting out of the car. 'Good day?'

Lexi ducked her head, nodding shyly. 'Lex, we're going to head back home tonight, OK?' Ava said, getting out and putting her arms around her daughter. 'We'll go to Emily's and get packed up, then make our way over later this evening.'

'No.' Panic crossed Lexi's face, and her cheeks drained of colour. 'I can't go back there, Mum.'

'Honey, it's fine.' Ava squeezed Lexi's arm, and Emily

admired her patience. Honestly, if Sophie acted like that, she wouldn't have time for it. But then, Sophie never behaved that way. From the very beginning, she'd been so independent and easy-going. 'You'll be fine. It's probably safer at our place than at Emily's.'

'No.' Lexi was shaking her head. 'I can't go back there. Not until they find the person who did this.'

Emily met Ava's eyes over the top of their heads and raised her eyebrows. 'You're both welcome to stay at ours as long as you want. You know that. I don't mind at all.' She paused. 'I can understand why you don't want to go back, though, Lexi,' she continued, although she couldn't. That place was alarmed to the hilt, and Ava was right: it was much safer than at Emily's. 'It's hard – and scary – when someone close to you has died in those circumstances.'

Lexi flinched. '*Died?*' Her wide eyes swung towards Ava. 'I thought you said Mr Bhandari was OK?'

Ava swallowed, her features tight. Emily could see how angry she was that this had come out, but she was trying her best not to show it.

'Oh my goodness, I'm so sorry,' Emily said, pretending innocence. 'I forgot she didn't know.'

'He's dead? Mr Bhandari?' Lexi's face drained of colour.

Ava put a hand on her daughter's arm. 'He had another heart attack in hospital,' she said quietly. 'This time it was so big, he couldn't recover. Mrs Bhandari has gone to stay with her daughter for a while.'

Lexi's face was so pale that Emily thought she might pass out. God, that child was nervy.

'I thought you told me he was going to be fine?'

Ava bit her lip. 'I thought he was. I'm sorry.' She tried to draw Lexi close, but Lexi pulled away.

'I can't believe you didn't tell me. You lied to me.' Lexi

looked her mum straight in the face. 'There's no way I can go back there now, Mum.'

Emily tried to hide a victorious smile. Mission accomplished, although Ava wasn't best pleased. She'd make it up to her, though.

'I understand, Lex.' Ava's voice was soft. 'But staying away from home isn't going to help things.' She paused. 'And you don't need to worry. The police have told me they have a suspect in custody.'

'They do?' Emily raised her eyebrows in surprise. She hadn't heard anything about that. Ava met her gaze with a harsh look, and Emily got the message. They didn't have anyone. Ava was simply trying to get her daughter to come back home.

Lexi collapsed into her mother's arms as relief washed over her face. 'I'm so happy they've got someone.' Her voice was muffled as she leaned into her mum. She raised her head. 'Who is it?'

'Just some lowlife,' Ava mumbled. 'Probably one of those men on mopeds who swipe parcels or something. They might have seen the open door and taken advantage of it.' She tucked Lexi's hair behind her ears. 'So we can go back now, all right?'

'I guess so.' Lexi nodded, and Emily's heart dropped. *Shit.*

'Right, well.' Emily forced a smile. 'I'll see you tonight, then.' She'd have to think of something else now.

'See you tonight.' Ava handed her the car keys and headed down the street, leaving Emily standing alone, waiting for her daughter.

TWELVE
LEXI

I'm on autopilot as we walk to Emily's, not seeing what's in front of me. It was such a good day until this. I hung out with Sophie and her friends again at break, and we talked about music and the bands they like. I actually had something to say, but now... now, I'm trying to breathe. I'm trying to keep the tears from falling from my eyes. I can't believe he's dead. That he'll never come back to the house again. I'll never see him out in his garden, or hear him humming a song like an out-of-tune bullfrog. He'll never wave at me when I put out the bins. Put out my packages.

Oh God.

Poor Mrs Bhandari. She loved him so much. I used to watch them sometimes: from my room, I could see down into a small corner of their lounge. I remember how once I saw them dancing, Mr Bhandari's arm around her as he held her tight. They were barely moving, but they looked so happy. So different from Mum and Dad, who seem like they're miles apart. Well, they usually are.

At least she has her daughter, I think, dashing the tears from my eyes before Mum can see. I've never met her, but I've heard her voice mingling with theirs; their laughter like a happy family should be. I wince. *Happy family*. I wish I had that.

I glance at my mum, anger circling inside. I know she's trying to protect me, but how could she not tell me Mr Bhandari died? How could she lie like that, right to my face? Why does she think I'm not strong enough to hear the truth? I know I'm only eleven, but I'm not a baby, and knowing what happened is better than being in the dark. Her thinking that I can't handle it makes me feel like I really *am* weak.

At least they found the man. Mum wouldn't lie about that, I'm sure. He won't come back for me, if it is the same person who fought with Mr Bhandari, and it definitely sounds like it is. I bite my lip as another thought hits. Will he tell the police what I've been doing? I push the notion away. They don't care what an eleven-year-old is up to. Not when they have a murderer in custody. I shiver. A murderer. Because even if the burglar didn't kill him outright, he might as well have. Mr Bhandari is gone, and it's all because of him.

No. I gulp in air. It's all because of me.

'You OK, Lex?' Mum glances over at me. She puts a hand on my arm, but I move away. I don't want her to touch me. 'I'm sorry I didn't tell you about Mr Bhandari. You were already so scared, and there was so much going on. I didn't want to make it worse, but I would have told you eventually. And I only found out they had a suspect in custody today,' she added quickly.

'Right.' I try to calm down, but anger is still snapping inside. I trusted her, and now it makes me wonder what else she's lied to me about. 'So you're not hiding anything more from me?' Alfie's name beats like a pulse in my head. I get that she didn't want to talk about him before, and I didn't ask. But now I am asking her to be open and honest with me, maybe for the first time in my life. I'm asking her to trust me – to trust that I can handle it. Because whoever Alfie is, he's clearly someone important. I could tell by her reaction when I said his name. And why else would Dad have a whole folder with his name on his computer, if not?

He could be the reason for the coldness in our house. *He* could be the reason she's unhappy, not me. And that would change everything.

Something passes between us – something I can't identify – and then she shakes her head.

'No,' she says finally, giving me that fake smile I've come to hate. 'Nothing else, I promise.'

Another rush of anger surges through me. Why won't she tell me? She really must think I'm too weak. Well, I don't need to rely on her. If I want to find out something, I'll do it myself. I take a deep breath, wondering if I can break into that folder. Dad's not the most techie, which is why it surprised me he had a password-protected folder. I bet he used the same password he uses for everything else. I can probably get into it, no problem.

I'll do it tonight when we're back home, I decide. I walk faster towards Emily's, and Mum glances over at me as she matches my pace. I speed up more, desperate to get away from her; desperate for time to move on.

The sooner we get through the evening, the sooner I can find out who Alfie is.

THIRTEEN
AVA

Ava hurried after her daughter, regret and guilt swirling inside. She hated lying to her. Of course she'd kept things from her before, but that wasn't lying. It was protecting her. But telling her that they had someone in custody had *definitely* been a lie. As far as she knew, the police hadn't been able to make any headway over what had happened that night. It was just that she needed to get home.

She swallowed, picturing the look in Lexi's eyes when she'd asked if there was anything else she wanted to tell her. She couldn't have been asking again about Alfie, could she? God, she was going to kill Dan. Anger and disbelief slid through her as she remembered how he'd said they should tell Lexi what had happened. How could he think of exposing their daughter to such pain and loss? She froze, remembering that she'd forgotten to put the laptop in the storage room with the box. Emily had rushed them out of the house before she'd had a chance. She would put the laptop in there when they got back tonight.

They went inside Emily's flat, and Lexi hurried straight to the bedroom.

'Start gathering up your things,' Ava called, but her voice

was drowned out by the slamming of the door, quickly followed by the blasting of Sophie's terrible music. Sighing, she thought of Emily and her daughter, curled up in front of the huge telly with steaming pepperoni pizza, laughing at whatever film they'd chosen to watch. She wrinkled her nose as she stared around the tiny space. There wasn't even a TV, and it certainly didn't lend itself to cosy family nights in. Was that why Emily spent so much time at work and Sophie so much time in her bedroom? In a way, she could almost understand. Anything was better than staring at the four walls in this depressing place.

Her phone buzzed and she jerked, grimacing as it clattered from her lap to the floor. 'Shit.' She reached down to grab it, but she couldn't see it. Sighing, she got down on hands and knees. Was it under the sofa? She peered into the dark space. She didn't want to reach under there. She plunged a hand in, eyebrows rising in surprise when she touched metal. She ran her fingers around its contours. A metal box.

She pulled it into the light. It was a safe, with a combination lock on it. She winced as she lifted it. Whatever was inside was super heavy. She tilted her head. Why would Emily have a safe here? And what did she have valuable enough to keep inside? Ava shoved it back under the sofa. It was none of her business. If she lived in this place, then she might have a safe too.

Ah, here was her phone. She squinted at the screen, wondering why Emily was texting her. Then she scanned the message, her heart sinking.

Sophie ill with stomach bug. So sorry. Probably best if you stay away for now – wouldn't wish this on worst enemy. Hopefully better tomorrow.

Christ, she thought, sitting back on the sagging sofa. This was going from bad to worse. Honestly, she wished she'd never swapped houses in the first place. She wanted to get back home, but she wasn't about to expose Lexi to what sounded like a horrific flu. Lexi was already tired and rundown as it was after everything. It wouldn't take much for her to pick up a virus.

Sighing, she texted Emily back that she wished Sophie well and that she'd check in tomorrow. Then, she got to her feet and put on the kettle, thinking even the tea here was flat and unappealing.

'Lex?' she called. There was no answer, so she knocked on the door. 'Lex, we can't go back home tonight. Sophie's ill. But do you want to go out to the cinema? We could catch that new Disney one you've been wanting to see.' If they couldn't go home, at least they could go out. A film at the cinema on a school night was a rare treat, and she knew Lexi would jump at it.

But Lexi's face when she opened the door was cold. 'I'd rather stay in,' she said. 'And that Disney film is for babies.' The door closed again.

Ava turned and sank onto the sofa. Lexi was clearly upset about Mr Bhandari, not that Ava could blame her. In the past, though, her daughter had always come to her when she needed comfort. But ever since Lexi had asked who Alfie was, there was a barrier between them that had never been there before. She wanted to talk to her daughter, but what if she started asking more questions?

She sighed, rubbing her eyes. The best thing was to leave it alone. Once they got home in their familiar environment, she was sure all of this would fade into the background – for Lexi, anyway. The hustle and bustle of getting ready for the class party would be the ideal distraction.

The phone buzzed, and Dan's name flashed up again. She shoved it under a pillow. She'd talk to him once he was back. He knew how she felt now, and anyway, this wasn't a conversation they could have over the phone, with so much distance between them. She needed him to be in their home and to understand what he was risking; that even if he found the space empty and cold, it was their daughter's safe place. If he couldn't handle staying quiet, then that was his issue. Telling Lexi about the past simply wasn't an option.

Because then, no wall would be strong enough to contain the wreckage. Then, everything would be blown apart.

FOURTEEN
EMILY

Emily set down the phone after reading Ava's message, relief flooding through her. She couldn't stay here forever, as much as she would like to. But maybe she could stretch out Sophie's illness, at least until the class party and Dan came home. A shiver of pleasure went through her at the thought of being here to help and organise the whole thing. She and Ava had always worked well together. She smiled, remembering when Dan had been on a work trip and they'd spent hours assembling the nursery furniture. It'd been tedious and tiring, but Emily hadn't been able to remember having so much fun. Standing side by side, pouring Prosecco in the shining sun, was bound to bring them together more.

She stared into the mirror. God, she looked so different to the woman who'd got pregnant all of those years ago. Anger bubbled up as she recalled the moment she'd stared at the test, unable to believe her eyes as panic gripped her. He'd told her he was using a condom. How could this be? True, she'd had her eyes closed. She'd lain there as she'd thought he'd been putting it on. He had been drunk, though. She'd been drunk too. God, what an idiot she'd been to think he was any different.

He'd been the one to start talking to her that night, buying her drinks as he asked questions about her life. For the first time, someone seemed interested, and she'd lapped it up. When he'd asked her back to his room, the thought of taking photos didn't even enter her mind. She didn't want to threaten him; to be that person with him. She wanted him to want *her*. She wanted to feel that from someone, from someone like him: wearing an expensive-looking suit, heavy gold watch, heady cologne, not to mention good-looking and groomed, miles from the rough men she'd grown up with. It didn't matter that he was wearing a wedding ring. For men, she knew that meant nothing, anyway.

But that moment of being wanted hadn't lasted. As soon as he'd finished, he'd rolled off her and asked her to leave. She'd crept away, humiliated and raging at herself. What had she been thinking? For God's sake, she didn't even have photos to blackmail him.

Then a few weeks later, she'd found out she was pregnant. Once she'd calmed down, she'd come up with a plan to use it to her advantage. She'd go to see him. She'd show him the test and tell him she was pregnant with his child. She'd tell him that she'd let his wife know what had happened, and then she'd demand a lump sum to leave. He would pay to get rid of her, she was certain of it. Look how fast he'd got rid of her after they'd slept together. Once she had the money, she'd terminate the pregnancy and be one step closer to the life she wanted.

Hands shaking, she'd gone back out to the reception desk and looked up the record of the man she'd been with that night. He was from a London suburb, so on her next day off, she'd booked a train and headed to his house to tell him. It wasn't exactly something she could say over the phone, and she didn't want to give him the opportunity to hang up and block her – or to accuse her of lies. She patted her handbag, where she had several tests clearly showing she was going to have a baby.

London was noisy and busy, the heat and rush of the underground overwhelming her. But when she got off the Tube close to where he lived, it was like a different world. She wandered in the direction of his address, her mouth dropping at the sprawling houses. She paused in front of an estate agent's window, shaking her head at the million-pound price tags some places had. Forget Norwich; this area was next level. A bit of hope and optimism burst through her. If he lived here, then he clearly had a lot of money – maybe more than she'd thought. This could be a shortcut to the world she'd dreamed of. Perhaps even better.

She turned onto the street and walked down it, then paused as the number of his house came into view. As she waited, the door opened and a woman came out... a *pregnant* woman, her belly obvious from a distance, proudly on display under her jumper. Emily blinked as she watched the woman get into the car, then expertly back away. This man had slept with her when his own wife had been pregnant? What an absolute piece of shit. But then, given what she'd seen from men over the past few years, nothing surprised her anymore. This could work in her favour, though. If he had a pregnant wife, he'd pay more for her to be out of his life.

Anger spurring her forward, she hurried down the walkway and rang the doorbell. She waited and waited, but no one came. She rang again, that anger growing with every second. She knew he was home. She could hear a TV blaring inside and see the lights. Did he know she was there?

'Open up!' she yelled, conscious of her voice echoing down the quiet street. 'Open the door!'

But it remained firmly closed, and her mind raced frantically. Of all the scenarios, she'd never thought of one where she couldn't talk to him. She got out her phone and punched in the number she'd scribbled down from his reservation record, listening as it rang and rang then disconnected, without clicking through to voicemail. She wasn't going to give up, though. She hadn't come this far for nothing. She'd kept banging on the door, kept shouting, until he'd had no choice but to open it.

But then it had all fallen apart.

She went up the stairs now and said goodnight to Sophie, then padded into Ava's room and closed the door. She inhaled the clean fresh floral scent that seemed to permeate the air, even after a few days of Ava not being here, as if her presence lingered. Then she went into the bathroom and stood under the shower, slathering herself in Ava's products one final time.

When she came out, she opened the heavy drawer and took out a pair of Ava's silk pyjamas. She knew Ava didn't like her wearing them, but after today, she wanted to feel as close to her as possible. As she slid them across her skin, it was like a comforting hug. She pulled back the duvet and crawled into the bed, letting the house wrap around her one more time while pledging this wouldn't be the end.

If she had her way, it would be the beginning.

FIFTEEN
EMILY

Emily jolted awake at the noises coming from downstairs. Someone was inside. She froze in the darkness, her heart beating fast as she listened to footsteps echoing on the marble tiles. Could it be a burglar? Slowly, she reached to where she'd put her mobile on the bedside table. The footsteps continued as her mind raced. Should she call the police? But the alarm hadn't gone off, and she was certain she'd set it. That meant whoever was downstairs had the code to the alarm.

'Ava?'

Emily gasped as Dan's voice cut through the silence. What the hell was he doing here? Hadn't Ava said that he wasn't coming back until the day of the party? Oh God. What would he do when he found her in this bed? In his wife's bed, wearing her pyjamas and smelling like all her products? She knew she should call out; that she should say something, but the words were jammed inside her. Her pulse raced as he came into the bedroom. She stayed unmoving in the dark, holding her breath as he eased into the en-suite. Then, as slowly as she could, she crept from the bed. She'd go into the guest room now, where she should have slept in the first place. Then she'd come out and make her presence known.

'*Emily?*' Dan flicked on the light when he came out of the en-suite, and she froze. Oh shit. 'What the hell are you doing? Where's Ava?'

Emily's heart pounded. 'I'm sorry,' she said. 'Ava isn't back yet. She's still at my place.'

Dan blinked. 'At your place? What do you mean? Lexi told me she was coming here tonight. I tried to ring Ava to say that I was on my way, but she didn't answer.'

Emily swallowed. 'They were supposed to come home, but Sophie was ill, so they stayed at mine. I didn't want Lexi to get sick.' She forced a smile, praying he wouldn't notice that the covers of the bed were rumpled where she'd been sleeping.

But he wasn't looking at the bed. He was staring at her with a strange expression as if he was realising something for the first time. Emily ran a hand over her face. With her hair in a ponytail and no make-up, she knew she looked about ten years younger. Fear darted through her. It couldn't... he couldn't...

Emily grabbed her suitcase. 'I'll get out of your way now, OK? I—'

'Wait. *Wait.*' Dan put up a hand, and she froze again. She wanted to run, but his gaze pinned her in place. 'I can't believe I didn't see it,' he said quietly as if he was speaking to himself. 'I can't believe it.'

Emily's heart beat faster.

'I knew I'd seen you before,' he was saying. 'But I didn't know where.' He shook his head incredulously. 'I do now.' He met her eyes, staring harder.

She clenched her jaw, praying he didn't remember.

'You came to the house. You asked if I'd ever been to Norwich.' He rubbed his head. 'And then you—' His face twisted.

'Please don't tell Ava.' Emily cut him off. He couldn't tell her. She couldn't stand it if Ava blocked her out again – permanently this time, because no way would she want to be friends if she knew. The thought was unbearable.

'How could you even *dare* to be a part of our lives after what you did? And why would you want to be?' He let out a puff of air. 'Are you some kind of crazy stalker?'

She held his gaze, her mind flashing back to the moment she'd realised Ava lived in the house she'd visited months earlier – that Ava had been the pregnant woman she'd seen from afar, leaving that day. She knew it had been a risk moving to Richmond, but the town had matched her vision perfectly of where she wanted to live. A great job had come up at a reputable hotel, and she hadn't been able to resist applying. Never in a million years had she expected to run into Dan again, let alone the woman she'd spotted at the house.

When Ava had taken her back home one evening to show her the nursery, she'd nearly died when she'd seen it was the same place. She'd shrunk back, praying Dan wouldn't recognise her, relieved when he barely gave her a second glance. She did look different than the woman he'd met, though. Her face had filled out, her hair was much lighter, and she was wearing makeup. She'd worried he might realise who she was the more time she spent with Ava, but he didn't seem that interested. His whole world was centred around his wife.

His voice started shaking. 'You need to leave now. You need to get out of this house.'

Emily shook her head. 'I'm so sorry,' she said. 'Honestly. Don't tell Ava. Don't tell her what I did. She'll be so upset. It will hurt her, you know it will. And you don't want to do that, right? Haven't you both been through enough?'

Dan jerked back, and she flinched at the anger on his face. 'Don't worry about us,' he said in a cold voice. 'I'll tell her whatever I want. It's not up to you to decide. And I want you out of our lives. For good.'

Emily shook her head again, harder this time. He couldn't do this. Not now – now that she finally had the chance to reconnect with Ava. Maybe she could talk to him and explain. That she needed some way to survive, some way for her and her daughter to survive. He was a father. He'd understand. He had to.

'Dan...' She tried to touch his arm, but he shook her off. 'Look, I understand you're upset. I'll go now, if you want. We can talk about this later, when things are calmer. I can explain. I'll explain everything.' The words tumbled from her in desperation. 'Just promise you won't tell Ava until we talk.' She pulled her suitcase from the corner and started gathering her things, eager to show him she'd do whatever he wanted if he'd only give her this chance.

She glanced up at him to see if he would agree, but his face was still hard as he reached for his mobile. Fear shot through her. Was he going to call Ava?

'Don't. Please, don't.' Her hand shot out to grab the phone before he could make the call.

He jerked in surprise. 'What are you doing? Give that back to me.'

'No.' Emily gripped the mobile tightly, her heart thumping so loudly she was sure he could hear it too. 'Not until you promise you won't call her now.'

'This is crazy.' He met her eyes. '*You're* crazy. And there's nothing you can say that would make me want to have you in our lives. You need to give me that phone, and then you need to go.'

The two of them stood in silence for a minute. She couldn't give him the mobile. Not if he was going to call Ava. Not if he was going to make sure she'd never be back in her life again.

'Right.' Dan let out an incredulous laugh. 'Well, if you won't give me the mobile, then I'll activate the alarm downstairs. The police will be here in minutes. I'm sure they'll be interested in what you've done.'

Emily sucked in her breath as panic rose. *The police*. He couldn't do that. Her mind raced as he moved from the bedroom and into the dim light of the corridor towards the stairs. Eager to stop him reaching the steps, she kicked the suitcase across the polished floorboards and out to the corridor. It rolled easily towards him, skidding in front just as he was about to step down. He stumbled over the top and, as if in slow motion, swayed in the air before tumbling down the stairs, one after the other, until he landed in a heap at the bottom.

Fuck. Holding her breath, Emily flew down the steps. Her hand went to her mouth as she stared at him. He was lying so, so still, with blood seeping from his head. What the hell had she done? Was he... she swallowed. Was he still alive? She hadn't meant for him to fall. She'd simply wanted to stop him. And now... Gingerly, she knelt beside him, sighing with relief when she noticed his chest was moving up and down. Thank God.

But what was she going to do? Not only would she never see Ava again, but she could forget ever having the life she'd been striving for. He could go to the police, say she'd attacked him in his own home, and charge her with assault. She could end up in prison, and Sophie... She froze at the thought of her daughter down the corridor sleeping. Could she have heard anything? She padded up the stairs and eased open the door to Sophie's room. The light was off and everything was silent, thank goodness.

She went back down to Dan. His eyes were still closed, and a huge bump was rising where he'd hit his head, but thankfully the blood wasn't flowing as quickly, and he didn't seem hurt anywhere else. She gazed at him, fear zinging through her. She'd made things so much worse. How could she convince him to stay quiet after causing him to fall down the stairs? If he'd been angry before, now he'd be downright furious.

She needed time to think, and Dan... Dan needed time to calm down; time to see she hadn't meant to hurt him, both then and now. He could wake up any second, though. He could put an end to everything, and she couldn't have that. What could she do? She breathed in, an idea slowly coming into focus in her head. The basement. There was that storage room down there – the storage room to which she still had the key. She could put him in there, maybe. He'd recover in the dark, cool space. He'd come to his senses, and she'd have a chance to think of a way to keep him quiet.

She looked at the man stretched out in front of her on the floor. He was tall and solid. He must weigh treble what she did. How was she going to get him down the stairs?

She lifted his arm and tugged, but he barely moved. She grabbed his legs and tried to pull him, but he was so heavy that he only slid an inch or two. She tried to roll him, but he was too bulky to turn over. She bit her lip, her mind spinning. Maybe she could put him on something and drag him that way? She went back upstairs and took the duvet from Ava's bed, then managed bit by bit to get it under him. Slowly, sweat dripping off her now, she dragged him to the door by the basement stairs and opened it up. Her heart sank as she peered into the darkness below. The stairs were narrow and steep. There was no way she was going to get him down there on her own.

She needed Sophie's help, but how could she explain what had happened? Sophie knew she worked hard to make a good life for both of them, but she didn't know the half of it. Emily had never told her anything about the past and all she had done, and Sophie never asked... not about any other family; not even about her father. She had Emily, and that had been enough. How could Emily begin to explain all she had been through?

Besides, Sophie was only eleven, for goodness' sake, and although she was mature, this was too much. But she didn't have a choice. Unless she wanted Ava to know everything, she needed to get Dan in the basement. Perhaps she could spin the story somehow, so that she wasn't the one at fault? After all, Dan had surprised her. She hadn't planned on any of this happening. It wasn't like she'd got herself into this deliberately.

Maybe she could say that Dan had attacked her? That he'd hit her, thinking perhaps that she was a burglar, and that she'd had to defend herself? In light of the attack next door, that made sense. She'd tell Sophie that he'd been in such a frenzy of panic and fear, he was like another person, and that now she was worried what he would do to her. If they put him in the basement, then he could recover, she'd talk to him when he was calmer, and together they'd sort it out. Otherwise...

Sophie would agree, Emily thought. She wouldn't want her mother to get hurt.

She scooped up Dan's mobile from the floor and shoved it into her pocket, thanking God that he and Ava were in the midst of an argument and wouldn't be talking much, if at all – not that they talked much, anyway. Then she went down the darkened corridor to her daughter's room. 'Soph?'

Sophie stirred in bed, then opened her eyes. 'Mum? What time is it?' Her mouth stretched in a yawn.

'It's the middle of the night. But...' She bit her lip. 'I need your help. Nothing to be scared about, but something happened.'

Sophie's eyes widened. 'What?'

'Dan came home early,' Emily said, trying to keep her voice calm. 'He...' She swallowed. 'I heard a noise, so I got up to see what it was. He must have thought I was a burglar, because he tried to grab me. We fought and I managed to shove him away, but he fell and hit his head. He's knocked out.'

'Oh my God. Mum!' Sophie sat up. 'Are you all right? Is he? Where is he now? Did you call the police?' The questions tumbled from her like an avalanche.

'I'm fine,' Emily said, putting a hand on her daughter. 'And he's OK too.' 'OK' might be pushing it, she thought, but he was better than she'd feared initially, anyway. 'He's downstairs. He's still out.' Hopefully. 'And I didn't call the police,' she continued. 'The thing is...' She paused, trying to think of how to say something that was plausible. 'Well, Dan, he's always been aggressive. Ava was afraid of his temper. He was in such a state that he didn't stop hitting me, even when I told him who I was.'

'You need to tell the police, Mum.' Sophie's eyes were wide. 'You can explain it all. Ava gave us permission to be here. You were defending yourself.'

Emily swallowed hard against the rising guilt. She hated lying to her daughter like this. 'I know. But I'm worried what he'll be like when he comes to. I mean, I did push him. If he's going to be angry, then we need to get him to a secure location. And I'm worried about what he'll say to the police if he speaks to them before properly calming down. He could tell them that I attacked him first.'

Sophie's eyes were filling with tears, her face twisted in fear. 'No. He wouldn't do that, would he?'

'I don't want him to do that, either, but I can't be sure. Not when he's in so much pain, and not in his right mind.' She paused. 'So I was thinking we can put him downstairs, in the basement where it's nice and cool and there's no light that could hurt his head, and give him time to recover. There's a door we can secure to make sure he stays safe. Then we can all sit down and have a proper conversation once he's better.'

Sophie stared at her. 'You want to lock Dan in the basement?' Her voice rose on every word, and Emily drew back. If you put it like that, it did sound crazy. But what choice did they have? She wasn't going to let this ruin her friendship with Ava... ruin her life. God, how could she have been so *stupid*?

'Yes,' Emily said. 'I do. Until this whole situation cools down a bit.'

Sophie kept staring. 'And you think locking him up will help cool it down?'

Emily nodded. 'Soph, I know it sounds insane. But we have to. He's going to be furious when he wakes up. We need to have some kind of control over him before he calls the police.' Sophie was silent, and Emily could see her words were starting to make sense. Some kind of sense, anyway. 'Ava thinks he's away for a bit longer, so we still have time. Neither she nor I had any idea he was coming home today.'

Sophie was silent for a minute, then nodded. 'Fine.' Emily helped her out of bed, and then the two of them went back down the corridor. They froze as they heard groaning coming from below. Oh God. Could he be awake? Was he trying to get up?

They edged down the stairs and to the basement door, relief pouring into Emily when she saw Dan's eyes were closed and he was quiet again. But they had to act fast before he came to.

'Help me get him down the stairs before he wakes up,' she said. Sophie stayed frozen, and Emily reached out to take her arm. 'Come on.'

She snapped on the basement light, and together, they worked to heave Dan down the narrow stairs: Emily at the bottom to prevent him from tumbling forward, and Sophie keeping his head stable at the top. Thankfully, although he groaned a few times, his eyes stayed closed.

Finally, they reached the bottom. Emily took the key for the storage room from her pocket, then opened the door. 'Right, let's get him in here.' They dragged him across the floor, then threw in some blankets, pillows and a jug of water.

'What if he needs to go to the toilet?' Sophie said, making a face. Emily shoved in a bucket that was in the corner, then closed the door and locked it.

'That will have to do for now,' she said. 'I mean, he won't be in there long. Just until morning.' She bit her lip, praying he'd agree to stay quiet... or she'd come up with something to keep him quiet.

'Right. Let's get to bed,' she said to Sophie. As they climbed the stairs back to their bedrooms, Emily thought of the dark red stain on the duvet, and she wondered if she'd be able to sleep at all.

She shouldn't, anyway. Not before she thought of something to fix the mess she'd made.

And she'd better think fast.

SIXTEEN
LEXI

My eyes fly open as the alarm on my mobile chirps from under my pillow. I turn it off quickly, cursing when I realise it's seven thirty: the normal time I get up for breakfast, and not the earlier time I'd thought I'd set it for. After Mum said we weren't going back last night, I decided I'd sneak home this morning to check Dad's computer. Mum will be furious I've left on my own, but I'm furious at *her*. Anyway, it will be so much easier to nose around Dad's things while Emily is still there. I'll tell her I need something for school, and she'll let me be. She's always super nice to me. I think she knows I don't have friends, since she used to try to get me and Sophie together for playdates when we were younger. I would have loved that, but of course Mum said no. She never lets me go anywhere.

How am I going to sneak past my mother now? Usually by this time, she's clanking around in the kitchen, the radio blaring and every curtain wide open as if she's trying to *force* happiness in. Mum always says she wants to be the first person to see her daughter's face every morning, a sentiment that used to make me go all warm and fuzzy inside. Now that I'm older, it annoys me, because I know that it doesn't make her happy. I shake my head, anger inside me rekindling as I think of how she lied to me, right to my face.

I sit up, eyebrows rising at the silence. Am I in luck? Is my mother having a lie-in? I slide from the covers and pull on my school uniform as quietly as I can, then take my backpack and ease into the lounge. I pause for a minute to write a message saying that I've forgotten something I need for class today at home. Mum's on the sofa under a blanket, her huddled form looking smaller and more deflated than I've ever seen. When she's awake, she seems like a soldier to me, as if she has a hard coating, ready to defend. Sometimes, I'm not sure if she's defending me or herself.

Seeing her like this makes me feel weird, so I hurry past her and open the door as quietly as I can. As I close it behind me, my heart pounds, waiting for her to shout out after me, but all is silent as I go down the stairs and into the dim grey light of the rainy morning.

It feels so strange to be out here alone while Mum is sleeping, I think, as I walk towards my house, the rain pelting my face. They've arrested whoever they think burgled Mr Bhandari, but I can't help glancing from left to right and looking behind me. God, I can't believe he's dead. Tears push at my eyes, and I try my best to hold them back.

Finally, I get to my house, expecting to open the door to light and the scent of toast and pancakes, like it always is in the morning. Instead, the curtains are drawn and it's dark inside. Are they not home? Maybe they've left already. Sophie is part of the dance club, and they're performing at the end-of-year concert. They might have an early practice. Or perhaps Sophie's still poorly and they haven't got up? I stand in front of the camera, and the door clicks open.

'Hello?' I call quietly, for some reason scared to be too loud. This doesn't feel like my home anymore. It's a strange place, and in a way, I feel like I shouldn't be here. But that's silly, I tell myself, as I walk towards the stairs. This *is* my home, even if I'd rather be somewhere else.

As I'm thinking that, I hear a curious sound coming from the basement. I tilt my head, trying to listen more closely. It sounds sort of like voices, followed by a scrape then a bang. My heart beats faster. Who's down there? Is it the burglar? Where *is* everyone?

'Oh!' Emily's voice comes from behind, and I swing round to face her, relief flooding through me as she closes the basement door. Thank goodness it was her down there. Maybe she was talking to herself or something. 'Lexi, hello! I didn't know you were coming by. I wish you would have called – Sophie's got the flu, and I don't want you to get sick. Everything all right?'

I nod. 'I'm sorry to barge in like this without telling you, but I need something for school, if that's OK? I forgot I have an assignment due today, and...' I stop talking as I realise she's not listening, so I go upstairs and into Dad's office as fast as I can. I slide into the chair and open the computer, remembering the last time I was here when I deleted the footage from the doorbell camera. I was so worried about me when I should have been worried about Mr Bhandari.

As quickly as I can, I navigate to the 'Alfie' folder. I put in the password Dad usually uses, but to my surprise, the folder doesn't open. I sit back, my mind spinning. What else would he use? On a whim, I enter my birthday, and... success! The file clicks open. God, sometimes Dad is so predictable, even when he thinks he isn't.

I sit back as photo after photo fills the screen, the thumbnails so small I can't quite make the images out. Holding my breath, I click onto one, and a picture of a tiny baby fills the screen. Who's that? I wonder. It must be Alfie, but... Quickly I scroll through one, then another, then more and more, my mind tumbling through various scenarios. Is this someone Dad knows? Obviously, I tell myself. But why is it a secret? And why did Mum act that way when I said Alfie's name?

I'm about halfway through the folder when one photo makes me stop. It's a picture of two babies, cuddling into each other in a cot. One of the babies looks like Alfie and the other...

The other looks like me.

I sit back in the chair. The other *is* me; I recognise the pink baby blanket that's wrapped around me. And Alfie has one exactly like it, but in blue. We're the same size and we look the same age. Is he... I almost don't want to think it, it feels so crazy. Instead, I click through more photos of us together, until I get to one that shows Mum, in hospital looking like she's just given birth, holding two babies.

Not one, but two.

Me and my brother. My *twin* brother.

I can't breathe. I can't do anything but stare at the screen. How can this be? How could I have a twin and not know anything about it? How could my parents not tell me? How could Mum look me in the eye and say she's not hiding anything else?

'Lexi?' Emily's voice floats up the stairs. 'Everything OK?'

I slam the computer lid shut. Everything's not OK. Everything's far from OK, but I don't know what to do. In a daze, I go down the stairs, smile at Emily, then grab my backpack and head to school. I have a brother.

I have a twin, and I don't know what happened to him. All I know is that he's not here. He's gone, and I don't know where.

I'm going to find out, though. I need to find out.

Because that could explain why I feel the way I do: alone, like there's something missing. Why Mum's so cold all the time. Why Dad can't bear to be home. Why I can't wait to get away. That could explain everything.

And if I have to rip apart this whole place – destroy this so-called family – to uncover the truth, then that's what I'll do.

SEVENTEEN
AVA

Ava awoke the next morning, stretching out on the uncomfortable sofa. *Please God, may Sophie be better today.* Please may this be the last morning here. She couldn't wait to get back to her place! To lock away anything that could harm her daughter, and to push Emily back to the fringes of her life. They'd been close once, but they never could be again. No one could understand what Ava had been through now – not even Dan. How could he?

She took in the barren, cold lounge once more, picturing Emily sleeping on this sofa for *years*. Of saving and scrimping, doing everything possible to make a life for her daughter. She sighed, thinking maybe there was one more thing they shared, after all. They both wanted the best for their daughters.

'Lex?' She poked her head around the corner, squinting in the dark. 'Lex?' She paused, but everything was silent. She snapped on the light. 'Lexi!' Her heart pounding, she scanned the room, but the bed was empty, and her daughter was nowhere to be seen. What the hell? Where was she? There was no way she could have snuck out without Ava noticing... was there?

'Lex!' She pounded on the bathroom door, then pushed it open. It was empty. She was gone. But where on earth would she go? And why?

Ava spied a note on the breakfast bar, and she streaked over to it, picking it up with shaking hands.

Need something at home, it said in Lexi's neatly slanted cursive that Ava had paid a fortune for her to take extra classes for. *Will go to school from there.*

Over my dead body you will, Ava thought, shaking with anger. How could she do this? When had Ava ever given her daughter permission to be out on her own? Lexi knew she wasn't allowed, no matter how much she begged or threatened to ask her father. Panic flashed through Ava at the thought of Dan, and how he'd wanted to tell Lexi about Alfie. How he'd wanted to show her the photos on the laptop – the laptop she'd forgotten to lock up.

Could he have told Lexi where to look? Was that why he'd been trying to call her last night? She didn't think he'd do that after their conversation, but could that have been why her daughter had left without saying a word? It was so unlike her. *Something* must have triggered her behaviour.

Ava threw on a coat and ducked into the pouring rain, cursing this whole situation as she rushed towards the house. If Lexi was planning to go to school from there, then she couldn't have left too long ago. Maybe Ava could catch her if she hurried. A quick glance at the tracker she'd installed to show her daughter's location confirmed she was still at the house.

Had she found the laptop? Was she looking at the photos this very second? Had she realised she had a brother? A *twin*?

Cars splashed past her and by the time Ava got to her place, she was absolutely drenched. She squished up to the door, conscious she had never looked worse. She hadn't even brushed her hair that morning. She glanced up at the camera and the door clicked open. She knew she should knock and wait, but if Lexi was in there, she wanted to get her out as fast as possible.

She stepped inside, blinking at the sight in front of her. Was that... was that Dan's tie? What was that doing here? He had a terrible habit of yanking off his ties and chucking them on the coat rack before coming inside. She'd spent years telling him to take the tie off upstairs where it belonged, but eventually she'd given up. In the grand scheme of things, it had seemed of little importance. She stared, her mind whirring. She didn't remember it being there before, but maybe Emily had found it under the side table in the entry and hung it there. There were probably no fewer than a dozen ties scattered around the place at any one time.

'Sophie!' She drew back in surprise as she noticed the girl sitting at the breakfast bar with a spoonful of cereal halfway to her mouth. Sophie's eyes widened and her face went pale, and Ava's heart sunk at the realisation that she may not have been ill at all. 'I thought you weren't feeling well! Your mum sent me a message that you were very poorly.'

Sophie's face went from white to red. 'I was feeling bad, that's true,' she stammered. 'Mum said I should stay home today and not go to school.'

'But your stomach is better now?' Ava eyed the huge bowl of cereal in front of her, and Sophie went redder.

'Um, yes, yeah. Much better, thanks.'

'Right.' *Had* Emily lied to her? Ava tilted her head. Whatever was going on, it wasn't Sophie's fault. The poor girl looked mortified – and terrified too. 'I'll talk to your mum about it. Don't worry. I'm only here because Lexi said she was going to drop by and get something before school. Have you seen her?' She poked her head in the direction of the stairs. 'Lex? Lexi! Are you up there?'

'Ava!' Emily's face drained of colour as she came into the room from the basement, quickly closing the door behind her.

Ava furrowed her brow, puzzled by their strange reactions. Why did they seem so worried she was here?

'You're looking for Lexi?' Emily asked. 'She left a few minutes ago.'

Ava's heart sank. She had missed her. She got her phone from her pocket and sure enough, Lexi was almost at school. Bloody tracker, she cursed. Sometimes, it took ages to update.

Emily put down the laundry basket. 'And not to be rude or anything, but you should probably go too. I don't want you to get sick.' She grimaced over at the laundry. 'We had quite a bad night last night.'

Ava peered at the basket, making out her favourite duvet cover with a huge brown stain. Oh God. So Sophie *had* been ill after all, then. Maybe that was why they looked so off-kilter: they were afraid she'd be upset about the duvet. What on earth had that child been eating? And why had she been in Ava's room? Ava tilted her head. Perhaps she'd been sick on Lexi's bed and needed a new place to sleep. It seemed Emily hadn't been lying, after all. She felt bad thinking that now. How many times had she thought Lexi was down for the count only for her to perk up thirty minutes later?

'You know what?' she said. 'Don't worry about the duvet. These things happen. Probably best to get rid of it. I'll buy another.' She paused. 'Did Lexi say why she was here?' It felt weird asking Emily, but she didn't have a choice. She needed to know.

'I think she said she had something due for school today and she needed to get it. Something like that.' Emily shrugged. 'If you leave now, you might be able to catch her.'

'OK.' Ava sighed in relief. She'd obviously read too much into this; Lexi might have forgotten about Alfie by now. Still, the very fact her daughter had run out without her sent chills down her spine. Anything could have happened, and she hadn't woken up to notice her leaving. At least she'd made it here all right, but that couldn't happen again. They had to come home, to a place that was secure, where she could trust her daughter was safe.

Where she could keep her safe – from everything.

'Look, I'm sorry,' Ava said. 'I don't want to force you out of here, but we need to get back to normal. Lexi needs her home back and everything she's used to. All of this has really thrown her.' Her heart pounded as she thought of her daughter in the wet, grim morning on her own; of how she could have found out about her brother. Thank goodness she hadn't.

'Sophie's fine now, and even if she had been ill, I've already been exposed to any germs simply by being here,' she continued. 'Do you think you could head back to yours this morning? I can run you up to school – I'm going to go there now to check on Lexi. You probably have everything already packed from last night, before Sophie got sick, right? And if you'd prefer to keep Sophie home today, then I can drop you both at yours. I need to go back to grab our things, anyway.' The words tumbled out of Ava in her haste to get to her daughter. She had to see her to make sure she was all right.

'Don't worry about tidying anything else up here,' she said. 'I don't mind doing it. I was planning to deep-clean before the party tomorrow, anyway.' She prayed there wasn't anything nasty lingering, but the place seemed fine.

Emily and Sophie both had that same fearful expression again, and Ava raised an eyebrow. What on earth was going on here? *Had* Sophie been ill? 'Is there more laundry downstairs?' she asked, moving towards the basement door. 'I can get it for you now, if Sophie needs her things. I—'

'That's fine!' Emily cut her off before she could reach the doorknob. 'I can get it. Anyway, it's probably still drying.' She took a deep breath. 'Look, I understand you want to get back. But wouldn't it be better to stay at my place today while I air out everything here? I'll do the deep-clean too. I'd hate for you both to catch what Sophie had.'

Ava barely heard the words. She understood that Emily didn't want to go. But she needed to be back in this house again now, within its familiar confines. She couldn't wait any longer.

'Look, you two have been such a big help,' she said, desperate to end this conversation and get to her daughter. 'Why don't you both come to the party? And as a thank you, why don't you stay for a meal here afterwards? I'm sure Dan would love to see you again.' Dan would love no such thing, but Emily wouldn't know that. 'If he's back on time, of course.' He hadn't said he wouldn't be, but his words about how he couldn't take it anymore had stuck in her mind. What exactly would he do? What had he done already? God, she'd almost prefer it if he didn't come home. Staying away would definitely make things easier.

Emily's face lit up, and Ava could see her words had hit the mark. 'That would be great. Thank you.' She glanced at her daughter. 'We'd love that, wouldn't we, Soph?'

'Wonderful.' Ava forced a smile. 'Right, I need to get going and talk to Lexi.' She looked at Sophie. 'Do you want me to take you to school?'

'Sophie can come home with me,' Emily said, crossing the room and putting a hand on her daughter's back. 'Don't worry about us. We'll be out of your way soon.'

Ava held her gaze. 'Great. I mean, thank you.' She drew in a breath. 'I'll go pick up some groceries and run some errands after seeing Lexi at school; give you a chance to pack up. I'll catch you later, then.'

Emily smiled. 'See you at the party. I can't wait!'

Ava nodded, thinking the party was the last thing on her mind right now.

EIGHTEEN
EMILY

'What are we going to do, Mum?' Sophie was staring at her with wide eyes. 'We can't leave Dan in the basement! What if Ava finds him? We could both be arrested!' Panic rang in her voice. 'Maybe we can talk to him now that he's had a chance to calm down and recover?'

Emily clenched her fists, telling herself to stay calm. She was close to getting back into Ava's life; to reigniting the glow inside that chased away the dark hollowness. Ava had even invited her to the party and then for dinner! She'd been right to believe in Ava's words all of these years. They'd only needed more time.

She couldn't let Dan blow it now. She'd lain awake all night, trying to conjure up something – anything – that might make him change his mind. But after a sleepless night, she'd realised that, even if he was feeling better, simply talking to him and trying to explain was never going to work. Hadn't he said himself there was nothing she could say? She needed something more if she was ever going to convince him to keep his mouth shut.

Thankfully, as morning broke, she'd come up with an idea that might keep him quiet. It was the only thing she could think of; the only thing she could offer.

The only thing she still had from that disastrous night so long ago.

Her mind swept back to the moment when she'd first come here. The moment the door *did* open, after she'd banged on it for what felt like hours. A man had stood on the threshold, his gaze friendly and inquisitive.

'Sorry, sorry, I had the TV up so loud that I couldn't hear you,' he had said. 'Can I help you with something?'

She'd gazed at him, confused. This was the right address. She was sure of that: she'd triple-checked on the hotel system. But this man wasn't the one she'd slept with. At least, she didn't think so. The lighting had been dim, but...

'Are you Dan?' she'd asked haltingly. 'Dan MacDonald?'

He'd tilted his head. 'Yes. Why? Who are you?'

She'd stared, her mind spinning. Could she be wrong? *Could* this be him? But try as she might, she knew it wasn't. The man she'd slept with had light hair, and he had dark hair. He'd been toned and slim, and this man was more on the stocky side.

'Were you at the Swan Hotel in Norwich about six weeks ago?' She could barely get out the words.

'No, but...,' He had paused, then blinked. 'Is this about my card? I had a new credit card stolen, before it got to me. The bugger took the envelope with my address and the card and used it for ages before I realised. One of the places was a hotel in Norwich. He must have checked in using my details.' His eyes had snapped. 'Does he owe you money? I'm afraid you'll have to get in touch with the bank about that. I hope you haven't come all this way...'

His words had flowed around her, and it was all she could do to keep standing. The man she'd slept with had been a con artist, like her. He wasn't someone who was rich, despite how he'd looked. He was someone taking advantage of others, exactly like she was. She'd slept with him for nothing.

And worst of all, she'd never get any money out of him. She didn't know who he was. She had swayed on her feet, and Dan leapt forward to grab her arm.

'Hey!' he had said, his voice rising in alarm. 'Are you OK? Come in, sit down.' He had navigated her over to a sofa, and she sank down onto it.

'I'm fine, I'm fine.' She'd closed her eyes to try to stop the room from spinning. 'I'm feeling dizzy, that's all.'

'Oh, I understand.' He had smiled. 'My wife is pregnant. She gets dizzy all the time.'

Emily could hear in his voice how proud and excited he was, and she could see he would be a great father.

'Let me get you a glass of water. You relax.'

She had nodded and breathed in, still trying to absorb what he'd told her. He wouldn't be giving her money. This wouldn't be a shortcut to all she'd wanted, and the pregnancy she'd believed would be her trump card was worth nothing. Her dreams had seemed further away than ever. She had felt more disposable than ever. She'd needed something to make all of this right again, but what, she didn't know.

She had got to her feet and staggered towards the door, rage propelling her forward through the haze of nausea. On the table by the door was a little glass dish, with keys and two rings – two expensive-looking rings. Even if this wasn't the man she'd been seeking, she couldn't help feeling he owed her something. He had everything, and she had nothing. In a flash, she had slid the rings into her pocket and was out the door. It was only when she'd got on the train and looked at them more closely that she'd realised it was a wedding band and engagement ring, and guilt tinged inside. The woman's rings, she'd guessed. Why had she taken them off?

It didn't matter. She'd sat on the train to Norwich, her brain working furiously to figure out her next steps. She'd end the pregnancy. That was the only option. She'd sell the rings and save the money. But somehow, neither of those things had happened. As her belly grew, people *noticed* her. They smiled, they chatted, and for the first time since her mum remarried, they were interested in her. She loved being seen, and the thought of ending it... well, she couldn't. Yes, it would be more of a struggle getting the life she wanted with a baby in tow, but maybe this child could help open doors.

She'd kept the rings, too, inside a little black pouch. They were an insurance policy for if things hit rock bottom. She'd found other ways to make money, anyway.

She stared at her daughter now, thanking God the rings were in a safe back at her flat. She would offer them to Dan in exchange for him keeping quiet. Given what Ava had told her when she'd talked about how upset she'd been at losing them, those rings had a value beyond the financial one. But what if he refused to take them? Or if she gave them back, and he still told Ava what she'd done?

She chewed her lip, thinking of his words earlier that morning when she'd gone to give him food and water.

'You can't keep me hidden forever,' he'd rasped, wincing as he'd taken a sip. 'Sooner or later, Ava will notice I'm missing. You'll need to let me go.'

He was right: she couldn't keep him hidden forever. Bartering with the rings was a risk, but it was the only thing she could think of at the moment, and at least it was *something* she could try. If he turned them down, she'd cross that bridge when she came to it.

Ava should be gone from the flat for the next few hours. She'd nip home now and grab them from the safe.

'Soph, I need you to stay here. I'll be back in thirty minutes, tops.' Hopefully, anyway.

Sophie was shaking her head. 'No way, Mum. I'm not staying here alone with him. What if Ava comes back?'

'Then you chat with her; distract her.' Emily grabbed her mobile and hurried out the door before Sophie could answer.

She raced back to the flat, her heart beating fast. After being at Ava's, this place seemed more of a dump than ever. She knelt on the floor to look under the sofa. Where had she put it? Yes, here it was. She slid out the metal safe, then punched in the code and combed through the contents to find the pouch.

She lifted out the plethora of phones, jewellery and cash she'd managed to forage from the spa locker room at the hotel. Taking things from her workplace wasn't the best strategy, but blackmailing men was way too risky with a child waiting at home. And what choice did she have? Her haul might never be enough for the private school fees, but Sophie did still need money for school trips, dance lessons, piano – all the things that Lexi did, in hopes of keeping in touch. She was very careful not to get caught, only entering the locker room when a guest complained of a maintenance issue or there was something to be fixed, and even then using an old swipe card that had belonged to a long-gone employee. And she only took the things to the pawn shops months after she'd lifted them. Half of the time, people didn't even bother checking back after making a complaint.

Furiously, she pawed through the safe, panic rising as she didn't uncover the pouch. It had to be here. She knew she'd put it in here. Granted, she hadn't seen it for ages, but she hadn't looked. There'd been no reason. Finally, after emptying the contents and combing through each item one by one, she sat back. The rings were nowhere to be seen. But where else could they be?

She shifted, her mind working. There weren't many options. She didn't have a bedroom to put things in, and... She got to her feet, throwing open drawers and upending the contents, but the rings weren't there. Was she going crazy? She had to find them! She tilted her head. Maybe she'd left them somewhere? Back in the hotel where she'd lived in staff accommodation in Norwich?

She shook her head. No. She was sure she'd put them in the safe, but, somehow, they were gone. *Shit*. What the hell was she going to do now?

She didn't have time for this! Ava could return home any second, and Sophie was so jittery, Emily wasn't sure she could delay Ava for long. Sooner or later – probably sooner, rather than later – Ava would go to the basement to do laundry or something. If she heard any noise from the storage room, that would be the end of everything. She couldn't let that happen.

First things first: she had to find a new place to stash Dan while she thought of another way to keep him quiet. Could she bring him back here? she wondered, before dismissing the idea. There were too many people around, and she had nowhere to put him. She could hardly shove him in Sophie's room, which shared a wall with a family who were always home and sure to pick up on any little noise. She needed an empty place, with no one nearby, where she could keep him for a day or two.

She jerked as an idea hit. She had the key to Mrs Bhandari's house. She could put Dan there.

Her mind spun as she thought through the logistics. She could take Dan in the side door and put him in the basement. She bit her lip. He was hardly going to go willingly, was he? Unlike last time, he wasn't unconscious. She had to find something to subdue him.

She blinked, thinking she had the answer. She had plenty of sleeping tablets; she'd used them tons of times to knock out the men. She'd slip some of those into Dan's water – just enough to get him drowsy and docile – then quickly hustle him into the Bhandaris'. She'd need Sophie's help once more, but Sophie was so scared now that she'd do anything.

The sooner they locked Dan away where he couldn't destroy everything, the better. Then she would think about what to do. *You can't keep me hidden forever.* Her gut clenched as his voice rang in her head. She'd come up with something.

She had no other choice.

NINETEEN
AVA

Ava pulled into the drive later that morning and got out of the car. Finally, she was home. Every bit of her jangled with nerves and exhaustion. She couldn't wait to get Lexi back here and have that closeness again with her daughter in the comfort of their own familiar space.

Lexi had been mortified when Ava had pulled her out of class, staring at the ground and refusing to talk. As Ava had gazed at her daughter, she realised she had no idea what was going on inside her head. That same uncertainty and fear coursed through her, and she'd waited for Lexi to speak – to apologise for leaving and explain why – but she'd said nothing. The silence had swirled between them, the air a foreign vacuum.

She'd pulled her daughter into her arms, then said goodbye and got back into the car. Everything would be fine, she told herself, repeating it over and over like a mantra. All she had to do was go back home. She'd take the laptop and lock it in the storage room as soon as she got inside. This time she wouldn't forget.

A flash of something inside the Bhandaris' caught her eye as she got out of the car. She squinted, but whatever it was must have disappeared. For a second, she felt fear flood through her as she thought once more of the burglar. Then she remembered the cat, and she laughed. She hoped Emily had remembered to feed it – and that she'd left the key. Her heart sank as she scanned the table and the counter. The key was nowhere to be seen.

Ava grabbed the first few bags of groceries from the supermarket and went into the house, wrinkling her nose at the scent in the air. It wasn't bad, it was just... not hers. After throwing open the windows, she breathed in the fresh clean smell of wet grass, then hurried up the stairs and into Dan's office. She paused as she stared at the computer. An image of the folder slid into her head. What exactly was on there?

Pain sliced through her, and she turned away, trying to keep the memories from enveloping her. She'd been so happy when they'd found out they were having two babies in one go. Dan had grinned for days, making endless jokes about 'two for one' offers and how potent his sperm must be. She'd rolled her eyes and told him that had nothing to do with it, all the while loving that they would have their family ready-made in one go. They'd only wanted two children anyway, and this way, she wouldn't have to take two sets of maternity leaves. It was hard enough to get one from her GP practice. Plus, as an only child herself, she loved that her kids would have built-in playmates. And as different sexes, perhaps they wouldn't be super-competitive either. She couldn't wait, calming images of rocking two babies, one in each arm, floating through her head.

Reality had proven very different, though. While Lexi had been an easy baby, going to sleep and feeding with no struggle, Alfie was a different story. Everything was an issue. He'd barely sleep. He couldn't feed, even after he'd got his tongue tie snipped. Nothing would keep him happy, and although Dan was happy to help, eventually Ava had to bunk in the nursery with the twins so Dan could go to work the next day without feeling like a zombie.

Ava hated to admit it, but sometimes she'd wondered what life would have been like if she'd had only one baby – Lexi. Emily seemed to be coping beautifully with Sophie, unlike her, who was constantly tired and frazzled. And part of her missed her old life as a competent GP, who people looked up to. Now, she was completely clueless at something that should have come so naturally.

What she wouldn't give to have those precious few months back again, she thought now. How could she have ever wished them away, wished her child away?

She swayed as pain washed over her, so strong it took away her breath. She reached out to grasp onto something, trying to steady herself. What was she doing? She couldn't think about this. She *shouldn't* think about this. She yanked the power cable from the computer as if she could unplug the memories from her brain. Then she opened the desk drawer to find the keyring with the key for the storage room. The sooner this was locked away, the better.

Hmm, that was funny, she thought, rifling through the contents. The keyring didn't seem to be here. She knew she should have checked to make sure Emily had put it back in the right place! Sighing, she glanced around the room, taking in the mess. Trying to find it in here would be like searching for a needle in a haystack. Half-heartedly, she slid open drawers and surveyed surfaces, but it was nowhere to be seen.

Ava stared down at the laptop, unease pricking her gut. The storage room was the ultimate secure vault – a place where she could lock away anything threatening. But now she was cut off. She was outside of it, with something that could ruin everything. The feeling that the secrets she'd tried to keep hidden for so long were slowly seeping out swept over her, and she put a hand on the desk to steady herself once more.

She straightened up, telling herself she was silly. She might not have access to it, but the storage room *was* locked. She'd seen Emily lock it first-hand. Everything was contained. Nothing from the past was escaping, and Lexi would never find the laptop. She'd make sure of that.

She hurried into her room and shoved the laptop to the very back of her wardrobe, under stacks of old jumpers and blankets. Then she went back downstairs and stood in the middle of the kitchen, trying to calm herself. First things first, clean everything. Emily had clearly made an effort, but there were still bits of something on the granite backsplash, and even through the trainers she only wore inside the house, she could feel grit on the floor.

She slid off her rings, noticing that they were easier to remove than the last time. Made sense, given she'd barely eaten anything the past few days. Maybe she'd get them made a little smaller. The last thing she wanted was to lose another set. Dan would be so dismayed. Or would he? Would he even notice?

Ava sighed, thinking of her husband. With the party fast approaching, she really should call and remind him what time it started. She was still so upset, though – and worried what he might tell their daughter if she couldn't convince him to keep quiet. The laptop might be hidden now, but he wasn't. It wouldn't be the worst thing in the world if he didn't make it, would it? Being away so much, he missed a lot of Lexi's school events. Lexi was used to it – used to only her being there. They were so close that she didn't need more. Fresh anger spurted through her. After all she'd been through, how could Dan think to threaten that closeness?

She wouldn't call, she decided, as she furiously scrubbed

the floor, harder and harder until her hands ached. If he wanted to come, he would. She filled her mind with the house, Lexi and the day ahead. That was all that mattered.

She would cling on to it for all she was worth.

Nothing – no one – would take it away from her.

TWENTY
LEXI

I'm still shaking with anger when Mum comes to get me from school. When she pulled me out of the classroom this morning to make sure I was OK, she looked *crazy*: her hair was dripping, her face was pale, and her eyes were wide and panicked. Everyone stared when she burst in, and I wanted to disappear. Although she seems like her usual self again – nice hair, make-up, much calmer – I don't feel anything like normal. Everything is different. Everything has changed. My family wasn't only the three of us. I have a brother. I have a *twin*. But what happened to him? I want to ask Mum, but there's no point. I know she won't tell me the truth. I can't trust her anymore. This is something I have to do on my own.

'Hey, honey.' She stretches out her arms to put around me, but I scoot away. 'Ready to go? I've got all your favourites. I thought we could have a lovely meal, then set up a sundae bar!' Her face glows, but instead of excitement, all I feel is fury. What, does she think I'm a toddler? That a sundae bar is going to make up for having a brother she never told me about?

'Forget it, Mum.' My voice is cold, and I see her flinch. 'I'm not hungry. I want to hang out in my room.'

She gives me a sidelong look as we climb into the car, and I know she's wondering what on earth is wrong with me. There's no way I'm going to tell her. She's not the only one who can keep secrets. I can see she's gearing up to ask a million questions, though, so I decide to stop her before she can start.

'I think I might be getting my period,' I say, and she's on me in an instant, smoothing my hair and patting my back.

'Are you having cramps? Any spotting? Let's get you home and into a warm bath.'

I turn to look at her, trying to keep the annoyance inside me before I burst. I knew this would work. A few girls in my class have got theirs already, and Mum is constantly on the lookout. But I don't want her to be. I don't want to tell her anything. She always wants to know everything about me, but how fair is it that she expects me to tell her everything, and she tells me nothing?

I'm going to find out what she's hiding, though. I'm going to find out about my brother, and I know where to start. There's a ton of old boxes and things downstairs. If Mum saved anything, I'm pretty sure that's where it will be. I don't care how long it takes me. Tonight, when she's asleep, I'm going to look in those boxes. I'm going to find out *something*. Like where he is now. What happened to him.

And why no one ever talks about him.

'I'm fine,' I say, making my tone happy and bright. 'You don't need to worry. I know what to do. And I'm sorry I upset you this morning. I won't do that again. Let's have that sundae bar. It sounds good.'

Relief and happiness cross my mum's face, and for a second, I want to say I'm *not* fine and crawl into her arms. But what's the point? It won't change anything. The only one who can do that is me.

I feel more alone than ever.

We turn onto our street, and as we pass the Bhandaris'

house, I can't help looking at it even though I don't want to. Instantly, pictures flash into my head: the man's face, twisted and angry; Mr Bhandari's gentle eyes wide when he spots the shadow in the dark; his crumpled shape on the floor and Mrs Bhandari's scream when she sees him. How can he be dead? I don't think I've ever known anyone who died, actually. A shudder goes through me, and I wrap my arms around myself.

Mum pulls into the driveway and opens up the garage, and we drive in. It feels weird to be home, and not in a good way. The thought makes me sad. Shouldn't I be happy to be back? I know Mum is. Maybe I take after Dad more than Mum, because I can see when he yanks off that tie that he's not happy to relax, like you might think. I can see how it's like his connection to the outside world, outside of here, and when he takes it off, that connection is gone. I pause for a minute, realising I haven't heard from him today. Usually, he texts in the morning to say hello, but there's nothing. He must have started meetings early.

The house is sparkling and smells of the fresh organic cleaning wipes Mum always uses, but I miss the mess from when Emily was here. The house looked real, then: like the kind of places people actually live in, not the showroom Mum keeps it like.

The night goes on forever, with Mum making way too much food and trying to get me to eat more ice cream than a human ever should. Then she wants to sit with me and watch what she thinks is my favourite show, but secretly I only watch because everyone at school does and it's all they talk about. I bite my lip, thinking of Sophie and her friends. Will she still talk to me now that this swap is over? I hope so. It was so nice to be able to laugh with people at lunch instead of staring down at my book. Maybe I can stop feeling so alone all the time. At least at school, anyway.

. . .

Finally, it's time for bed, and Mum gives me an embarrassing session on period products, cuddles me and then turns off the lights and comes upstairs with me. It sounds weird – it is weird – but she still insists on tucking me in and staying upstairs with me once I'm in bed. I wish she would have a few glasses of wine and chill by the TV in the lounge, like the other mums do.

I lie in bed and close my eyes. When I can't wait any longer because I'm about to go to sleep, I slide out of bed as quietly as I can and open the door, my heart lifting when I notice the light under her door is out. I tiptoe past her bedroom and down the stairs, skipping the one that always creaks.

It's creepy in the lounge in the dim light, with shadows from the trees casting dark patches on the floor, and although I shouldn't, I look over at the Bhandaris' once more. It's dark there and nothing is moving, and I tear my glance away before those pictures start playing again.

I open the door to the basement and hit the switch, but the light doesn't go on. I freeze for a minute in the pitch black. I know there's nothing down here, but my heart is still beating fast. I pause and listen, and silence swirls around me. I'm scared, but I'm going to do this. I need a light first, though.

I creep back upstairs and grab my mobile, then flick on the torch and go down again. I head straight to the storage room where most of the boxes are and try to open the door, but it doesn't budge. My heart sinks when I notice the doorknob has a hole in the middle for a key. How am I going to open it now? I've no clue where the key might be.

But just as I think that, a memory comes into my head of Dad and me together, that day I bought my old phone off eBay. He opened his desk drawer to get something for work, and I saw a keyring inside. I remember asking Dad what the keys were for, and he shrugged and said stuff in the basement. I hold onto that image now as I head upstairs and into the office. It feels like someone is guiding me. Like someone wants me to find out. Like my brother is willing me forward.

Inside the office, I open the drawer and the keys are there, glistening in the light of my torch, as if they were waiting for me. I grab them and go down to the basement, then cross the room and try a few in the lock. I know one will work. I know it.

My heart lifts as the lock clicks. I push the door open, excitement running through me. A strange scent stops me in my tracks. What is that? I tilt my head, trying to identify the smell. It's like sweat mix with unwashed clothes, and it's awful. It must be something in one of the boxes, I tell myself. It's been locked away in here so tightly that the whole space reeks.

I try to hold my breath as I scan the room, my heart sinking as I clock all the junk scattered about. God, this is going to take ages. Where should I start? I walk around the room, peering at the labels scrawled on boxes in Dad's very messy handwriting and Mum's neat block printing. Then I see a box in the corner, on top of all the others. It's different from the rest: while the others were simple cardboard ones, this is thick white textured material, kind of like a gift box for jewellery, but much bigger.

There's no label, but something tells me this is what I'm looking for. It's taped shut, and I bite my lip, hesitating for a second. Do I want to open it? Do I really want to know? Then I think of my mum's face as she lied straight to my face about Mr Bhandari and everything else she kept from me, and anger swirls inside. Yes, I do want to open this. I want to find out.

I leave the room to grab a knife from the workbench, then go back inside and slit open the box like I've seen my dad do so often with Amazon deliveries. The smell is still swirling around me, though less intense than when I first came in here. Maybe it's not something in the boxes, after all? But I don't have time to think about it too much, because all my attention is focused on the white box in front of me.

I put it on the floor and sink down beside it, eager to see

what's inside. My pulse races as I lift the flaps, praying there's something that can help me learn more. I take in a little blue blanket right on top as if it's protecting the contents, and my eyes widen. It matches the pink one I have in my baby box, and I know it had to belong to my brother. Gingerly, I reach out to touch it, picturing the soft fabric swaddling Alfie. My heart swells in my chest like it's going to break through, and I clutch it close. Finally, I set the blanket aside and look back in the box.

The next thing I spot is a tiny blue cardigan like the one I have too – although much less worn than mine. Then there's a stack of photos. I pick up one of the two of us together in Mum's arms. God, she looks tired... but so happy as if there's a light coming from inside her. Sadness goes through me as I think that I don't remember ever seeing her like that. I reach for another one, a picture of three babies in the swimming pool, Mum, and... I squint. Is that Emily?

It is! She looks almost exactly the same, but she and Mum have their arms around each other, and they both have huge smiles. I leaf through the photos of them together with the babies. There are tons of them. I thought they only knew each other from my school, since Mum never sees her anywhere else. By the looks of things, though, they must have been very good friends at one point. I wonder what happened.

I set aside the pictures and keep searching. There's so much stuff here, but it's not telling me anything. I'm not really sure what I want to know, if I'm honest – what I'm looking for. Something more. Something that tells me what happened to my brother. Something that explains why no one ever talks about him. I'm his twin, and yet I know nothing. A flash of anger goes through me again, like a lightning strike, making my insides burn.

I continue to rifle through, my fingers touching a solid file at the very bottom. I lift it out, then open it up and scan the documents. There's a birth certificate, and I stare at the neat typing.

Alfie George MacDonald. I run my fingers over the paper as my mind repeats the name. Alfie. Alfie and Lexi. The names go well together, and sadness pushes out the anger. I've always felt so alone, but I didn't have to be. I could have had a brother right beside me, at home and at school. I could have had a *friend*. I swallow and carry on reading. He was born a few minutes after me. I was his older sister.

I lift the birth certificate, and the next paper underneath makes me blink. I blink again, hoping I'm wrong. Maybe it's too dark in here. Maybe I didn't see the words correctly. I can't breathe now as I hold the torch closer, my stomach twisting as I read the words once more. I wasn't wrong. This is a death certificate. A death certificate for my brother – for Alfie.

My twin is dead.

I drop the paper like it's on fire, and it flutters to the floor. I don't want to hold this. It's so final, so... brutal. There's no way to change it, no going back for a do-over. My brother is gone, and I'll never know him. Even though, in the back of my mind in a little place I didn't want to let grow, I knew he had to be dead, I still had hope. And now that's vanished.

I swipe the paper up off the floor, my nose wrinkling as I see a smeared rusty-brown patch, right by my foot. It's odd, because everything else in here is tidy, with not a mark on the floor. What is that? I scooch closer to take a look, and the scent of metal hits my nose. Was that part of what I was smelling earlier? It smells like... like blood.

I shake my head. It can't be blood. Why would there be a patch of blood here, in the shadows, almost all the way under the shelf? Could an animal have got inside, maybe, and got hurt? Unless the animal could open a locked door, there's no way. Maybe something spilled. Either way, it's not important now. All I can think about is what happened to my brother. How did he die?

I shine the torch on the paper, desperate for any shred of

information, catching my breath when I spot the date of death. It's only three months after our birthday. The word 'our' echoes in my mind, and I swallow at that thought that, for those few months, I had someone in the world who was always beside me. Actually, not only for those few months. We were together in Mum's belly too. Alfie was with me, all the time, and now he's gone. That's why Mum is so sad.

Maybe that's why I always feel so alone too.

Tears push at my eyes and I wipe them away, then look at the certificate once more. There's not much on there, but the cause of death says... I squint, my heart racing. Sudden Infant Death Syndrome. SIDS. I tilt my head. Isn't that when the baby stops breathing in the middle of the night? And nobody knows why? I never could understand how that could happen. It doesn't make sense.

But it happened to my brother. I wince as I picture Mum leaning down to pick him up, only to find... I push the image from my head. It's sad. It's awful, but I know it happens. So, why wouldn't they tell me? Why don't they talk about him – ever? That's not normal. Not at all.

I put the certificate by the side of the box and look through the rest of the contents. There's a bunch of clothes, little shoes and a whole stack of cards. I flick through them: they're from people saying how sorry they are. I glanced at the names. People I don't know and don't think I've ever met. Judging by this huge pile, my parents had a lot of friends. Now, they don't seem to have any – or at least Mum doesn't. Dad, I'm not sure. He's away so much he could be best mates with a whole colony of aliens on Mars for all I know.

I stare into the box, feeling like I don't want to close it up again. It's wrong to do that to my brother. I want him to come with me, and so I reach in to take something. My fingers touch a cold metallic object and I pull it out, eyes widening when I clock that it's one of those little gadgets with lots of tools that fold out. A Swiss Army knife, I think it's called, and a memory weaves into me of when I turned ten. Mum gave me a necklace, one I'm still wearing.

'Double digits,' she'd said, as she put it around my neck and did up the clasp. 'This is a real milestone birthday. My parents gave this to me when I turned ten, too, along with another little gadget. A Swiss Army knife.' She made a face. 'I think they wanted a boy, but Dad gave it to me. He said his father had given it to him at that age too. Not sure exactly what he expected me to do with it.' She smiled, but her eyes were sad. 'Don't worry, I won't inflict it on you. Be careful with the necklace. It's a real diamond.' She'd wiped away tears that leaked from the corner of her eyes, and I remember thinking how she was getting so worked up over this birthday. But it wasn't just the birthday. I know that now. She was thinking of Alfie, who she should have given the knife to. I close my fist around its solid weight. He can't have it, so I will. I'll carry it with me, to remember him and keep him close.

I take the blue blanket that matches my own, too, and tidy up the box as best I can. I place it back on the stack, then close the storage-room door behind me. As I climb the stairs in the dark, I try to get a grip on how I feel. I've learned more about my brother, but somehow, it feels like I know less. I know I had a twin. I know he died of SIDs. I know details, but I still don't understand why Mum and Dad kept so quiet. I still don't know anything about *him*. What he was like as a baby; how he cried. Where he's buried. There's this whole part of my life that's completely missing, and I want to fill it in. I need to fill it in so that maybe I can start to feel whole again. Maybe I can be happy.

There's no point asking Mum. Dad's always been the one who understands; the one who gets me. He'll tell me what I need to know. What I should have known ages ago. He has all that stuff on his computer, after all. He must look at the photos;

think of Alfie often, instead of keeping it all boxed up and out of the way like Mum. I know he'll be back tomorrow afternoon for the party, but I don't want to wait. I don't want to go to the party, anyway. I'll take the train to Brighton and talk to him there. I've got more than enough cash hidden in my bedroom for the ticket. I hunch over in the dark kitchen and text him to say that I'm coming and to tell me his hotel, then go upstairs.

I put the keyring back in his desk drawer and go to my room. Then I open the drawer at the back of my own desk, where I stashed the cash in an old envelope inside some ancient exercise books. It was the only place I could think of to hide it where Mum might not check. I yank out all the broken pens and bits and bobs I've shoved there. Then I take the stack of books and leaf through them, looking for the envelope. Finally, it falls out of one of them, and I open the flap.

My heart sinks. It's empty. There's nothing inside.

I blink and sit down on the bed, trying to understand. I had almost £500 in there. It can't have simply disappeared. No one else has been in this room besides me and Mum, and Mum wouldn't have taken it. If she had, she wouldn't have left the empty envelope – and I definitely would have heard about it.

But actually... I swallow as it hits me. There was someone else inside my room. *Sophie.* She had plenty of time to look through my things and take the money. Maybe she didn't think I would notice for a while, and that's why she kept the envelope there. She wouldn't do this, though, would she? She wouldn't take my money, all the while laughing and chatting with me at lunch?

Maybe that was why she was so nice – because she didn't want me to suspect her. Maybe she didn't want to be friends with me, after all. Because it had to have been her who took this cash, no matter how much I don't want it to be.

How could she steal from me like that?

Anger and hurt flood into me, along with the feeling that

I'm alone once more. I want to run to Sophie's now and confront her. I want to grab the cash back before she spends it, but of course I can't. Mum would have the police looking for me if she discovered me missing in the middle of the night, and anyway, I don't want to get in a fight in front of Emily. She'd wonder how I got all of that money and why I'm hiding it in my room, and I don't want her to tell Mum. I'll talk to Sophie tomorrow in school, away from the teachers.

I'll get the money. I'll go to Dad. And I'll find out all I can about my brother and fill the empty space inside me, even if I can never fill it in for my family.

I can't wait for morning to come.

TWENTY-ONE
EMILY

Emily hurried into work the next morning, conscious that her absence yesterday – without so much as a phone call – would not go down well with her manager. He ran the hotel with an iron fist, always making a huge point of saying how he expected punctuality and respect from his employees. Yesterday, she'd given him neither.

She'd meant to call and say she wouldn't be in. But then they'd had to move Dan.

She let out her breath, still unable to believe what had happened. At least he was safely stowed away at the Bhandaris', although she couldn't keep him there for long. Her heart lurched as she remembered how, despite how groggy and disoriented he'd been from all the tablets she'd given him, he'd opened his eyes wide and stared straight at her when she tied his hands with a bit of rope they'd found.

'What the hell do you think you're doing?' he'd asked, the words emerging fuzzy and unclear. He'd squinted at her as she'd helped him sit up. 'Jesus Christ, Emily. This is insane. You have to let me go.'

'Come with me,' she'd said, trying to manoeuvre him to his feet. He refused to budge, though, staying limp on the ground.

'Come on.' She jerked his arm, and he winced, attempting to move away. He must still be hurting from his fall down the stairs, she thought, pulling his arm even harder. Maybe this would get him to stand.

Dan let out a cry and scrambled to his feet. 'OK, OK. Please, stop.' He swayed as if he was going to fall, and Sophie rushed forward to take his other arm.

He groaned as he saw her daughter. 'Sophie. I can't believe she dragged you into this.'

Emily glanced at her daughter's tense face. Sophie hadn't wanted to help. She'd wanted to talk to Dan now that he was calm, but Emily knew that never would be enough. So she'd promised Sophie that if she did this one last thing, she could have whatever she wanted when this was all over. Sophie had raised her eyebrows and asked if she'd meant it, and Emily nodded quickly. Whatever her daughter asked for, it couldn't be more challenging than this.

'I'm so sorry,' Dan slurred at Sophie. 'You shouldn't have to do this.'

Guilt had pierced through her, but anger quickly rushed in to take its place. Why was he apologising to her daughter? What did he know about the sacrifices she'd made to get to where she was? What did he know about anything? Rage surged, and she yanked him forward despite the fact he was in pain and unsteady on his feet. He swayed and crashed heavily into the side of the narrow staircase, his head knocking into the sole lightbulb. It sputtered and went out, and Emily cursed as she and Sophie forced him up the stairs. She'd fix that later.

They manoeuvred him out of the house and the short distance across the drive to the Bhandaris'. With every step, she expected him to struggle and try to get away, but he was too groggy and hurting too much, wincing as he trudged slowly forward. When she opened the door and ushered him in, he stopped and looked at her.

'Why are you taking me here?' he said, his words still garbled from the drugs.

Emily didn't answer. She closed the door behind them, and she and Sophie eased him down the basement steps towards the furthest corner of the room. They lowered him to the floor, and he collapsed in a heap. Emily used the moment to tighten the ropes.

'I'll be back to bring you some water and something to eat,' she said, grabbing Sophie's arm and taking her up the stairs. This wasn't a long-term solution. She could keep him drugged and under control for a day or two, maybe, but she *had* to think of something.

One thing at a time, she'd told herself to quell the panic clogging her mind. She'd returned to Ava's and cleaned the storage room as quickly as possible, then swept up the shards of the broken bulb in the stairs, cursing that she hadn't a clue where the new lightbulbs were. She put the keyring back in Dan's desk drawer, in case Ava might notice it was missing and start to wonder what she'd been up to – not that she could ever imagine something like this. She didn't need them any longer – not now that Ava had started inviting her to things again. The day had passed and then the night, and she still hadn't come up with any ideas. The panic inside was swirling faster and faster, threatening to engulf her completely.

'Thanks for joining us this morning,' her boss said sarcastically as Emily went behind the desk and clicked on the screen.

She turned to face him. 'I'm very sorry,' she said, arranging her face into the calm, professional expression she knew he wanted. 'I had a family emergency.'

'One that stopped you from using your mobile?' His tone was cold.

If only he knew. 'Actually, yes.' Her mind raced. 'My daughter and I were mugged. Our phones were stolen.'

'Oh.' His face softened, and she held her breath. Had she convinced him? 'I'm sorry to hear that. I hope you're OK?'

'Yes, fine, thank you,' she responded. 'And I'm so sorry I didn't get in touch. I can assure you it won't happen again.'

'Good.' He nodded curtly, then gave her a long look. 'Speaking of thefts, we're getting closer now to finding who's responsible for all of those thefts from the spa.'

Emily froze. 'Really?' Her voice came out raspy, and she cleared her throat.

'Yes. Police think it's an inside job. We're checking through all swipe cards that accessed the club now, and cross-referencing. Shouldn't take too long to pin down who it is.' He shook his head. 'Can you imagine stealing from the place you work in?'

'No, that's awful.' She managed to sound believable, or so she thought. Was it her imagination, or was he giving her a rather strange look? She was being paranoid, she told herself. Of course he didn't suspect her. If he had, he'd have turned her in by now. Thank goodness she'd used an old swipe card, but she'd have to stop taking things from the spa now, taking things from here, full stop. It had only really been a stopgap, anyway.

'Look, I was going to tell you this yesterday, but Yunis is leaving next month to start a new position in Spain.'

Emily raised her eyebrows. Yunis was the deputy general manager of the whole hotel. If he was leaving, could that mean there was a chance she could finally move up? She'd been waiting for something for months.

'I'm going to put your name in as the next deputy manager,' her boss said, smiling. 'You'll need to have an interview, of course, and it will mean longer hours and a lot more responsibility – but there'll be a salary increase. Does that sound like it might be of interest?'

Emily grinned, excitement stirring inside. 'It does! I'd love it. Thank you so much.' What perfect timing! The extra money might compensate for not being able to steal items from the spa locker room, although she'd still need to think of something to pay for Sophie's school. If she sorted out this mess with Dan and got back in Ava's life, though, maybe Sophie could do one year at the comprehensive while she saved like crazy. Maybe Sophie wouldn't even need to go to private school, and Emily would finally have enough for a better place. And deputy GM! It was a huge step towards who she wanted to be. People would have to acknowledge her then. They'd have to respect her.

Her boss strode down the corridor towards his office, and Emily felt determination flooding through her. She *was* on the right track, both at work and with Ava. If she kept this up, soon she might have everything she'd ever wanted.

She couldn't let anyone stop her now.

TWENTY-TWO
LEXI

I toss and turn all night. It feels like I can't sleep for longer than five minutes, and whenever I open my eyes and see that only a short time has passed, I groan and flop down again. I can't stop thinking about the money Sophie took and how I thought she liked me. I can't stop thinking about my brother – Alfie. And I can't stop thinking about talking to Dad. I need to know my brother. I grab the little blanket I took from the box and hold it close to me, wishing I could remember him.

Finally, it's time to get up. I glance at my mobile, heart sinking when there's still no message from Dad. He must be really busy, but I'm sure he'll text me soon, and I know he'll make time for me once I'm there. I push the blanket under my pillow, roll out of bed and put on my uniform. My gaze falls on the Swiss Army knife on my bedside table, and I gulp. I have to put it somewhere fast before Mum sees it! I slide it into my pocket, thinking I'll find a safe hiding spot before school. Then I brush my hair and go downstairs. Mum's in the kitchen making my usual breakfast, and by the efficient way she's clanging about, I can tell she's relieved to be back. I wonder how she can stand to be in this place, though, after what happened. I bite my lip. *Did* it happen here? I know so little, and finding out about my brother has only made me feel more in the dark than ever.

I choke down my pancakes, dodging Mum's questions about how I'm feeling and if my period has actually started. I pretend as best I can that I'm happy and jolly and super excited for this horrible party. I'm glad I won't be here. I don't want people to see my room or all the stuff that's crammed in there. I don't want them to hear the cringey songs she's picked out, or the lame cakes she's going to bake from scratch and not order from the Cupcake Corner, the place where everyone gets their cakes from. It makes me feel even more that the house isn't somewhere I want to be.

I think she buys my act, although I can feel her watching me when she thinks I'm not looking. I grab my schoolbag and head to the car. Mum chatters away on the short distance there, but I turn on the radio and tune her out. All I can think about now is Sophie. Sophie, and my money. I have to get away from here. I have to get to Dad.

'Bye, Lex. Have a good day!' she trills as we stop by the school, and I smile brightly and get out. I barely see her face as she smiles back at me.

The sun is shining and the air is warm. Everyone's running around the playground, but I sit on the bench in the corner, squinting into the sun. I'm so, so tired after being awake all last night, and my emotions are spinning inside like a mini tornado. I take a deep breath to try to make it stop, but if anything, it spins faster.

'Hi, Sophie!' Sophie's friends call to her, and I glance up to see Sophie hurrying across the playground towards them. She looks as exhausted as I feel, with dark circles under her eyes, and I wonder what kept her up last night. Maybe she feels bad because she took all my money. Well, she should.

Jealousy and rage shoot through me as I watch her chat with friends. Why should she have all those friends when she's such a bad person – when she's *stealing* from me? And how could she make me think I might be her friend too? Well, she won't have friends for long once everyone finds out what she's done.

Before I can stop myself, I get to my feet and cross the playground to where Sophie is standing.

'Hey,' I say, my voice loud with anger.

Sophie swings around, and a strange expression comes over her face when she sees me. I stare for a minute, and then it clicks. She looks *guilty*.

'I know what you did,' I say, conscious that everyone is looking at me. Any incident in the playground is always big news, but I don't care. I'm not the one in the wrong here.

Fear passes over her face, and she starts to tremble. She should be afraid, I tell myself. I had a lot of money there. 'I'm so sorry,' she says, and tears fill her eyes. 'I'm really sorry. Please don't tell anyone. My mum—'

'I won't say anything if you give it back,' I say, cutting her off. I bite my lip as I glance at her pale face and shaking body. I mean, I want her to feel bad, but she seems like she's about to faint. 'I need that money.'

She jerks. 'Money?'

I grab her arm, dragging her away from her friends. 'Yes. The money you took from me. The money I had in my room and which is now gone.'

I wait for her to answer, but instead she lets out a laugh and shakes her head. Anger goes through me. What, does she think this is *funny*?

'Money. You're talking about money.' She meets my eyes. 'I don't have your money, Lexi.'

'Then what were you apologising for?' I ask, still unable to believe it. She must have the cash. She has to. It's gone, and she was the only one in that room.

'Oh, I thought it was something different.' She shakes her

head. 'Never mind, it doesn't matter. But I didn't take your money.'

'I don't believe you.' I stand my ground. There's no way she could have not taken it. She as good as admitted it earlier, despite changing her story now. Maybe she expects me to back down, but I'm not going to.

She shrugs. 'Believe what you want.'

She turns to go, but I grab her arm. I'm not letting her get away. I need that money.

'Give it to me. Or tell me where it is. Now.' I shake her arm furiously, satisfaction shooting through me when I realise my grip is so strong that she can't break free. I'm not as weak as people might think I am.

'I don't have it.'

Strangely, she doesn't keep resisting my grip. She goes limp, sagging in my arms, and I yank her up before she falls. Has she fainted? Fear goes through me as kids circle around us, yelling and screaming, and I'm about to let her go when a sharp voice cuts through the crowd.

'Stop! Break it up!' Miss Malik somehow manages to get through the kids, and I let Sophie go. I step back from her and try to catch my breath. My heart is pounding, I'm drenched in sweat, and my head is throbbing. I'm going to be in so much trouble. Slowly, I raise my head and take in Sophie's face. She's staring straight at me with such a guilty, sick expression that I *know* she's done something wrong. That must be why she didn't fight back. She feels bad.

'Girls!' Miss Malik is staring from me to Sophie and back again, her eyebrows raised. 'What on earth has got into you two?'

We both stand silently. Neither one of us answers.

'Come with me.' Miss Malik takes each of us by the arm and leads us into the school, towards the head teacher's office. Oh God. I'm going to be in so much trouble. 'You go in there.' She points at the Calm Zone, a small room outside the office where the bad kids are sent to calm down. I've never been inside it. 'And you, there.' She gestures to a bench in the corridor for Sophie. 'I'm going to let Mrs Peters know what happened. And I don't want to hear a word from either of you.'

We both nod, and I glance up to see that Sophie looks as worried as me. She doesn't need to, I think, as I duck inside the Calm Zone. Emily is barely around, and she probably won't care – not like my mum. I bite my lip, wondering if Mrs Peters will tell her what I've managed to hide from her for so long... what Dad hid from her for so long. She doesn't know that I was caught that day selling stuff at school. She was at the doctor and they couldn't reach her, so they rang Dad at work and told him.

I can still see his sad eyes when he asked me why, and I said it was because all of the things Mum bought didn't make me happy. That they only made me feel sad. He sighed and said he understood, and that maybe we should keep this to ourselves, as long as I didn't do it again. I didn't do it at school, anyway. Guilt pours through me as I think of Mr Bhandari. I wish I'd never done it at home either.

And now the money is gone. I gaze out to the corridor at Sophie, barely able to see her through the tears in my eyes. What does it matter? Even if Mum doesn't find out I was selling things, this fight will put a stop to everything. She'll be watching me like a hawk. I won't be able to go find Dad, and once he's home where the silence is so heavy, I'm not sure he'll be able to talk to me about Alfie. I won't get more money, and I'll never be able to get away from here. I'll be trapped, in a home that's sad and cold, beside a house where a murder took place. A murder I helped happen.

I'll be sad and cold. Forever.

I need to get out of here before Mum comes. I need to go to Dad and tell him what's happened. He'll understand. He can explain it to her. He'll talk to me and tell me everything. I get to my feet, looking up and down the corridor.

'What are you doing?' Sophie hisses as I flash by her towards the door.

But I don't look back. I keep going. I'll go to the train station, then call him and ask him to transfer me the money for the ticket.

I need to find Alfie, even if I am eleven years too late.

TWENTY-THREE
AVA

Ava turned into the drive after dropping off Lexi that morning, loving that she was home again. Thank goodness, because she only had a few hours to get ready for the class party this afternoon. God, it was so hard to believe that Lexi would be moving to secondary in September! Even if the school was small, down the street and relatively sheltered, it was going to be a big adjustment. They'd stay close, of course. That wouldn't change. Without her daughter, what would she do?

She had Dan, but... She bit her lip, recalling their argument. She didn't really have him, did she? Even if she did convince him to keep quiet and he decided to stay, knowing that he wanted to tell Lexi about Alfie put even more distance between them. How could she ever reach out for someone who'd threatened everything? Could they ever share a life again?

At least Lexi was all right, still protected from the pain and loss that had threatened. In light of what she'd said about her period maybe starting soon, her strange behaviour made sense now. And maybe Lexi had gone home that morning to get some period supplies. Ava had told her where they were, in case she ever needed them. She'd probably been too embarrassed to tell

Emily, although Ava didn't get why she hadn't told her until later. Still, she had told her, and they were back on the same page again.

She went inside the house, mentally running through a list of all she had to do: finish tidying up, do the laundry, buy tablecloths, pick up the tables and chairs she'd rented, go to the wine warehouse – the tasks were endless.

First things first: making sure Lexi's bedroom was clean. She didn't think Lexi would invite girls up to her room, but if she wanted to show off her clothes or gadgets, then she might. Ava frowned, thinking that Lexi never had anyone over. She couldn't really say she minded too much, though. She liked having her daughter to herself. Still, it would be good for Lexi to have a few friends her age – anyone but Sophie. She sighed, thinking how Sophie always seemed so mature and friendly. She'd be the ideal friend for Lexi when she started secondary, but Ava couldn't open the door for Emily any further. Cringing, she remembered how she'd invited Emily and Sophie over for supper after the party. God, she'd wished she'd never done that, but she'd been desperate to get Emily to leave.

She straightened the pillow on Lexi's bed, then blinked as she spotted something underneath. A swatch of fabric, the same blue as the sky. An image flashed into her mind of her baby boy, wrapped in that same colour. She shook her head so hard it hurt her neck. She must be imagining things. That blue blanket couldn't be here. It was only because she was thinking of him so much these days. The blanket was inside the sealed box in the storage room, not here on Lexi's bed.

But despite telling herself that, her heart still pounded as she moved the pillow to reveal exactly what she'd seen inside her head. Slowly, as if she was in a dream, she reached out, jerking back when her fingers touched it. It *was* real. It was the same soft fabric, the exact shade, and the right size. And it was here, now, under her daughter's pillow.

But *how*? The storage-room door had been locked. She distinctly remembered Emily locking it when they'd finished tidying the basement. Lexi would have no idea where to find the key. *She* hadn't been able to find the key. Had it been there all along? Could she have missed it somehow? She'd been so rattled by the laptop, but...

It couldn't be the same blanket. It wasn't possible! Panic charged through her, and everything was a blur as she raced into Dan's office and threw open the desk drawer. She sank back as she spotted the keyring. How could she not have seen it before? It didn't matter. Pulse racing, she grabbed it, then went downstairs and into the basement, not pausing to try the light. The darkness didn't threaten her. It was already inside her, the fear almost suffocating her. She flew across the space towards the storage room, her heart pounding as she put the key in the lock.

She opened the door. The air was musty and a strange scent swirled around her, but she barely noticed as she crept towards the stack in the corner as if it was a bomb about to go off.

Then she took in the ripped tape and gaping flaps, and her heart exploded. She leaned against the wall, hunching over as the pain coursed through her. The box had been breached, its contents rifled through. And the memories she'd so carefully contained, away from her daughter, spewed out like a noxious cloud, enveloping her before she could think to move away.

Her son's face the morning she'd found him filled her mind, and she wrapped her arms around herself as if she could brace against it. It was too late, though, and the scene scrolled through her head like a film in technicolour, unfaded by time. He'd always been the first to awaken, crying at six o'clock sharp as if his internal alarm clock had gone off. But that morning had been blissfully silent, and when she'd jerked awake, she'd noticed with surprise it was seven and the house was still silent. She'd sat up in a panic when she'd realised that instead of sleeping in the nursery, like usual, she was in bed beside Dan. God, she really must have been tired.

For a second, she allowed herself the sweet luxury of lying there, eyes wide open, listening to the birds chirp as the sun filtered through the window. When was the last time she'd had a moment to herself to *breathe*? she wondered. Alfie must have exhausted himself after crying so much last night.

Finally, she slid from the covers, got dressed and brushed her hair, loving that she had the time to do this instead of rushing around while the babies were kicking on their mats. She put her hair in a ponytail and smiled at herself in the mirror, thinking that for the first time since she'd given birth, she actually recognised herself. Humming a little tune, she peeked into the nursery. Everything was quiet. She was almost afraid to go in in case she woke them up, but she braved peering into Alfie's cot.

He wasn't there. He wasn't there, and what met her...

She jammed the box flaps closed, then dashed out and slammed the door, squeezing her eyes tightly to try to stop the film from playing. She couldn't bear what had come next. The dreadful realisation. The knowledge that she was to blame, and that her daughter must never, ever find out.

Dan had agreed, at the first and only discussion they'd had at Alfie's funeral. They'd decided on a small memorial service in a place around the corner from the playground Alfie would have spent hours in if he'd lived. Dan had offered to ask his parents to hold baby Lexi at the back of the room, but Ava had shaken her head.

'I don't want Lexi anywhere near this,' she'd said, her voice cracking. It was silly, she knew. Lexi was only three months old. She didn't know what was going on, but somehow Ava felt like the sadness would seep into her and taint her.

Dan had nodded. 'I understand,' he said. 'She's too young.' He put a hand on Ava's shoulder, but for some reason, Ava flinched. 'Don't worry. We'll make sure she never forgets her brother. We'll keep his memory alive for her.'

Something had twisted inside of Ava. 'I don't want to keep the memory alive for her,' she hissed. 'What memory? She won't remember anything, anyway. To tell her what she's lost is cruel.'

Dan's face went pale, and he nodded and moved away, and Ava felt guiltier. He'd lost something, too, of course. He was grieving too... because of her. But she couldn't bear for her daughter to feel that same loss. She had to protect her. That was the one thing – the only thing – she *could* do.

And now she'd failed. Lexi knew she had a twin. A brother, who should have been by her side and wasn't. She'd always feel like something was missing. She wasn't protected from loss. She'd always feel that sadness.

Because of her.

The vibration of her mobile jolted her back to the present, and she fled the room and locked it behind her. Hands shaking, she slid the phone from her pocket. Was it Dan? Anger surged through her as she realised he must have told Lexi about the box and where to find the key. How else would she have known?

She leaned against the door. She'd told him how she felt. So how could he do that? How could he go against her wishes as if they meant nothing? And how could he leave Lexi to face all of this on her own? God, she couldn't *wait* to talk to him now. She didn't want to hear his explanations; his justifications. She only wanted to let out rage. She'd tried so hard to protect her daughter, and he'd ruined everything.

She glanced at the screen, adrenaline pumping. But it wasn't him – it was the school. Why were they calling? Was Lexi OK? She tried to calm down, telling herself they were probably ringing about the party. It wasn't a school event, they'd taken great pains to stress to her, but they wanted to make sure she had permission to collect their kids from school if their parents weren't picking them up. Ava had done all the forms weeks ago.

'Hello?' she said, trying to focus. All she could think about now was Lexi. Lexi, opening the box, finding out about Alfie, clutching the blanket...

'Mrs MacDonald, please can you come up to the school? Lexi's been in an incident with another student, and she'll need to spend the rest of the day at home.' Mrs Peters, the head teacher, spoke calmly and firmly.

Ava nearly dropped the phone. *What?* 'Is she all right?' Her heart was beating so fast that for a second, she felt like she might faint.

'She's fine.' Mrs Peters' voice was soft now. 'She's sitting in the Calm Zone with Miss Malik.'

Ava slumped onto the floor. Thank God. 'What happened?' She couldn't imagine. In all of her years at the school, Lexi had never been called into the Head's office. She'd never even had a detention, for goodness' sake. She was the type of child teachers forgot was in the room. Whatever had happened must be related to finding out about Alfie. It had to be. It must have been such a shock, and... Her gut clenched when she realised that, despite her certainty, she'd had no idea her daughter had found out until she'd discovered the blanket. She'd been so sure she would know, but instead she'd put it all down to period pains.

Maybe she didn't know her as well as she'd thought.

'I'd rather discuss it when you're here,' Mrs Peters said. 'Can you come now?'

'I'm on my way.' Ava hung up quickly, then went up to the bedroom. She tugged off the old jogging bottoms and pulled on a pair of jeans, twisted her hair into a knot and hurried back out to the car. As she drove the short distance, her mind spun. Had Lexi broken down? Started crying, got upset? Was that why she was waiting in the Calm Zone, whatever the hell that was?

Ava pushed the pedal down, and the car shot forward. She

had to get to her. She'd hold her as tightly as she could – tighter than ever before. She'd pour whatever it took into her daughter to abate the confusion and pain she must be feeling. She'd find some way to make up for this failure. She had to.

She parked and rang the buzzer to get into the school, jiggling her keys impatiently. Finally, she was inside, and she raced to the Head's office.

'Oh!' she said, eyebrows rising when she spotted Emily, clad in her work uniform, sitting on the chair. What was she doing here?

'Ava, hi.' Emily smiled, but she seemed... tense, maybe? Could this be about something that had happened between Sophie and Lexi? They'd seemed to be getting on, but perhaps they'd argued. That wouldn't be the worst thing in the world.

'Please, have a seat.' Mrs Peters pointed to a chair beside Emily's, and Ava sank into it. What on earth was going on?

'I'm afraid your daughters were involved in a fight in the playground this morning,' Mrs Peters said, and Ava's mouth dropped open. A fight?

She shook her head. 'No. That's not possible. Lexi's never hit anyone in her life.' The thought of her quiet, sensitive daughter doing something like that was laughable.

Emily was about to speak, but Mrs Peters put up a hand. 'I've talked to numerous children who saw what happened, as well as some teachers. Apparently, the girls were arguing about money. Lexi thought that Sophie had taken some cash she'd hidden in her bedroom, and Sophie denied it.'

Ava couldn't believe what she was hearing. 'Money? Money hidden in her bedroom?' Her voice was rising, and she was shaking her head back and forth. 'No. That's not right. Lexi doesn't hide money in her bedroom. Why would she? And I don't give her cash. Where would she get it from?'

Mrs Peters was gazing at her steadily. 'Maybe from the items she sold here?' she said quietly. 'As you know, we had to have a firm word with her about selling them at school, as they were causing quite a bit of trouble.'

Ava stared. 'Items she was selling?'

Mrs Peters shifted, an uncomfortable look sliding over her face. 'I had your husband in here a few months ago to discuss it after her teacher saw her. It hasn't happened since, I can assure you of that.'

'Right. Yes. Of course.' The words trickled from Ava's mouth, and she nodded slowly, trying to pretend she knew what the hell the Head was talking about. Lexi had been selling things? The things she'd given her? Yes, she'd noticed a few items missing here and there, but she'd never thought in a million years that Lexi would be *selling* them. A memory clicked into her head of Sophie saying how Lexi wanted to get rid of her stuff. For a fundraiser, she'd said, but that clearly hadn't been true. So, what did Lexi need the money for? She had everything she wanted – and more, clearly, if she was selling off her things.

Ava swallowed, the betrayal hitting her hard, adding to the rage already inside. Dan had known? He'd known all of this, and he hadn't told her? How could he do that? How could he keep this from her? *She* was the one who knew everything about her daughter. Well, she'd thought she was, anyway.

'Look, I know the big leavers' party is this afternoon at your house, Mrs MacDonald,' the Head said. 'And it's the last full week of school. I don't want to do anything too punitive at this stage.'

Ava let out a breath. Thank God. The last thing she needed was Lexi entering a brand-new school with this hanging over her.

'So as long as the girls apologise to each other and agree to get on for what little time we have remaining, then I think we should let this go. It would be best if the girls go home now to cool off.' Mrs Peters paused, glancing back and forth between them. 'All right?'

Ava nodded. 'That's fine with me. Thank you.'

She looked over at Emily, expecting her to be nodding and agreeing too, but her face still had that strange tense expression. Maybe she knew Sophie had taken the cash. She must be embarrassed and upset. Money had always been a tense subject with Emily. She remembered when they'd had lunch in a posh café, a few weeks after they'd first met. Emily had wanted to treat her, but when the bill came, she'd gone white. Ava had offered to pay, but Emily had turned red and shrugged her off, saying she had the money. From where, Ava didn't know. Maybe Sophie's father chipped in? He was yet another thing Emily had always been close-mouthed about.

The Head stood up. 'Right, if you'd like to take your children home now...' It was clear she was finished with them, and they all got to their feet. 'I'll take you to them.'

She strode forward, and Emily and Ava followed behind.

'The girls are waiting over here. Sophie's here, and Lexi's... Oh.' Mrs Peters' brow furrowed as she took in the empty Calm Zone. 'Where's Lexi? Did Miss Malik take her somewhere?'

Sophie shook her head. 'No, Miss Malik was called away for a second. And Lexi just took off.'

Ava gaped at her. 'Took off? What do you mean? Where did she go?' Oh God. Poor Lexi. She must be terrified that she'd be in a world of trouble, especially since she hadn't told Ava about selling the things she'd given her.

Mrs Peters looked at Sophie. 'Are you sure? Did she say where she was going?' Sophie shook her head, and the Head put a hand on Ava's arm. 'Don't worry. She's most likely in the school somewhere, maybe in the toilet.'

Ava nodded, unable to speak.

'She has her bag,' Sophie said. 'And that has her phone.

Maybe you can try calling her?' She dropped her head. 'I didn't take the money,' she said quietly. 'I promise I didn't.'

Ava nodded again and slid out her mobile. She didn't have time to deal with that now. She punched in her daughter's number, praying that she would pick up and talk to her, even if she was only hiding out in the loo. But she didn't answer, and worry ballooned inside.

'I'll check the school,' Mrs Peters said, striding off down the corridor. Ava gripped the phone, her mind spinning. Then she remembered that tracker on Lexi's phone. She pulled up the info, zooming in on the blue dot on the map that showed her daughter's location.

'She's at the train station!' she said, panic flying into her once more. Where on earth was Lexi going? Was that why she needed money? She couldn't get on a train to God knows where alone. Ava let out a cry, her head spinning. All of these secrets. How could she not have known any of this about her daughter?

'Look, don't worry about the party or anything you need to do to get ready for it,' Emily said, the same friendly eager look on her face again now. 'I'll take care of it all. The list is on the fridge, right? Sophie can help. I'll make sure she stays where I can see her,' she added quickly. 'We can hold the fort until Dan arrives.'

Ava didn't have time to think about it or to care. Whatever had happened between Lexi and Sophie was nothing compared to her finding out about Alfie. Everything else had paled into insignificance. She needed to get to her daughter. She needed to do whatever she could to fix this.

'Yes, fine, thank you so much,' she said tightly, hardly looking at Emily or Sophie now. 'I'm not sure Dan's coming, so if you could stay until I get home, that would be great. Thank you. Bye.'

She hurried to her car. Speaking of Dan, she grabbed her mobile and jabbed at his contact. It clicked through to voicemail once again, and her heart dropped. Where *was* he? No matter how angry she was at him, this was their daughter. Lexi needed him. Why wasn't he answering? Was he on the train home already?

'Dan, please ring me. Something happened at school, and Lexi...' She swallowed, barely able to believe this was happening. 'I know you spoke with her about Alfie. She opened the box in the basement with all of his things, and she must be so upset.' Fresh anger and panic shot through her. 'Lexi ran out of school. It looks like she's at the train station. I'm on my way there now. Just... just call me. Please.'

Her voice was cold, even to her own ears. She never could forgive him for what he'd done, but she couldn't waste time thinking about their future now. All she could focus on was finding Lexi and bringing her back. Back home – back to her – where she belonged.

Back to where she would try to make up for failing to protect her daughter.

Again.

TWENTY-FOUR
LEXI

Trains whip by me as I sit on the metal bench at the station, the wind cool against my hot cheeks. I've called Dad at least ten times now, but he's still not answering. It hurts that he kept this from me, this huge secret that has changed everything. But I don't think he wanted to keep it silent. I can see that from his laptop folder. He wanted to keep Alfie's memory alive, unlike Mum who boxed it all up. He'll tell me whatever I want to know, I'm 100 per cent certain of that.

I pick up the phone and call him again, but it still rings out. I duck my head, my eyes filling with tears. For a split second, I think that I'll go home and get my cash before remembering once more that I don't have any. That Sophie's taken it. Because no matter how much she might be denying it, she had to have. It couldn't have disappeared into thin air. Anger pours into me, followed by panic. I have to get out of here. I can't stay. I have to get to Dad.

But how?

My mind races as I think about how to get money – fast. I could sell something, I guess, but I don't want to go back home. Mum might be there waiting. Is there anything on me that someone would buy? I look down at the mobile in my hand. I could fetch a lot for this, but I still need to talk to Dad and find out where he's staying. I scrabble through my bag. Pens? Broken pencils? Who would give me anything for that? I have my old phone that I bought off eBay, but it was only worth £20 when I got it and I'm sure it's less now.

My fingers go to my necklace and run along it, like they always do when I'm thinking, and my eyes widen. This is worth a lot of money, I know that for sure. All the girls in my class were so jealous, but that wasn't why I wore it. It's worth a lot to me. It's the one thing that made me happy when Mum gave it to me, because I could see how much it meant to her too. I blink back tears as thoughts swirl through my mind. If I sell it, I'll have more than enough to get to Brighton to see Dad. Maybe enough to make up for some of the money Sophie took.

But... can I do it? Can I sell this necklace that's so special to me – and my family? I swallow as I picture handing it over to someone. Then I think of my parents and all they kept from me. My family is broken right now. I'm broken right now. And while I may not ever fix my family, I can fix me. I need to do whatever I can to get to Dad, even if it means selling the necklace.

How can I sell it? Maybe a pawn shop? I know there's one off the high street. I'll go there now. My phone starts ringing, and I jump, praying it's Dad. But Mum's name comes up, and I send it straight to voicemail. I don't want to talk to her. I play the message as I hurry down the station platform towards the exit, my heart pounding as she tells me not to get on any train; that she's on her way.

How does she know I'm here? I look around me for a minute as if she can see me now. I feel that way often: like she's always there, always watching, although I know she's not. And while sometimes it feels comforting – like the night Mr Bhandari was killed – usually it's annoying. I look at the phone in my hand as a lightbulb goes off in my head. It's the iPhone. I remember she installed the tracker so she could see where I am at all times, alongside the child protection filter to block dangerous websites, including social media. It's the reason I bought the old phone off eBay.

I can't take this phone with me, I realise. I have to ditch it quickly, before she catches up to me. I swallow, thinking I still don't know where Dad is staying. There can't be too many big hotels for conferences in Brighton, can there? Whether I talk to him or not, I'll find him somehow. I put it down on an empty bench at the deserted end of the platform. Maybe someone will take it, and Mum will think I've got on the train. Or it'll stay here. Either way, she won't know where I am for once in my life.

I hurry out of the station and down the road, towards the pawn shop. My heart is aching at the thought of selling this necklace, but I don't really have a choice, do I? I need money, and I need it quickly.

Finally, I'm at the pawn shop, and I go inside. A man behind the counter glances up as a bell tinkles when I enter, surprised to see me there.

'Hello.' I swallow and scrabble at my neck to get the necklace off. 'I'd like to sell this, please.'

The man tilts his head. 'How old are you?'

'Sixteen.' I clear my throat and put on my best mature face, praying he either doesn't have good eyesight or has no idea what a sixteen-year-old looks like these days.

'Nice try, kid.' He nods towards my jumper. 'Never heard of a sixteen-year-old who goes to St Mary's Primary School.'

Damn. My heart drops as I realise I'm wearing my school uniform complete with a huge crest with the name of my school. What an idiot I am. Tears spring into my eyes, and panic fills me again. What am I going to do? I don't want to stay here. I want to get away. I want to get to Dad.

Maybe... An idea floats into my head. 'Can you tell me how much this is worth?'

The man looks at me as if trying to see if I'm a good kid or not, then nods. 'OK. Let me see it.'

I take off the necklace and drop it on his palm, holding my breath as he stares at it, then takes a little thing like a magnifying glass and looks at the diamond. 'Someone loves you a lot if they've given you this,' he says, shaking his head. 'I'd say it's worth about a thousand.'

I jerk. A thousand pounds? I mean, I knew it was expensive, but... I bite my lip as his words echo in my brain. My parents do love me a lot. I know they do. It's just... I wish I felt it. 'Thanks.' I force a smile and go out to the street, then duck into an alley between the shops and get out my old phone – I keep it zipped in a side pocket under some tissues, the one place Mum doesn't look. It's a last resort and I don't know if I'll be able to sell the necklace in time, but it's the only thing I can think of.

Quick as a flash, I snap a photo of the necklace, then log into my Facebook account and list the item for sale on Marketplace.

Then I sit back, cross my fingers and wait.

TWENTY-FIVE
EMILY

'Come on.' Emily took Sophie by the arm and hurried her away from the school. 'Let's get out of here. We have to go to Ava's and get the house ready for the party.' And make sure Dan was knocked out with more drugs, she thought, but Sophie didn't need to know that. Right now, she couldn't think of anything else to do – she could hardly move him somewhere with half the school next door. At least her boss at work had left before the school had called and she'd had to leave. She'd put a junior colleague in charge, saying she wouldn't be back in today.

'I don't want to go there, Mum. Lexi won't want me at the party.' A tear slipped down Sophie's cheek, and she swiped it away as Emily continued to propel her along the street. 'And what are we going to do about Dan?'

'I'll take care of it, don't worry,' Emily said. Thank goodness Ava wasn't sure if he was coming to the party today. His absence wouldn't be any cause for concern, although she could see from his mobile that he did have quite a few notifications today for missed calls and texts. Hopefully, Ava would think his lack of response was down to work or anger, and nothing else.

'I can't believe Lexi would think I actually took that money,' Sophie said, another tear trickling down her cheek.

'I know it wasn't you. She'll forget about it soon, don't worry. She shouldn't have so much money in her room, anyway. Where on earth did she get five hundred pounds?' Emily muttered as she strode down the street. She couldn't wait to be back inside the house again. She'd decorate and put on the very best party she could. Whether Ava could come or not, she'd be grateful for what Emily had done.

Sophie jolted to a stop. 'How do you know it was five hundred pounds?' she asked.

Emily's heart dropped. Oh God. She hadn't really been paying attention to what she'd been saying. She tilted her head, meeting her daughter's eyes. 'Well, I don't. I'm only guessing.'

But Sophie's eyes had narrowed. 'You took that money.' It wasn't a question.

Emily tried to get her daughter to keep walking. They didn't have time to waste on this. She forced a laugh, hoping it sounded believable. 'Of course I didn't. Why would I do that?' She shook her head, remembering her surprise when she'd discovered the envelope of notes during a rifle through Lexi's things to see how much stuff she had. How had Lexi come across this much money? And why was she hiding it? Maybe Ava and Lexi weren't as close as she always made them out to be. Lexi would definitely notice it was gone, but she wouldn't be able to say anything to her mother if she didn't want her to know it had disappeared. It had been a risk worth taking, and she hadn't stopped to think that Lexi might blame Sophie – or that she'd dare to fight her over it, if she did. She'd have to think of a way to bring the girls together again, although that was hardly her top priority at the moment.

'Mum, stop.' Sophie held her gaze. 'I've seen the stuff you steal. I've seen the safe you put it in.'

Emily jerked. What? Sophie knew she'd been stealing things?

'And I know you're doing it for me,' she said. 'So I can go to private school. I know it's a lot of money.'

'It is.' Emily nodded, relieved Sophie understood, even if it wasn't really for that. She could never steal enough to cover those costs – at least not enough watches and phones. 'It is a lot of money.' She paused. 'But look, you don't need to worry. I'm not going to take anything anymore. I'm getting a promotion at work, so I won't have to.' And if things worked out with Ava, then she might not need to put Sophie in private school. She wouldn't need to rely on school to stay in Ava's life.

Sophie stopped. 'A promotion at work?'

'Yes.' Emily hurried her forward. 'I'm going to need to spend more time there, since I'll be mainly on night shifts. But you're used to that, right? You don't need me around.'

'Mum.' Sophie's voice was small. 'You know what you said about if I help you, you'll give me anything? Whatever I want?'

Emily glanced at her daughter. 'Have you thought of something?'

'I want you to stay home with me.' Her voice was low, and for a minute, Emily wasn't sure she'd heard Sophie correctly. 'I don't want you to work every night. I don't want to be home alone all the time.'

Emily's mouth dropped open. What? That was the opposite of what she'd expected. Sophie loved being independent, having the whole place to herself each evening.

'I know you want us to have a good life, but I just want to have family around. Like you did.'

Emily started. What did she mean? Sophie had no idea how she'd grown up. How did she know that she'd had family around? Even if she had, she'd still felt as invisible as someone living alone.

'All I want is to be with you and spend more time together, like the movie night we had at Ava's. That's it. I don't care about anything else.'

Emily blinked. She couldn't mean that, could she? The movie night had been fun, yes, but it had been a one-off. Sophie would get sick of her if she was around all the time. They worked so well the way they were now. Anyway, she couldn't turn down this promotion; this chance to have people look up to her and listen to her... and to get more money. It was the best thing for both of them. 'I'm sorry, Soph. I'll spend as much time with you as I can before my new job starts, but I have to take this.'

Sophie's face slammed closed. 'Right. So you lied. You said if I helped you, you'd give me anything. But now you won't.' Her face was flushing red again. 'You don't even want to be with me *now*.'

'Of course I do!' Emily touched her daughter's arm, but she jerked back. 'Look, why don't we talk about all of this later? Let's focus on helping Ava with the party.'

'I'm not going,' Sophie said. 'I'm going home.'

Emily held her gaze for a minute, then shrugged. 'All right.' She could hardly force her to do something. She'd never had to do that, and she never would.

Sophie turned, hurrying back towards the flat. Emily watched as her daughter got further and further away. She just needed to cool off, Emily thought. Typical teenage strop; she was getting closer to that age. Better that she didn't go to the party, anyway. Emily could do what she needed without Sophie interfering, and she wouldn't have to worry about any tension between her and Lexi.

She bit her lip, wondering what on earth had prompted that comment about her family. God, she hadn't thought of them for ages. Why would she? It only made her angry. Angry that they'd never noticed she was hurting. Angry that instead of trying to help her, they'd only added more to the burden she was expected to carry.

Emily drew in air as she remembered the last time her mother had got pregnant. She'd been thirteen, and she'd managed to secure a role in the school production. She'd loved being under the lights onstage, if only a few seconds, and she couldn't wait for her mum to see her. But when she'd handed her the ticket to come, her mother had shaken her head.

'Em, I'm so sorry, but I can't be more than a foot from a toilet right now,' she had said, turning green as she spoke. Her hand had slid down to her stomach, and Emily had felt horror growing inside. No. Her mother couldn't be pregnant. Not again. For God's sake, Emily's brother had only turned one! What was *wrong* with her parents? And every time her mum was expecting, she was throwing up almost the whole nine months. Emily had always had to drop everything to help out, and when the baby had come, anything she had ever wanted mattered even less.

'No, Mum. You can't be serious.' Her voice had sounded so hard that she barely recognised it. She couldn't take this. She couldn't do this again. She had already had such a tiny, tiny piece of her mother's heart, and now she was about to have less.

To have nothing.

'The more kids, the more love,' her mother had said merrily, rubbing her growing belly, and anger had stirred inside at her selfishness. It was more for them, but less for everyone else. 'It's still very early days, but I'm going to need your help with this one more than ever. You're old enough now to babysit and help around the house. Laundry, cleaning, things like that. We'll a need to pull together.'

She'd rushed to her room, unable to look her mum in eye. If she could have run away then, she would have. Bu knew if she wanted any chance to have the life she needed noticed, she had to at least finish GCSEs. In the mea though, there was something else she could do, she'd thought, the idea forming in her mind. Something that could stop this from happening; from going any further. She could stop the baby being born.

She'd racked her brain, spending ages researching how to end a pregnancy, finally finding a kind of tea that might cause problems. She'd served it to her mum each day, telling her it helped with sickness and praying it would work.

And one morning, her mum had gathered them close, tears running down her face, and told them that she wasn't going to have a baby, after all. Emily had had to try hard to hide her happiness. She felt guilty, of course, when she saw how sad her mother was, but she knew it was the right thing. And besides, there was no way of telling if it had been the tea she'd been giving her mother that had caused the miscarriage. It could have happened, anyway. Her mum had never got pregnant again, and life had continued.

Shame she couldn't make Dan go away as easily, she thought now. God, it would be so much simpler if he just... *disappeared*. She blinked at the notion, allowing herself to work through that scenario even as she knew she could never go that far. Could she? She had his phone from when he'd been knocked out that first night. She could try to guess his password d use it to text Ava that he'd decided to go away for a bit; to some space after their fight. It would take a while until Ava to think that something might be wrong. Maybe she'd be was gone, and she wouldn't try to find him. She dn't seem to want him around much.

herself drift into a daydream where she and Ava erating about men over a glass of champagne. e on their own with teenage daughters at school. Ava would draw her more and more into her

ed on the present, she told herself as she went

inside Ava's house. She had to get everything ready for this party. And – she eyed the list on the fridge – it seemed there was a lot to do. Then she'd go pay Dan a visit.

By the time the party started, everything would have fallen into place.

One way or another.

TWENTY-SIX
AVA

Ava drove the short distance to the train station, her heart pounding. Please be there, she repeated over and over. *Please.* She parked and got out, then pushed through the station barrier and raced over to the platform, following the tracker on her phone. She was getting closer and closer, but... Oh God.

She came to a halt when she spotted a mobile on top of an empty bench. She picked it up, her heart sinking as she turned the sparkly pink case over in her hands. There was no mistaking it: this was Lexi's, the latest iPhone Ava had bought her a couple of months ago. Why was this here? Had Lexi forgotten it before getting on a train? Had she remembered her mother could track her and decided to ditch it? Now she was all alone on her way to God knows where.

Or – Ava froze as the thought entered her mind – maybe she wasn't alone. Could she have been talking to someone and arranged to meet them? She must have been so upset by Alfie; she wouldn't have been thinking clearly. You always heard such horror stories. Until now, Ava had been confident that could never happen to her family.

But then, she'd never thought what had happened to Alfie

could happen to them either. Shouldn't she know better by now?

What was she going to do?

She sank onto the bench, clutching the mobile in her hand as every cell vibrated with pain and panic. Lexi was out there somewhere, without her phone, without her family, without *her*. Her daughter was missing, hurting and vulnerable, and as angry as Ava was at Dan, it was all her fault. It might have been Dan who'd told her, but she was the one who'd caused this horrific chain of events.

Because no matter what Dan said, she was to blame for Alfie's death. It hadn't been SIDS. She knew better than that, and she should have been more careful. If only she hadn't been so tired. If only she'd been *thinking*. How she wished she could roll back time to that night and change it all. Everything – everyone – could have been so different.

She jerked as a thought hit. Could Lexi be on her way to see *Dan*? Had he decided not to come home for the party, and Lexi was going there? But if she had no money... She punched in his number now, but once more it went through to voicemail.

Lexi's iPhone bleeped, and she blinked in surprise as Sophie's name came up on the screen. Why would Sophie be trying to get in touch, especially after the fight they'd had? She entered her daughter's password and opened the message.

Need to talk to you. Can you meet me at my flat in an hour?

Ava stared, her mind swirling. Obviously, Lexi wouldn't get this message. She wouldn't be going to the flat. But maybe Sophie knew something more than Ava did. Judging by what she'd learned that day about Lexi selling her things, there was a lot Ava didn't know. Perhaps Sophie could give her a clue about where Lexi had gone – and why. She'd head to Emily's flat now and talk to Sophie; see what she could uncover.

She had to find her daughter.

She rushed off the platform and over to the car park. Then she got into the car and navigated through the traffic towards Emily's place. As she passed by her street, her gut clenched at the thought of Emily in her house once more, doing everything she should be doing for this party. She sighed, gripping the steering wheel. She should have cancelled it. She shook her head. It was too late now. Emily would do what she could to get the place ready. Anyway, if she did find Lexi soon, then she could take over when she returned.

She parked on the street outside Emily's block of flats and hurried out, praying the parking warden wouldn't give her a ticket. It was the least of her worries now, though. She raced to the door, sweat clinging to her brow as she breathed in the hot and humid air. It was still morning, but already the air hung like a wet blanket around her, making everything seem weighted down.

She buzzed Emily's door, tapping her foot impatiently as she waited. No answer. She buzzed again, her heart sinking. Where was Sophie? She glanced at her watch. It was only about fifteen minutes since she'd sent the text about meeting back here. Had she gone somewhere else in the meantime? Ava couldn't afford to wait. Lexi could be miles and miles away by that time.

As she stood there, a woman with a buggy came out the door, then held it open for Ava. Ava nodded her thanks and darted in, then ran up the dingy stairs to Emily's flat. She pounded on the door, her pulse racing.

'Sophie! Are you there?' She waited, but there was no sound. 'Can you open the door? I'm not angry at you. I want to talk.' She strained to hear, but there was nothing, and she sighed. 'Please, if you're in there, I just want to find out if you know anything about where Lexi might have gone. Please.' She waited again, then reached out and tried the handle. To her surprise, the door opened easily, and she raised her eyebrows. Maybe Sophie had her headphones on and hadn't heard her knocking and ringing.

She pushed the door open further, wincing at the mess inside. It was nothing like the flat which had greeted her that day when she and Ava had stayed. This one had things strewn everywhere, dishes piled on the counter.

'Sophie?' she called, edging inside. 'Are you in here?' She almost tripped over a pair of shoes. God, how did Emily stand this? 'Sophie?'

The door to her bedroom was open, and Ava glanced in, her heart dropping. The room was empty – she wasn't lounging on her bed with her headphones, like Ava had hoped. She glanced at her mobile. Thirty minutes now since Sophie had sent the text. Should she wait? She sank onto the bed for a minute, almost too tired to stand. Sophie's room was like a different world: even though the dark sparkly paint was hardly her cup of tea, it was neat and tidy – neater than Lexi's room by far – with everything in its place. Strangely, though, a few drawers were wide open, with clothes removed and piled neatly on the end of the bed. Ava tilted her head. Was Sophie going somewhere?

She squinted at a metallic box, recognising it as the safe she'd seen under the sofa. It was wide open, with a jumble of phones, jewellery and watches inside. What the *hell*? What was all of this? Was Sophie stealing from other places too? Well, whatever she was doing was none of her concern now. Unless... she swallowed, thinking of Lexi. Unless Lexi was somehow involved? Was that why Sophie had been texting her? Was that why they'd been fighting?

A door opened and closed, and Sophie came into the flat carrying a suitcase. She must have gone to the storage unit to get it.

'Sophie!' Ava's heart lifted. Thank God. Now, maybe, she could find her daughter. 'Thank goodness you're here.' She held up Lexi's phone. 'I found this at the train station, and I read your message that you wanted to meet here to talk.'

Sophie's eyes were wide as she came into the bedroom. She looked terrified. 'None of this is... I didn't—'

'Look, I meant what I said. I don't care if you took the money.' Ava cut her off. 'I really don't. I only want to find Lexi.'

'I don't know where Lexi is.' Sophie swallowed.

'Why did you want to talk to her, then?' Ava was desperate now. Sophie must know something. More than she did, anyway. There was something going on. 'Was there something you wanted to tell her?'

Sophie bit her lip, and Ava wondered what on earth she had to say. 'Look, Sophie, whatever you know, it's OK to tell me. Everything's going to be all right. Tell me. Please.'

Sophie drew in a deep shuddery breath. 'Fine.'

But as she was about to start talking, they heard the door open.

TWENTY-SEVEN
LEXI

It's weird being on the street in the middle of the day when I should be in school. I'd rather be there than wandering around town, waiting for someone to buy a necklace I really like. No, scratch that. I don't want to be in school. I don't want to be anywhere near here. I want to be with Dad. I've got to talk to him.

I've got to get this money.

I glance at my phone. Still no message or money, and I don't have much time left. Mum's probably already sent out multiple search teams. Honestly, I feel more like a fugitive on the run than a girl who ran out of school.

Girl who ran out of school. The words ring in my mind as I slump against the wall. I can hardly believe that's me. I got in a fight. In the playground, of all places. I was sent to the Head, and I took off. Now I'm here on the street. Trying to sell my jewellery. Who *am* I?

That's the thing, I think, staring out at the cars driving by. I don't know who I am. All the stuff Mum throws at me – how overprotective she is – means I haven't had a chance to explore what *I* like. I eat what she gives me, since she says it's best. I wear the clothes that she buys and watch the shows she wants to. And still, inside, I feel empty. When she stares at me, I'm only half here.

At least I know why now. To her, I *am* only half here. And she's tried so hard to fill that space she's pushed me down too. Maybe I can never fill all that space for her, but I can at least fill it for me. By finding out about Alfie – by finding myself.

My mobile pings, and my heart lifts. Finally! I click onto the screen, my heart beating fast as I take in the message from a woman saying she's interested in the necklace, and she needs it for a party tonight. Can we meet as soon as possible? I couldn't have asked for anything better, I think, typing a message that we can meet. I bite my lip, thinking even if it is a woman, I should be careful. I text back to meet me in the café by the bridge, then sink down to wait. She says she's not far and she'll be there in half an hour.

Half an hour! It feels like forever, but I know it's not that long, and I'm lucky to have found someone who wants to move so quickly. My heart is racing with all that's ahead of me, but I try to relax. The day is hot and hazy, and the normally heaving pubs have just opened for lunch. The river path is deserted, with few people ambling slowly by, and the café is quiet. I'm the sole customer sitting outside.

'Hey.'

I glance up, shielding my eyes against the sun. A man is above me, and I scrabble to my feet. The sun is so bright I can't make out his face, and I wonder why he's talking to me.

Then I squint, and it clicks. It's *him*. The man who got upset when the iPad I sold him wasn't working. The man who got in a fight with Mr Bhandari. The man who I thought burgled Mr Bhandari... and as good as killed him.

What's he doing here? Didn't Mum say he was arrested? Fear judders through me, and I jerk away. 'Aren't you in prison?' The words pop out of my mouth, and I want to take them back. What a stupid thing to say. He's obviously not in prison.

He snorts. 'Prison? You trying to be funny?'

'I'm meeting someone,' I say, my voice trembling. 'She'll be here any minute. So I'm sorry, but I can't talk now.'

'Someone you're selling a necklace to, right?'

I blink. How does he know that?

'Yeah, that's me,' he says. 'I was waiting for you to pop up again on Marketplace so I could get back what you owe me. No one scams me.'

I try not to shiver as I hold his gaze. He's skinny, with tattoos up and down his arms, and he's wearing a baseball cap pulled low over his eyes so I can't see the top half of his face. He's got huge baggy trousers on – the kind I always wonder how they stay up – and a scent of sweat and something else, something sweet and cloying, hang off him.

As scared as I am, anger bursts through me. This is the man who terrified Mr Bhandari so much that he died. I reach for my phone.

'I'm calling 999,' I say, my voice trembling.

But before I can do anything, the man grabs the mobile from my hand. 'Piece of shit,' he says, throwing it onto the asphalt. 'Now give me that necklace.' His voice is low and gravelly.

I shake my head. Does he think he can take it? Is this what he thinks I owe him? No. No way. I can't give it to him. I need to get to Dad. 'I'll only give it to you if you pay me the money first.'

He snorts. 'Pretty brave for a kid, huh? How old are you?' he asks.

I swallow. I don't need to answer that. It's none of his business. And why does he want to know, anyway? 'Do you want the necklace or not?' I ask. My voice is shaking, and I cough to cover it up.

'Oh, I want it, all right.' His low voice sends shivers through me again. 'Anything else you can give me?' His eyes run over me. 'Watch? Cash?'

'I need to go,' I say, glancing around me. The café is deserted now and there's no one nearby. 'I—'

He wrenches my arm. 'You aren't going anywhere until you give me that necklace.' His lip curls as he looks at it. 'And I want more than that.'

My heart is pounding so hard I can barely hear anything now. I don't know what he means, but I know that I'm in terrible trouble. 'I don't have anything. Honestly. I don't have any money on me at all.'

He pauses, tightening his grip on my arm. 'Your house isn't far from here, right? I remember where you live,' he says. 'Dead posh. Bet you can get me lots of stuff from there.' He gives me a little shake. 'And if you say a word to anyone, it won't be good for you. Remember, I know where you live.' His eyes gleam, and I think once more of Mr Bhandari. 'Let's go.'

And before I can say anything more, he starts dragging me towards home.

TWENTY-EIGHT
EMILY

Emily paused for a second to catch her breath, glancing around Ava's house. Everything was almost ready for the party, with only one more thing on the list: she had to take care of Dan, and then she could wait for people to arrive. She rifled through her bag to find the bottle of pills. *Shit!* There were only a few left – nowhere enough to knock him out like she needed. Her mind spun. Were there more at home? She thought there might be another bottle in the medicine cabinet, where she'd stockpiled prescriptions over the years.

She glanced at the clock. She still had a bit of time before people started to come. She'd nip back to the flat, get the pills, and sort Dan out before anyone arrived. Hopefully, Sophie would be in her room with the door closed, and she wouldn't notice her coming and going.

As fast as she could, she hurried down the street. Her legs burned and sweat trickled down her back, but she didn't have time to waste. After what felt like forever, she was at the door to the flat. She paused, staring as it shuddered back and forth in the draught. It only did that when it wasn't fully closed... when it hadn't been locked properly. How many times had she told

Sophie to make sure to secure it, she thought, coming inside? She put her handbag down on the table, about to call her daughter's name, when she stopped.

Something wasn't right. There was a scent in the air, a fresh floral scent she'd know anywhere. Oh God. Her heart dropped when she glanced into the bedroom. It was Ava and Sophie, and the safe was beside them.

The safe was *open* beside them.

Her pulse raced, her mind clogged with so many thoughts it was difficult to grasp onto one. Somehow, Sophie had got the safe open. But how? Why? Had she guessed the code? Thank God Ava's rings weren't there. Imagine if she'd found them! She jerked as a thought hit. They weren't there, but she'd been so certain they had been. Could *Sophie* have taken them? Was that where they'd disappeared to?

'What's going on?' She tried to make her voice light and airy, but to her own ears, it sounded tight and nervy. 'Ava, why are you here? Did you find Lexi?'

'No, not yet.' Ava shook her head. 'I came to talk to Sophie and see if she might know more about where Lexi went. Look, I don't care if Sophie stole that money. I told her that too. But this...' She gestured towards the safe, and Emily's gut clenched.

'I had no idea she was taking all of that,' Emily said quickly, before Ava could say more. 'I'll talk to her. We'll sort it out. In the meantime, I should get back to the party. I came to check on Sophie and make sure she was OK.' Nothing could be further from the truth, but Ava wouldn't know that. 'And you need to find Lexi, of course.'

'Yes, of course.' Ava was still looking at the safe. 'But Sophie, what was it that you wanted to tell me?'

Emily froze. What the hell? What *was* Sophie going to tell Ava? It couldn't be about the rings, could it? She had no way of knowing who they belonged to, though. Could it be about Dan? No. Sophie wouldn't do that to her. She might have wanted to let him out, but not before he agreed to keep quiet. And she knew he hadn't done that yet.

Whatever Sophie had wanted to say, it could create more problems. That was the last thing she needed. 'Wait, is that *Lexi?*' She pointed out the window at a gaggle of girls walking down the street. From this distance, it was impossible to make out if one was Lexi or not, but they looked the right age. They didn't appear to be wearing school uniforms, but one had Lexi's mouse-brown hair and slight figure.

Sophie squinted. 'It might be. I can't tell.'

'I'll see you back at the house,' Ava said, grabbing her phone and jumping up. 'Thanks again for setting up the party.'

Ava hurried from the flat, and Emily sighed in relief. Spotting those girls on the street had been a stroke of luck. She'd known Ava wouldn't risk one of them being Lexi and not going after her. She'd managed to rid of her before Sophie could say anything.

'Mum...' Sophie shook her head. 'How could you tell Lexi's mum that I stole all of this?' She gestured to the safe, then dropped her gaze. 'I was only going to take one or two things, I promise. I'm sorry. I needed the money.'

'Look, none of that matters right now,' Emily said, trying to stay calm. They could talk later about what Sophie needed money so desperately for – about the fact that she'd been stealing from her mother. 'I need to ask you something. Did you take two rings from here? Gold ones, both with diamonds. They were in a small black pouch.' She crossed her fingers, her heart pounding. If Sophie had them, she could talk to Dan and hopefully, this whole saga would be over. 'Look, I don't care that you took them, but I need them back. They could change everything.'

Sophie dropped her head. 'I'm sorry,' she said again, her voice small. 'They were right at the bottom of the safe. I didn't think you'd miss them.'

Emily nearly collapsed in relief. 'So you did take them. Oh, thank God. Thank *God*. Can you give them to me?' *Please may Sophie still have them. Please.*

But Sophie was shaking her head. 'I can't.'

Emily's heart dropped. 'What do you mean, you can't?'

'I don't have them anymore,' Sophie said. 'I sold them.'

Emily drew back. *Fuck.* 'You sold them?' Her voice rose. 'How much money did you need? And what *for*?' She swallowed, trying to get her head around it all. OK, the rings were gone. At least she knew for sure. Right now, she had to get back to the party. And she had to deal with Dan. 'It doesn't matter,' she said, waving a hand. 'You can explain it to me tonight.'

'Mum...' Sophie met her eyes. 'I'm not going to be here tonight.'

Emily shook her head. She didn't have time for this. 'Fine. But you need to tell me where you're going. A friend from school or something?'

Sophie gestured around her room. For the first time, Emily noticed items piled on the bed and emptied drawers. She raised her eyebrows. Where the hell *was* she going?

'You asked me what the money was for.' Sophie straightened her shoulders. 'I needed it to find my family. Your family.' She paused. 'Our family.'

Emily stared. What on earth was she talking about?

'You never wanted to talk about them, so I never asked. I don't know why.' She shrugged. 'I guess I was used to our world with only the two of us. But the older I got, the more I started to wonder... the more I started to want more than just us.' She dropped her head. 'You were never here.'

Anger burst through Emily. Not this again! She was never here because she'd been busy working. Working for them, so they could have the life she wanted.

'I tried to find things out myself, but I didn't know where to start. I didn't know where your family lived. I didn't know who my father was.' Sophie sighed, and Emily thought that even she didn't know. 'But I couldn't find anything. Not my father, not my family. So I opened the safe – I just kept trying codes until I found one that worked – and I sold those rings. They were old and they didn't fetch much, but it was enough to hire a private investigator. They couldn't find my father, but they did find my grandparents – your mum and stepdad.'

Emily's heart dropped.

'I only wanted to see what they looked like at first. I searched on Facebook, and there they were. They seemed so normal. So nice.' She lowered her head. 'And that made me want to know more, so one day when you were working, I took the train.'

Emily gazed at her daughter, unable to believe what she was hearing. Sophie had taken the train to Norwich, all alone? How could she not have known any of this? 'I thought I would see where they lived and where you grew up. You never told me anything about when you were young.' She paused, waiting for Emily to say something, but she couldn't find the words.

'But when I got there, the street...' She breathed in, and Emily could almost see the picture in her head now. The row of identical houses, with old cars in the drive and stuffed bins out front. The shout of children playing in the street, and the smell of cooking.

'Well, it wasn't anything special. It wasn't like where Lexi lives. But the people there were happy. They were together. I could hear them inside their houses, talking and laughing. They didn't need more.'

Emily shook her head, thinking how wrong that was. They had wanted more: more kids, more love, like her mum had said. They might have been happy, but she hadn't been.

'I couldn't help ringing the doorbell.' Sophie's voice cut into her memories, and she met her daughter's eyes. 'I wanted to see them. My grandparents.'

Emily swallowed, picturing her mother opening the door to come face to face with her granddaughter.

'And when my grandmother saw me, she stared. She stared, then asked me who I was.' Sophie's face twisted, and Emily saw the anger there. 'She didn't know I *existed*, Mum. You never told her about me.'

Emily blinked, letting her daughter's words wash over her. Of course she hadn't told her mother that she was pregnant. She hadn't looked back after she'd left. There had been nothing there for her, and her mum had been so busy with all the other kids that although she had reached out a few times, it hadn't been long until she'd stopped trying.

'I told them who I was, and they asked me in. I liked them, Mum. And they told me I have aunts, uncles, cousins.' Her face was glowing. 'When I said goodbye, they asked me to keep in touch. I have, and they helped me realise something.' She paused. 'I realised how much I want to have that life. A normal life, with people around. People who are kind. And happy. Not pushing all the time, or trying to get more money. People who are *there*.' She dropped her eyes. 'That's why I asked if you would stay home with me instead of taking that job.'

Emily stared, frozen, trying to take in what her daughter was saying. She'd gone to Norwich. She'd gone to the place Emily had left. She'd met the family who hadn't been able to give her what she wanted – who had left her alone in the night, wishing for someone to talk to her. And her daughter wanted *that*? She thought those were the people who'd make her less lonely?

Sophie gestured to the clothes on the bed. 'I was going to stay with them for the summer. See what it's like.' She lowered her head. 'Maybe start school there, if they'll have me. That's why I opened the safe again – to get something I could sell to buy a train ticket.'

Emily jerked. *What?* Sophie was going to leave here... She swallowed. Leave *her?*

'Mum?' Sophie's voice was small. 'It's OK if I go? You don't mind? You're so busy that it might be a good thing, right?'

Emily flinched as it hit her that was exactly what she'd thought about her mum. But it wasn't the same, she told herself. Not at all. After all the kids, her mum had barely remembered her existence. Emily was doing all she could to build a life for her and her daughter that would make everyone recognise their worth. That was what someone who really cared about their child and their future did.

Silence fell between them as her mind spun. She didn't want to let Sophie go, but maybe it *was* a good thing. Sophie would soon see how invisible she'd be in a house crammed with people and limited resources, and she'd be back in a heartbeat. It would help her understand all her mum was trying to get for her, and give Emily the time and space to deal not only with Dan, but to start her new job without worrying about her daughter. It would put some space between Sophie and Lexi, too, giving them the time and space to forget their fight.

'Go.' Her voice was hoarse, and her heart twisted at the hurt on her daughter's face. She didn't *want* her to go, but it was best for both of them. Right now, anyway. 'And Sophie, don't worry about anything here. Dan and everything... I will make sure he keeps quiet.' Somehow.

'You *are* going to let him go, right?' Sophie let out a breath. 'It's just... well, I helped you because I didn't want you to get in trouble. I thought you were defending yourself. That you would let him out once he had a chance to calm down. But you still haven't.' She paused, her eyes lasering through Emily as if she could read her mind. 'I saw how you hurt him when we moved him to the Bhandaris'. You aren't going to do anything bad to him, are you?'

Emily was silent, praying she'd drop it. She could never

understand what was at stake here. 'I'll make sure he stays quiet,' she said once more. 'I promise. Don't worry, OK?'

Sophie held her gaze, a tear dripping down her cheek. She swiped it away, and Emily could see how much she was trying to be strong. She was so proud of how mature her daughter was, and Norwich would help her grow up even more – to see where she really belonged.

'I need to get back to the party,' Emily said. 'If you want, I can go with you on the train later this evening.' She hadn't returned to Norwich since she'd left, and she'd no desire to go now, but she could stay at the station and take the first train back to London.

'That's all right, Mum.' Sophie's voice was soft. 'I've texted Grannie the train time and she'll meet me at the station. You don't need to come.'

Grannie. Resentment flashed through Emily at the image of her mother's smiling face greeting Sophie off the train. Her mum would fold Sophie into her soft arms and hold her tightly. Emily could smell the laundry detergent she used and the scent of her favourite shampoo, and longing swept over her.

She pushed it aside. Longing for what? That hug would last for an instant, and then she'd be invisible again, nothing more than an unpaid skivvy helping out with the family. She'd left for a reason, she reminded herself. Sophie would soon find that out too.

'Right.' She swallowed, trying not to show the emotions churning inside. 'Text me when you get there.'

Sophie nodded.

Emily gazed at her daughter, words pushing up inside of her. She wanted to say she loved her. She did love her, of course. She didn't have to say it: it was obvious in everything she did, in how hard she worked. Besides, her mother had told her that a million times, but she'd done nothing to show it. If she had really loved her, then she'd have stopped having more babies.

'Bye.' Emily turned, blinking back the tears that had sprung into her eyes. Sophie would be back soon. This was all for the best.

And what she'd been striving for, grasping for, was finally within reach. All she had to do was keep a clear mind.

Over to the Bhandaris' to deal with Dan – keep him quiet, like she'd promised Sophie – and then, once that was done, she could enjoy the party.

And the start of her new life.

TWENTY-NINE
AVA

Ava rushed down the stairs and out of Emily's building as quickly as she could, desperate to catch up to the group of girls they'd seen from the window. It was a longshot that one of them could be Lexi, but she couldn't take any chances. If Lexi had left her phone at the station, then maybe she hadn't got on the train at all. She ran down the street, forcing her legs faster. Finally, she was close enough to the girls to see that none of them was her daughter. She bent over, trying to catch her breath. Where should she go now? What should she do?

Where was her *daughter*?

She looked up at the sky, feeling the world swing around her. She'd tried so hard to keep Lexi close and to shield her from grief and loss. She'd tried, but she'd failed. Lexi had uncovered the terrible truth about Alfie, and the only thing left had been to hold her tighter to alleviate that pain; to try to rebuild the walls around them higher and stronger. To try all she could to make things right again.

But her daughter had disappeared. How could Ava do that when she couldn't find her? How could she do anything now?

Her legs trembled as the remaining strength left her, and

she collapsed onto the grassy verge. The only thing that had kept her moving forward was gone, and that poisonous cloud of pain and despair was enveloping her once more. She closed her eyes, helpless to stop it seeping in; unable to hold back the brutal barrage of memories dragging her backwards in time. Back to that night – the night she'd been more tired than ever before. Three months of relentless night waking for not one but two babies had left her like a zombie.

She'd finally got them both to sleep, and she'd slumped down on the settee. But as soon as she'd closed her eyes, Alfie had started crying. She'd scooped him up and rocked him in her arms, but he wouldn't settle. Finally, when the urge to lie down and close her eyes was overpowering, she'd popped him in the cot with his sister. He always settled when they were together. That was the beauty of twins.

It would only be for a second, she thought. Just until he dropped off. She'd go get a cup of tea, and when she came back, she'd put him in his own cot – it was dangerous for the babies to sleep too long together; the threat of suffocation was terrifying. But she'd never returned to the nursery. Instead, she'd walked in a daze to her bedroom, flopping beside Dan in the blissful silence. That must have been what had happened, although she couldn't remember any of it.

And when she'd gone to the nursery the next morning... She let out a cry now at the memory. Alfie had still been in the cot with his sister, and he hadn't been moving. He'd been wedged against Lexi, and he'd been blue. Ava had screamed and picked him up, then lay him down on the floor and started CPR, even if she knew it was too late. He was gone. Her son was gone, a few short months after she'd given birth to him.

Lexi had still been sleeping soundly, untouched by anything as Ava held Alfie in her arms. In a haze of shock, Ava had been determined not to disturb her. She'd rushed from the room and into the bedroom, still holding Alfie, tears streaming down her cheeks as numbness wrapped around her. Dan's shouts and questions as he called the ambulance couldn't pierce through. She'd locked herself down – locked what she'd seen down – vowing never to tell her daughter what had happened. That she'd put them both together in the cot. That she never should have done that. That *she* was to blame.

Dan had cried over and over that she wasn't at fault. The autopsy had declared Alfie died of SIDs. He'd told her she could never be certain one twin had cut off the airways of the other, but she knew what she'd seen. She'd never, ever forget.

She couldn't change that she'd taken something – someone – away from her daughter. Someone she could never, ever replace. She'd tried so hard to give her the best life possible, although she knew she could never make up for it.

She winced as it hit her that, despite all her efforts, she'd failed at that too. All she'd learned about her daughter in the past couple of days didn't point to a child who was happy at home. It pointed to a child who couldn't wait to get away.

A child who had her own protective walls; her own secrets. Her own pain tucked away, like her mother.

Why hadn't she noticed? How could she not have noticed?

She rocked back and forth, realising that she hadn't noticed because what she'd done hadn't really been for Lexi. It had been for *her*. Focusing on keeping the pain away from her daughter had also meant that she could keep the pain and guilt away from herself too. To talk about it; to share it – that would mean reliving everything, and she couldn't do that. She couldn't bear to face her mistake, even if she'd never tell Lexi what had really happened.

But in trying to protect her daughter, she'd left her more vulnerable. She'd left her to find out she'd had a twin and that he'd died – all on her own, with no one around her. She'd left her with an aching wound inside, and nothing to bandage it. No matter how many material goods she threw at Lexi – no matter how tightly she clutched her or how high she built the walls – it could never be enough. It never had been.

Ava didn't know how long she sat there, weighted by the guilt and grief she'd set free by reliving that memory. The sun burned down and sweat dripped from her, but she barely noticed. Cars flashed by, the wind hot on her cheeks as they passed, but she didn't turn away. She was open and raw, an endless pit of darkness and despair inside. She'd failed both her children. She'd tried so hard, but it hadn't been enough. What kind of mother was she?

She drew her knees up and rested her head on them, unable to bear the pain. As she closed her eyes against the bright light, Alfie's face swam into her mind. The agony abated for a second and she held his image there, tracing it in her memory. She jerked as she realised it wasn't only the pain and guilt she felt now, but also love. She'd loved him so much she couldn't allow herself to remember it. It had been boxed up, along with the other emotions she was hiding from. But now... it had all come pouring out, and she could feel the strength of that love coursing through her.

A love that made everything else – even the memory of what she'd done – bearable.

Her eyes flew open as a thought hit. Maybe she did have something to give her daughter. *Alfie*. She could give Lexi Alfie. She'd go through the photos and all the mementos. She'd make Alfie come alive again, despite him being with them for a few short months. She shook her head, thinking how the very thing she'd forced Dan to keep silent for so long might be what helped her daughter heal. The haze of grief and shock had blinded her, but now she could see clearly. Now she could see Alfie clearly, and she wanted to share that with her daughter.

First, though, she had to find her.

Determination surged through her, and she got to her feet. Sophie knew something. She'd been about to tell her when

Emily had arrived. She'd go back to Emily's now and see if she could get Sophie to talk. She was about to turn and retrace her steps when she saw a flash of something that looked like Lexi's school uniform – and of Lexi's long sandy hair. She squinted, thinking she must be hallucinating; that she wanted to see her daughter so much she'd conjured up the image. But no, that *was* Lexi. She was being hurried along by a man that Ava didn't recognise, with a cap pulled down and baggy trousers. Who the hell was that? And what was he doing with her daughter?

'Lexi!' The yell echoed down the street, but Lexi and the man didn't turn. '*Lexi!*' As fast as she could, she raced across the pavement. She had to catch her daughter. She couldn't let her go.

The pair rounded a corner, disappearing from sight. Ava pumped her legs faster, ignoring how tired they were. Where on earth where they going? Who was this guy? Whoever he was, he certainly didn't look like someone she wanted her daughter hanging out with.

'Lexi.' The word came out like an anguished cry when she gasped for air. They ducked into an alleyway and she followed, streaking up the path and getting closer and closer.

'Lex!' Finally, she was near enough to grab her daughter's arm. She spun around, her face pale and eyes wide. She looked absolutely terrified.

'Who the hell are you?' the man said. He was slim and scruffy, yet something about his presence was menacing and evil.

Ava drew herself up despite the fear. 'I'm her mother,' she said. 'I'm her mum, and I'm taking her with me. Come on, Lex.' She tried to pull her daughter towards her, but the man gripped Lexi's arm tighter.

He laughed, a low dark snigger that made a shiver go through her. 'You're not taking her anywhere.' He stepped closer. 'Not until she gives me what she owes me.'

His foul breath made her want to retch, but she held her ground. She'd found her daughter. She wouldn't let her go.

Ava got her phone out to dial 999, but the man knocked it out of her hand before she could start dialling. She gulped as she watched it clatter down the pathway, then glanced around. No one was in sight, and high walls on either side meant they couldn't escape. 'Take the mobile,' she said, gesturing to it. 'And you can take this too.' She started to slide off her wedding ring, thinking this one had never felt right. 'It's worth way more than what my daughter could ever owe you.'

He paused, seeming as if he was wavering for a second. Then he shook his head. 'You have some expensive kit at your house. I want some of that.'

Ava's heart dropped. How did he know that? What had Lexi said? She frantically thought of what she could do now. Children would be arriving any minute at the house. She couldn't bring this man straight into that scene. God knows what would happen. Somehow, she had to stop it.

'Look, take us to a cashpoint,' she said. 'I have my card. I can withdraw whatever you want.'

The man met her eyes and his grip on her relaxed, and she could tell he was thinking about it. In that second, she jerked away from him, knocking him just enough off balance so that he crashed into the stone wall behind them.

'Run!' she shouted to Lexi, her heart pounding as the man looked at her with anger in his eyes.

'You little bitch,' he said in a low voice, rubbing his head with one hand and reaching out to her with the other. There was a sharp blow to her face, and he grabbed her. Before she could think to move away, he pushed her up against the cold stone wall and shook her so hard her teeth knocked together. 'You—' His eyes widened, and he clutched at his leg. 'What the fuck?'

'Come on, Mum!' Lexi appeared from behind her, her eyes

wide, and the two of them raced up the path as the man shouted and cursed after them. Finally, when there was no sign of the man and they'd turned onto their street, they slowed.

'What happened? How did you get him to let go?' Ava asked, hardly able to say the words.

Lexi drew out a small metal object, and Ava blinked. Was that the knife she'd planned to give Alfie on his tenth birthday? 'I used this to stab him in the leg. Not too hard. Enough so he would let go. I'd forgotten I had it in my pocket, but suddenly I remembered it was there.'

Ava met her daughter's eyes, thinking how brave she was – and how ironic it was that something she'd been planning to give to her son had saved them. Had saved them both, in the hands of her daughter. In a way, it was as if Alfie had reached through time and the two of them had worked together. They were a team, like they should have been.

'Mum!' Lexi's eyes were wide with horror. 'You're bleeding!'

Ava touched her lip, swollen from the man's punch. She could feel the crusted blood there from where it had split, and she looked down at her T-shirt where it had splattered. She met her daughter's worried stare. 'Don't worry. It's only my lip.'

'Mum...' Tears filled Lexi's eyes, and Ava took her in her arms.

'We can talk about everything later. We *will* talk about everything later.' She pulled back, then smoothed her daughter's hair. 'And I have to say, I've never been prouder. It's because of you that we're safe.' She blinked, thinking of what her daughter had done. She wasn't only brave; she was *strong*. Ava had been so wrapped up in thinking she had to protect her that she hadn't seen that either.

'Can we go home?' Lexi asked.

Ava drew in a breath. 'Emily's going to be there, getting ready for the party, if it hasn't already started by now. And Dad should be there too.' God, she hoped so, anyway. For the first time in ages, she really wanted to see him. She needed to see him, to tell him that he was right. It was time to talk about their son.

Finally, she was ready.

'OK.' Lexi took her arm, and the two of them went back to where Ava had parked the car, ignoring the curious looks of strangers at her bloody face and shirt. The attack seemed so long ago now. It had only been minutes, but so much had changed. That barrier between them had been lifted.

In almost losing her daughter, Ava had managed to find her again.

THIRTY
EMILY

Emily stood smiling in the middle of the front garden as the party swirled around her. Everything – even the weather – was perfect. The sun streamed from a brilliant blue sky, warm air caressed her, and the garden was a vibrant mix of colour and scent. The tablecloth for the trestle table she'd set up fluttered in the gentle breeze, and planes arched overhead on their way to foreign destinations.

Emily wondered what the passengers were thinking as they stared down at the party in full swing, with excited kids streaking by and mothers clad in floral dresses sipping their drinks. They must be envious, she thought. They must be wishing their lives could be like this; that they could live in such a beautiful part of the world, in such a beautiful house... like she and her classmates had wished that day. For once, she was the one on the inside with others coveting what she had. This was what awaited her if she kept on track.

Hurt twisted her stomach as she thought of her daughter, but she pushed it away. Sophie would be back when she realised what a mistake she had made. Nothing – no one – in Norwich could come close to this. Of course finding new family members was exciting, but Sophie would soon see it wasn't as good as she'd thought. She belonged here, in this place, with her mother. Emily tipped her head up, closing her eyes to feel the warmth of the sun on her face.

The sound of a car made her eyes fly open. More guests! But her heart dropped when she realised it wasn't a guest. A taxi was pulling in next door, and Mrs Bhandari got out of the backseat. *Shit.* Dan was in the basement, and she'd yet to give him the pills. By the time she'd got back from her flat, guests had already been streaming down the road, and she'd had only enough time to let herself in and grab the drinks from the fridge. If Mrs Bhandari went inside and discovered him in the basement... she closed her eyes again. She didn't want to think of that scenario. She'd slip away now that the party was in full swing and give him the meds to make sure he kept quiet. The old woman was half-deaf anyway and she wouldn't need to go into the basement, but Emily couldn't take any risks. She'd think about the next steps when the party was over.

She grabbed the bottle of pills from her pocket and was about to go next door when another car pulled into the drive. She squinted, making out the faces inside. Was that Ava? And Lexi, beside her? So she'd found her, then, Emily thought. She had her daughter back. She stared at the two of them embracing in the car, her stomach churning. She'd get her daughter back, too, she reminded herself.

Ava and Lexi were climbing out of the car now, and Emily's eyes widened. What the hell had happened? Ava's face was swollen, dried blood caked across the side of it, and her white T-shirt was covered with blood. Instead of trailing behind as usual, Lexi was walking beside her, her spine straight and her gaze intense as she approached. She went inside the house, and...

Her heart dropped as she noticed Mrs Bhandari approaching Ava, then Ava's surprise at whatever Mrs Bhandari was telling her. What exactly was she saying? The old woman had always been chatty, often too much for her own good. Emily tilted her head, remembering when Ava had first introduced her to the Bhandaris. They were so friendly and welcoming, but all she could see was a huge empty house for a couple who didn't need it. How was it fair that they had all this space when they could barely get up the stairs, while she was crammed into a tiny flat with a squalling baby? She'd pasted on a smile, though, and pretended to be grateful for the crumbs of advice they handed out.

She forced herself back to the present, focusing on the tasks ahead. Whatever Mrs Bhandari and Ava were talking about, she didn't have time to speculate now. She had to get inside the Bhandaris' and deal with Dan. Then she could cope with everything else.

She grabbed the key from her handbag and eased out the side door, cutting across the narrow grassy patch that separated the Bhandaris' house from Ava's. Then she unlocked the side door and pounded down the basement stairs, determination hammering inside of her. She'd make sure he stayed quiet. She'd promised her daughter as much. She couldn't let him destroy everything.

But... She scanned the floor where he'd been sleeping, her mouth dropping open. The space was empty, with no sign of him. Panic swept over her. What the hell? Where was he? Frantically, she scanned the space again as if she could have somehow missed a six-foot-tall man. He had to be here! Heart beating so hard she could feel her body vibrate, she combed every inch once more before slumping onto the floor in defeat.

He wasn't here. That much was for sure. But how could he have got out? There was no way to unlock the basement door from the inside. Mrs Bhandari obviously hadn't discovered him, or all hell would have broken loose.

Emily shook her head so hard it hurt. It didn't matter how he'd escaped. What mattered was that he could ruin everything.

She scrambled to her feet, fear propelling her forward. She had to find him. She had to stop him. But how?

She froze, thoughts tumbling through her head. He'd probably gone straight to the police. By now, he would have told them what she'd done. She closed her eyes, picturing Ava's surprise and hurt when she found out what had happened. The shock and betrayal would reverberate forever between them. All Emily had been hoping for – all she'd been waiting for, for so long – would never happen. Ava never would give her the warmth and belonging she desperately longed for; the sense that she mattered. Hell, *no one* would give that to her once the police caught up with her.

Rage swept through her, bubbling to the surface and exploding with such force that she couldn't hold it in. The scream reverberated around the closed space.

She reached out to the wall, trying to get a grip on the volcano erupting inside.

What was she going to do now?

THIRTY-ONE
AVA

Ava's eyes popped as she pulled into her driveway. In such a short time, Emily had worked a real miracle. The front garden was swarming with kids gathered in little groups chatting, laughing and dancing to Taylor Swift coming from the outdoor sound system Dan had installed at exorbitant expense. A trestle table had been set up along the side of one of her prized flower beds, heaving with drinks and goodies, and the laughter of mums swilling Prosecco drifted over. It was like an alternate universe, where the past few hours had never happened.

She and Lexi got out of the car, and Lexi ducked inside to have a shower and clean up before coming back down. Surprisingly, she seemed excited about the party now, despite the earlier fight with Sophie – and all that had happened since. Ava bit her lip as she thought of the girl. Why had she texted Lexi? And what had she been about to tell Ava, back in Emily's flat? She'd known Lexi was selling things. Had it been about that? A tap on her shoulder made her jump, and she turned to see Mrs Bhandari.

'Goodness!' the older woman said. 'What happened to you? Are you OK?'

Ava nodded. 'I'm fine.' She touched her face. 'It looks worse than it is. How are *you*?'

Mrs Bhandari sighed. 'I'm all right. As well as I can be.' She drew herself up. 'And I'll be coming home again soon. I just came to check on things and make sure my cat is all right. It was nice being at my daughter's, but it's not my home, my space. And my son-in-law is going to fit an alarm, so I don't need to worry. Oh, that reminds me. Would you happen to have the key on you?' she asked. 'The key my daughter gave you for taking care of the cat? I'd like to give it to her so that she has the spare.'

'Oh!' Ava jerked. 'Yes, of course.' She took the fob from her pocket, then glanced up at Mrs Bhandari again. 'I'm sorry; I'd forgotten I'd given it to Emily. Long story, but she was looking after the cat for us.'

'Oh, she didn't need a key. She has one, anyway. She must have forgotten.'

Ava drew back. Had she heard correctly? 'Emily has a key?'

Mrs Bhandari nodded. 'We stayed close even after she stopped coming to see you.'

Ava blinked. They had?

'She's been helping me a lot,' Mrs Bhandari was saying. 'I don't remember things like I used to, and she helps me make sure I pay all the bills and keep the accounts in order. I have my daughter, you see, but she's always very busy with her children.'

Ava nodded, trying to make sense of it all. It sounded so nice, so caring, and yet... Why hadn't Emily ever told her? Why keep it a secret?

'And she was such a comfort that night, when Mr Bhandari had his heart attack. The night of the burglary.' Mrs Bhandari's eyes filled with tears. Ava reached out to touch her arm, trying to understand. Emily had been there? She'd known about the heart attack? She'd sounded so surprised when Ava had told her the news. Why would she pretend?

'Not that they got anything of value,' Mrs Bhandari continued. 'The only thing they took was my husband's watch and some cash. He always talked about how much it was worth, but only to him. I bought it for next to nothing in a market. We didn't have much money back then.'

Ava drew in a breath at the mention of a stolen watch, thinking back to the watches she'd seen in the safe at Emily's. Could Mr Bhandari's watch be there too? Could *Emily* have been the one who'd taken it – who'd taken all those watches? Was that why she'd kept quiet about being there that night; about being close to them all of this time?

She looked up from where she was chatting to Mrs Bhandari and her gaze was drawn towards Emily, standing in the middle of the front garden. Her face was like thunder, and Ava blinked. Why did she look so angry? But as if a switch had been flipped, Emily quickly rearranged her face into a smile before darting inside.

'Let me find her now,' Ava said.

'Don't worry,' Mrs Bhandari responded. 'My daughter will come by when she's finished work to get the key. I don't want to keep the taxi waiting.'

Ava nodded. She waved goodbye to Mrs Bhandari, then headed towards the house. There had to be a logical explanation for this, although Ava couldn't think what. Once inside, Ava peered at the throng. Had Dan come?

'Emily? Dan?' She glanced around the packed room, but there was no sign of either of them. Then through the window she saw Emily using her key to open the Bhandaris' side door, and her brow furrowed. What on earth? Why was she going in there now? This whole thing was getting stranger and stranger, and her suspicion that Emily had somehow been involved in what happened the night of the burglary was growing.

She hurried from the house and followed Emily through the side door into the Bhandaris'. Inside the house it was dark and the air smelled musty and stale, although it had only been a few days since Mrs Bhandari had left. She paused in the gloom for a minute, wondering where Emily had gone.

'Oh!' The cat streaked out from behind the sofa, cutting in front of her as he ran down the corridor, and Ava rolled her eyes. That cat again! God, she really was tense. No wonder, after what had happened earlier today. Thank goodness she'd found Lexi. A shudder went through her at the thought of what could have happened.

She was about to head into the lounge to see if Emily was there when she heard a scream coming from the basement.

Without thinking, she rushed towards it.

THIRTY-TWO
LEXI

I watch from my room upstairs as Mum talks to Mrs Bhandari, then disappears from view. I'm so happy Mrs Bhandari is here, because I need to tell her how sorry I am. I need to say that it was my fault, that I brought the burglar to the door. I need to be strong now and tell her that I know who might have done it, words I should have said before. I never should have erased that doorbell footage.

I throw on my jeans and a T-shirt. I'm about to make my way downstairs when I hear a scream coming from next door. Fear jolts through me. Did the man come back? Is he here now? Who's screaming?

I need to see what's happening. I can't let him hurt anyone else. I charge down the stairs, my heart pumping fast. I almost trip because I'm going so quickly, but I grab the railing and steady myself. I fly out the side door and into the Bhandaris', skidding to a halt in the corridor. The basement door is wide open, and Mum and Emily are inside, talking on the basement stairs.

'Mum?' I edge down the steps. Something strange is crackling in the air around me, and my senses tell me to move carefully. 'Are you OK?'

'I'm fine.' Mum smiles, but I can see she's doing it to calm me down. 'I came to check on Emily. I heard her scream.'

I nod. 'I heard it too. That's why I'm here.'

'Why don't we go back to the party?' Emily says, a smile nailed on her face, but her eyes hard. She takes my mum's arm, and there's something about her grip that screams danger to me.

'Wait,' Mum says. 'There's something I want to ask you, away from everyone else.'

Emily meets her eyes. 'What?'

'Have you been stealing from the Bhandaris?' she asks slowly, and my mouth drops open. *What?*

'I know you stayed close with them. And I know you were there that night,' Mum continues. 'Mrs Bhandari told me, and she said his watch is missing. And you...' She swallows. 'You have all those watches in the safe. Did you take his too?'

Emily shakes her head. 'Don't be ridiculous.'

But Mum won't back down, and I'm so, so proud of her. 'Prove it, then,' she says. 'Let's go back to your flat. Let's look in that box, and—'

And then, before I can think to move, Emily flies past us up the basement stairs, slamming the door behind her. For a second, Mum and I stare at each other in the dim light as if we can't believe she's really done that. Mum tries the door, pushing and shoving at it. I join her, throwing my weight against it, but it stays tightly fastened.

'What are we going to do?' I ask, sinking onto a cold step. God, it absolutely reeks down here. It hits me that I've smelled this before – back at home, that day I went through the box and found Alfie's stuff. That room was like this, too, but with a big brown patch that smelled like... I wince at the memory. It smelled like blood. Fear darts through me, and I meet Mum's eyes. 'I'm scared.'

'It will be fine.' She eases down beside me and takes my hand. 'I can't quite work out what's going on. But we will. Together, we will. Let's sit tight for now.' She pauses, then tilts her head. 'So you went through Alfie's things? Did Dad tell you where to look?' Her voice is light, but her gaze is intense.

'Dad?' I shake my head, thinking it's time now for me to be open with her too. 'No, he had nothing to do with it. He's never mentioned Alfie.' Hurt zings through me again that he kept this from me, and I pause, trying to gather up the words. 'I saw the folder on Dad's laptop, the night after burglary.' I can feel my face getting hot at the lies I've told, but I want to make it right now. 'I went to erase the footage from the doorbell camera. I was afraid it might show me putting out packages, and I saw his name. When I asked you, I could see he was someone important. And I wanted to know who.'

Mum nods slowly. 'OK,' she says finally. 'OK.'

I twist my hands in my lap. I don't want to hurt her, but if I do want this family to be a team – to actually be together, and for each of us to be solid – I need to be honest. 'You never talked about him. About Alfie.' His name comes out loud and strong, and despite all the emotions inside, I'm proud of myself. He existed. He deserves to have his name said and not hidden away. 'And...' I pause. 'You give me all this stuff, and it's like you're trying to make up for something. For not having him. For only having me.' A tear slides down my cheeks, and I can see tears gathering in her eyes too. 'Like I'll never be able to make you happy.'

'Oh, honey.' She puts a hand on my arm. 'I'm so sorry.'

'And I wanted to know why. Why didn't you talk about him? What happened? So I went to the storage room, where all the boxes were. I thought there might be something there.'

Mum sighs, and although I was worried she might be angry, she doesn't seem angry at all. 'I should have told you,' she says. 'I should have talked about him... about Alfie.' She smiles, but tears streak down her face. 'But I wasn't only trying to protect you. I was trying to protect myself too.' She sighs and wipes away a tear, leaving a smear of blood. 'You see...' Her face twists. 'Alfie shouldn't have died. It never should have happened.'

I shake my head. What is she talking about? It's not like you can control SIDS.

'And I couldn't cope with it,' she says, her eyes faraway now as if she's seeing into the past. 'So I had to shut it all away. From you, from Dad, from *myself*.' She reaches out and pushes back a lock of hair from my face. 'I'm so, so sorry if that made you think you were never enough. I suppose it was my way of making up for all the guilt I felt. I didn't do right by your brother. I wanted to do right by you. To stop you from feeling you were missing something. To give you everything I couldn't give him.'

'Oh, Mum.' I throw myself into her arms, and she tightens them around me. Then I draw back. 'I know you love me. But...' I breathe in. 'I don't need you to protect me, or to give me all that stuff. It makes me feel like you don't think I'm strong enough. And I want to know about Alfie. He is a part of me, and a part of our family.'

Mum nods. 'I've seen how strong you are, how brave. I've never been prouder.' She smiles. 'And I can't wait to tell you about your brother. When we're out of here, we'll sit down and go through all of his things. Deal?'

'Deal.' I answer quickly, almost afraid she'll change her mind. 'But I want Dad to be with us. I want us to do this together.'

Mum shifts towards me, and for a second, I'm afraid she's going to say no – that our family will stay on separate sides, like we have been for so long. Then she reaches out to touch my arm. 'Of course,' she says in a gentle voice. 'I want that too.' She holds my gaze. 'You know, your dad did want to tell you about Alfie. He thought you should know. He didn't want to hide it away from you, but I asked him to keep quiet. I couldn't bear the pain, but it wasn't right for me to make him push his own pain down inside. He deserves to let that out too.' She pauses, wiping a tear that streaks down her cheek, and it hits me that although I knew she was sad, this is the first time I've actually seen her cry. Even though it makes my gut twist, I also feel like an enormous weight has been lifted. Seeing her true emotions instead of the fake shield she held up for so long makes me think we *can* be a family. A real one.

'That would be great.' I try to smile and enjoy this moment, but there's a knot of worry inside when I think of my father. 'Where is Dad? I tried to call him so many times, but he never answered. Then I left my phone on the bench, so I couldn't see if he responded, anyway. I did think it was strange, though, because he always answers my calls.'

Mum bites her lip. 'I'm not really sure,' she says. 'I haven't heard from him either. Not since Wednesday. I left him lots of voicemails and texts, but nothing.' She pauses, and fear goes through me. Is he OK? 'Actually, I remember seeing his tie yesterday morning and thinking he was home.'

'So, where do you think he is? Do you think he *could* have come home?'

Mum holds my gaze. Silence falls, and I can hear the party outside. It feels so strange that I'm stuck in here while everyone else is laughing and dancing at my house. While *Emily* is there, in control of everything.

I remember the weird feeling that morning when I went over to see Dad's laptop too. The sounds in the basement, and how Emily looked when she came up the stairs from the basement: definitely not happy to see me, and maybe a little afraid?

'The storage room,' I say slowly. 'When I went inside, it smelled the same as this. Like sweat and wee. I'm pretty sure there was blood there too. I thought it might be something from a box that leaked out, but...' I meet her eyes, and my heart starts beating fast. Could that be from *Dad*? 'Do you think he came home and Emily hurt him? And put him down there?' The questions fly out of me. It's crazy to think, but...

'I don't know.' Mum's shaking her head, looking as confused and worried as me. 'I'm not sure what to think about her right now. I don't know why she would, though. They barely know each other.' Mum's face is pale, and I can see the wheels turning inside her mind. 'She knew where the key to the storage room was, but how would she get him down there? I'm sure he wouldn't go easily, and then to move him over here? Not to mention he's so much bigger than her, and...' Her face twists, and she squeezes my hand. 'Wherever he is, I'm sure he's all right.' I can see the fear in her eyes, though, and I grip her hand even harder. As worried as I am, it feels like, for the first time, we're in this together. That we're a team, instead of her trying to keep me in the dark about everything. And vice versa.

But even as I nod and smile, I can't help wondering: if Dad *was* here, then where is he now?

THIRTY-THREE
EMILY

Emily hurried up the stairs of the Bhandaris' basement and out the side door. Her heart was pounding and her head was swirling, and even though she had no time to waste, she didn't know which direction to move in. Where could she go? What could she do? She had to do *something*, but... She looked up at Ava's house, the hulk of it looming over her. How had it all come apart like this? The sounds of the party she'd organised drifted through the air, and her gut twisted. She'd been on the cusp of all she'd wanted. Now, she was about to have nothing.

She shook her head, reminding herself that wasn't true. She may not have the world she'd been working on here, and she may not have Ava. She wasn't alone, though, because at least she still had her daughter. Sure, Sophie was about to leave, but Emily would go after her now, before the police came. They could make a fresh start somewhere they wouldn't be found. Emily was used to flying under the radar. Without the job promotion – without any job at first – she could be around more, like Sophie wanted. This time, they could work together to build a new life people would envy. At least she still had that safe full of jewellery and watches to get them started.

One watch, in particular, that should bring in a very tidy sum – if it didn't give the whole game away. Damn Ava for talking to Mrs Bhandari and asking all those questions! She'd have to make sure to sell it far from here, where no connection could ever be made. If only she'd heard Mr Bhandari coming down the stairs that night, then all of this could have been so different. If only she'd been more careful. She could have kept taking things from them for years to come. They'd been such a goldmine.

She'd never forget the day she'd been nosing around the Bhandaris' kitchen one morning early on, fetching some sugar for the tea Mrs Bhandari had served her and Ava. Ava had been massive by then and Mrs Bhandari moved at the speed of a snail, so she'd got up to get the sugar. There'd been an open bank statement sitting on the kitchen table anchored down by Mr Bhandari's glasses, so of course Emily hadn't been able to help sneaking a peek.

What she'd seen had floored her. Floored her and motivated her to stay in their lives – to make herself an indispensable part of their lives – and see how much she could get out of them. She knew they had a daughter they doted on and that she would never be able to get herself into their will, but in the meantime, she would take what she could. So she made a point of dropping by to help out with chores, run errands, go grocery shopping, pay bills. They were old-school, of course, paying everything in cash, and it hadn't been too hard to siphon off bits here and there. As they got older, they relied on her – and trusted her – more, and she'd started taking greater amounts.

They weren't using it, she'd told herself to quell the tinges of guilt she'd felt when Mrs Bhandari would hug her and say she was an angel in disguise. They didn't need it, and they couldn't take it with them. She *did* need it, though, and the bits and bobs of jewellery she managed to get from the spa weren't nearly enough to keep her going. The extra money she got from them had been a godsend.

The huge bill for Sophie's private school and for every term in the foreseeable future had made her reckless, though. She'd dropped by that evening after work under the guise of replacement light bulbs for the ones that had burned out in the lounge, but really she'd needed to write another cheque. She knew it was risky forging their signatures in their ancient chequebook. She'd only done it once before to pay the school deposit, but she was desperate. She'd got yet another email requesting payment for Sophie's first term, and she knew if she held off any longer, her daughter might lose her place. She had to pay it now.

She'd let herself in, relieved to see that the couple was upstairs. Maybe she could get in and out without them even knowing she was here, she'd thought as she'd opened the cabinet in the lounge where the cheques were. She'd filled out her name and was finishing up writing Mr Bhandari's signature when she heard his voice behind her.

'What are you doing?'

She'd gasped and swung around, her mind working to think of something to say. But what could she? Mr Bhandari might have terrible hearing, but his eyes were as sharp as ever. And she could see him staring at the filled-in cheque with a furrowed brow.

'You know, if you needed money, you only had to ask,' he said, shaking his head. 'We would have been happy to give it to you.'

She met his eyes, her mouth dropping open in surprise. Truthfully, she'd never thought of asking. No one besides Ava had ever given her anything.

'But to steal from us? From the people who treated you like their own daughter?' His face was so sad and disappointed that, for a second, she almost couldn't stand the guilt. Then she stared at the old man in front of her, hardening herself. They could have offered her money. They had more than enough, and she had nothing. She didn't need to feel guilty. She needed to feel *angry*.

'We would have given it to you. If you really needed it, we would have helped,' Mr Bhandari repeated. He nodded towards the cheque in her hand. 'Give that to me, and then you need to go.'

She shook her head. She couldn't let him have it. He might show the police what she'd done.

He reached out for the cheque, and rage swept through her. Rage at the past and the present; at what she'd been reduced to, only to have the life she deserved. Why should she have to leave? Why should people look at her with such disappointment and dismay? She was only doing what she needed to.

She batted his hand away, but he stepped nearer. She pushed him back from her, loving how his eyes widened as if he was seeing her for the first time – seeing how strong she was and how powerful she could be. A fearful expression crossed his face, and satisfaction flowed into her. He should be scared. He—

She blinked as he clutched at his chest, then crumpled to the floor with a thud. She stared at him lying there, a mix of emotions going through her. She didn't want him to die. Of course she didn't. But... maybe things were starting to go her way, after all. If he was gravely ill, then he wouldn't be able to report her to the police, would he? He might not remember any of this. She glanced at the cheque in her hand. She wouldn't be able to cash that, but at least she wouldn't be in jail. She would still need the money, though.

Quick as a flash, she knelt beside Mr Bhandari and took the watch from his arm. He was always going on about it, and although she didn't recognise the brand, it looked like it was worth a fortune. She was about to leave when she heard Mrs Bhandari coming down the stairs. *Shit*. Pulse racing, she shoved the cheque into her pocket, along with the loose cash that was in the drawer, then threw some of the contents of the cabinet drawers onto the floor to make it look like a burglary. She ducked out the door, holding her breath as she heard Mrs Bhandari scream and call 999. Just as she was about to creep away, the sound of the siren cut through the air, and she froze. The last thing she wanted was to be spotted hurrying away from here with a forged cheque and stolen watch.

She took a deep breath, then spun and opened the door. 'Anyone home? Oh my God!' Feigning surprise, she rushed to where Mrs Bhandari was crouching over her husband, trying to do CPR. The police and ambulance arrived, and it was then that Mrs Bhandari noticed the watch was missing. Police asked if anything else was, and Emily bit her lip as Mrs Bhandari clocked the mess on the floor and the missing cash from the open drawer.

'We must have been burgled,' she'd said, her eyes wide. 'That must have been why my husband had the heart attack. Emily, did you see anyone near the house?'

Emily had shaken her head, her eyes wide. 'No, no one.' She could almost feel the watch and the cash burning a hole in her pocket. 'Is he going to be OK?' God, she hoped not.

'Madam, if you'd like to come with us.' The ambulance driver was bundling Mr Bhandari into the ambulance, and Mrs Bhandari followed.

'Are you family?' the police officer asked. 'Can you stay in the house while we have a look around?'

'I'm a family friend,' she said. 'I don't mind staying for a bit. I have a key to lock up when you're done.'

They'd had a look around, but like she'd known, they hadn't been able to find anything. Eventually, they'd left and she'd hurried home through the dark night, then burned the cheque and put the watch into the safe. Emily shook her head now, recalling Ava's challenge to show her the safe contents and prove she didn't have it. Mr Bhandari might be dead, but somehow it felt like he was haunting her from the grave.

That same rage she'd felt earlier twisted through her, and for a second, she felt a mad urge to burn down the house – to set a fire and watch it spread – like she'd done so long ago at Lexi's birthday party. But that hadn't been to destroy anything, she thought. That had been so that she could put it out and save the day; to get back into Ava's life. Pain swept away the rage, and she sighed, reminding herself that while it was too late to save things here, she still had Sophie. She'd go back to the flat, grab her things as fast as she could, then slip away and try to track down her daughter. She had to move now, before anyone could stop her.

She was about to hurry away when she spotted two figures coming up Ava's drive. She squinted into the bright sun, trying to make them out. Her heart lifted at the sight of her daughter. Sophie! She was here! She hadn't gone, after all. She must have realised she did belong with her mother, not with people she hardly knew. A smile grew on Emily's face as she edged forward. She'd grab her now and they could take off together. Then she saw someone behind her daughter – someone who made her freeze in her tracks.

Dan. Oh God. Dan was here too. And behind him: two police officers.

Emily stared, unable to process what she was seeing; what her daughter's presence with this group meant. Sophie couldn't have been the one to let out Dan, could she? She wouldn't do that. She *wouldn't*. She may not know everything at stake, but she knew enough to understand what could happen if they let Dan go without convincing him to keep quiet. She wouldn't risk the police arresting her mother, no matter how angry or hurt she was. Besides, Emily had promised to take care of it.

But here she was, alongside Dan and the police, and that could only mean one thing. Her daughter hadn't gone to

Norwich. She'd gone to let Dan out of the basement. It had been her. Of course it had. No one else knew where he was, and he couldn't have escaped on his own.

Sophie had come back, but not to be with her.

How could she do this?

A pain unlike anything she'd ever known stabbed into her, so strongly she almost couldn't breathe. She bent over as it seared her insides, everything else fading but for the knowledge that her daughter had betrayed her. She'd tried to give her everything, and not only had Sophie wanted to leave, but she'd wanted to ruin it all. Emily had been so fixated on Dan that she'd never stopped to think the threat could come from her very own daughter.

She dragged herself behind a bush, peering out to see Dan, Sophie and the police cross Ava's front garden. Were they looking for her? What would they do when they couldn't find Ava or Lexi? She thought of how she'd locked them in the basement, and her legs started trembling. She had to get away from here.

As they were about to go inside Ava's, Sophie turned towards the Bhandaris' house, her gaze drawn as if by magic towards where Emily was crouching. Their eyes locked, and Emily gulped. Was her daughter going to turn her in? Would she alert the police? Would Emily leave this place in handcuffs, in front of everyone?

As they stared at each other, Emily could read every emotion in her daughter: sadness, hurt, anger... She jolted at the realisation that this was the first time she could truly see what Sophie was feeling – the first time she'd *tried* to see. She'd never taken the time, just as her own mother had never taken the time with her. She'd been so focused on doing what she wanted – on getting what she wanted – that she hadn't stopped to see it wasn't the best thing for her daughter. Even when Sophie had asked her to stay home, the same way she'd asked her mum not to have any more kids, she hadn't listened. She'd turned away from her daughter. She'd made the same mistake as her mother.

Sophie was right to leave. She was right to be angry with her.

Emily tried to telegraph all she could to her daughter in that one moment; to show her that she finally understood. That she did love her, despite not being the mother she'd deserved. That she was so, so proud of her, and that she knew she'd be OK. That whatever she chose to do now, Emily wouldn't blame her.

Sophie blinked, then dropped her gaze and turned away. Emily felt the energy drain from her as the realisation hit. Her daughter wasn't going to turn her in. Maybe, despite not giving Sophie what she needed, she loved her, after all. Maybe this was the love and acceptance she'd been seeking, right here in front of her the whole time. She'd been so blinded by her own desire to be important that she hadn't realised how important she was to the person she loved most.

Tears filled her eyes. She didn't know how, but her daughter had turned out to be so strong – and a much better person than her. She'd punished her mum for all the emptiness she'd felt, but Sophie had let her go. She did love her, but Emily didn't deserve it. Maybe she *wasn't* worthy. The agony inside as she watched her daughter walk away from her was almost too much to bear, and she slumped onto the ground. A branch snapped beneath her, the sharp snap ricocheting between the houses in the narrow space.

Dan's head swung towards her. She froze, her hands flying up to her mouth. Oh God. He hadn't seen her, had he? Her pulse racing, she tried to move even further behind the bush, but sharp branches blocked her way. Panic and horror rose as she watched Dan and the police get closer and closer. Frantically, she glanced from left to right, but in the gap between the buildings, there was nowhere she could go.

'Emily?' Dan's voice floated through the air, and the noise of the party went quiet. 'Is that you?'

She held her breath, praying they hadn't spotted her. Her heart was pounding so loudly she wondered if they could hear it too. She jerked back, the branches pricking into her. They couldn't find her. They couldn't. They—

Squealing tyres cut into her thoughts, and everyone turned towards a car roaring up to the house.

'Hey!' A male voice rang out, followed by slamming doors. 'Come out here, you little bitch.'

Emily stared as a short thin man with bloody trousers cut across Ava's lawn towards the front. Who the hell was this?

'You think you can stab me like that and get away with it?' He was practically frothing at the mouth, but before he could open the door, Dan and the police were on him, dragging him back. 'Called the cops, did you? Doesn't matter. I'll tell them what you did. I'll...'

Emily didn't pause to hear the rest. His voice faded as she backed out of the bush and ran as quickly as she could down the street, not even looking back to see if anyone had noticed. Faster and faster her legs churned, desperation driving her forward.

Towards what, though, she didn't know.

THIRTY-FOUR
AVA

Ava and Lexi perched on the steps in the gloom of the basement. Lexi leaned against her, and despite the awful circumstance they found themselves in, somehow they felt more solid; more together. Now they only had to find Dan, and they would be a family again.

A family. The thought reverberated through her head, and she realised that ever since Alfie's death, she hadn't been able to think that way. It had been too painful, because 'family' had always included Alfie. She'd tried to hide from that by burying herself in her daughter – by burying her son away in the basement – but instead, she'd almost lost them. Now, finally, she could have them back again. Each of them, here, occupying their own place. And Alfie would always have his place too. She wasn't afraid to remember him now.

She drew in a breath, thinking how ironic it was that now that she was ready to talk about her son – to do what Dan had always wanted – he was nowhere to be seen. She'd been so angry when she'd thought he'd told Lexi about Alfie, but even if he hadn't, he'd been right. Panic rattled through her. Had he returned home early after they'd argued? Why? She thought back to his words about how he couldn't go on like this. Had he been planning to say he was ending their marriage? A fierce desire to wrap her arms around him and hold him close washed over her as all the emotion she had buried beneath the memories of her son came bursting to the surface. She prayed it wasn't too late... that the distance between them *could* be bridged.

She turned to face Lexi, pushing back a bit of her hair. She would wait for Dan to go through the photos and the box of Alfie's things, but she couldn't keep Alfie from her daughter one second longer. She couldn't bring him back, but she could help him come alive in Lexi's mind... in her soul. Lexi *was* strong enough. She'd proved that today in spades. Ava had to be now too.

She blinked, surprised to realise she was smiling as she thought of her son – of his life, and not how he'd died.

'I want to tell you about your brother,' she said quietly, and Lexi's eyes widened. 'I want to tell you about Alfie.' Silence swirled between them, and then... then she started talking. About how happy she was when she was pregnant, the bet with the doctor, the first time she'd held them both in her arms. On and on, images and stories bubbled out of her, like a spring with an infinite source. Little details she hadn't remembered trickled up, as clear as if it had been yesterday, the happiness alongside them shiny and new. It felt like her son was here with her, and with Lexi clutching her arm, that the three of them were together once more for the first time since that night.

It made her long for Dan more than ever, and that same fear she'd felt earlier swept over her. Where on earth was he? She tilted her head, Lexi's theory about Emily hurting him when he came home early running through her mind. Could he have surprised her, and she struck out at him by accident? Was the blood Lexi had seen his? Or was it something more... a secret Emily had been hiding, like her relationship with the Bhandaris? Despite all the time they'd spent together, she realised now there were large parts of Emily's life she'd never known about. She swallowed, trying to quell the rising panic. He had to be OK. *They* had to be OK. They couldn't lose each other now.

She got to her feet, hauling her daughter up with her. 'Come on, Lex. Let's give this door another try. Maybe after another few shoves, it will open.' She didn't want to sit around and wait any longer. They had to get out of here. They had to find Dan.

Lexi nodded, and the two of them started up the stairs. But just as they were about to throw themselves against the door, they heard voices and footsteps. Ava could see the fear on Lexi's face. She'd been terrified that Emily would return and do something to them. But this didn't sound like Emily. This was more than one person. Before they could move, the door swung open.

She stared, at first unable to believe her eyes. Was that Dan? Standing there, looking down at her now? Was he real or was she dreaming? She hesitated for a second, unsure if she could trust what she was seeing.

'Dad!' Lexi streaked up the stairs and threw herself into Dan's arms. Relief and happiness poured into Ava. He was real. He was here, and he was real. Tears came to her eyes as she watched her daughter and husband hug. God, he looked awful, Ava thought, taking in his pale sweaty face and the massive bump on his head. *Had* he been trapped in here? Then all the questions cleared from her mind, and she got to her feet. The next thing she knew, she was in his arms.

'I'm sorry,' she whispered as she drew him close. Sorry for what had happened to their son. Sorry for forcing him to bury his pain. Sorry for pulling away when he needed her most. It was only two words, but it encapsulated so much. It encapsulated her heart, and she hoped with every cell that he understood.

That he didn't push her away now, like she'd done to him for so long.

It felt like forever, but then he tightened his arms around her – so tightly she could feel his heart beating. They stayed like that for a minute as if they were recharging; as the batteries that had been drained of everything except survival were now replenished with the love and light that had been taken away.

'What are you two doing down here?' Dan asked when he finally let her go. 'I was coming to show the police where she'd held me.'

'Emily locked us in,' Lexi said. 'Have you found her?'

Dan shook his head, wincing. 'Not yet. The police are looking. Come on.' He ushered them up the stairs, his movements slow and deliberate like he was afraid he'd topple over. They went back to their house, blinking into the bright sun. The garden was empty of people now, and Ava looked at the detritus of the party. Everything felt so different, and yet it looked the same. But she was different, she thought. She glanced over at Lexi, thinking she seemed different too. Older, somehow. More confident.

'I'm so glad you're all right,' Dan said, as they followed the officer into the cool of the house. 'When we couldn't find you here, I was terrified what might have happened.'

'We?' Ava asked, still trying to take in everything.

'Sophie and me,' Dan said. 'She's the one who got me out of the Bhandaris' basement and took me to the police. She said she was worried what Emily might do to me. Such a brave girl.' He met her eyes. 'I have so much to tell you.' He shook his head. 'I'm sorry I couldn't keep you both safe from all of this. If only I'd known...'

Ava put a hand on his arm. 'It's not your fault,' she said, realising he'd said those exact words to her when she'd told him about Alfie. He'd said it so many times, but she hadn't been able to take it in. She should have kept her son safe. She never should have left him in the cot with Lexi. But even if it was her fault, she couldn't let the pain keep her from remembering him.

He deserved that. They all did. 'I have a lot to tell you too.' She nodded towards the back garden. 'Would you mind crashing out there?' she asked. 'I could really do with the fresh air.' The cool shade and the gentle breeze swirling around her were exactly what she needed, not the conditioned air inside the house.

Dan nodded. 'Of course. Me too.'

They went around the side of the house and into the back garden, settling onto the settee on the terrace under the shade of a huge sun umbrella. Ava looked up at the house. It had shielded her for so long, enabling her to block out everything else but her daughter. She didn't need that anymore, though. Lexi didn't either.

'So, first things first, *are* you OK?' Dan gestured towards the blood on her face; on her shirt. 'Did Emily do that to you?'

Ava shook her head. 'No, no. That's a whole other story. Once Lexi's cleaned up, we'll talk about it together. As a family.' Warmth flooded through her at the thought. 'So... what happened to you? Are *you* all right?'

Dan shifted towards her on the sofa. 'It started on Wednesday, the night I came home. I knew you'd been at Emily's, but Lexi had told me you were going back home that evening. And I...' He sighed. 'I didn't feel good about how we left things. I wanted to talk. When I got here, though, Emily was in your bed.'

Ava winced, imagining the scene.

'And when I saw her that night, something twigged inside my head. I remembered something from so long ago.'

'All right,' Ava said slowly, wondering what he was going to say.

'Remember when you lost your rings?'

'Yes.' What did this have to do with anything?

'Well, you didn't lose them,' Dan continued. 'They were stolen. Stolen by Emily.'

What? 'I don't understand,' Ava said. 'We didn't know her then. Why would she take my rings?'

'You remember I told you about that woman from Norwich who showed up here, thinking I was someone else? The man who stole my credit card?'

The memory was hazy, but Ava nodded.

'Well, your rings went missing after that, right? We thought she might have taken them, but we couldn't be sure.' He shook his head. 'I always thought Emily looked kind of familiar, but I figured it was because I'd seen her at the hotel, like you said.' He let out air. 'But that wasn't it. It was because I'd seen her that day, here at our house. Before you met her at the antenatal clinic.'

'And you only recognised her a few days ago?' Ava asked. She shifted on the sofa, shielding her eyes from the sun.

'It wasn't until the other night, seeing her without her make-up, that I knew it was her.' He paused. 'She begged me not to tell you, but of course I had to. I went to grab my mobile. She snatched it away and wouldn't give it back, so I went to go downstairs and activate the alarm. But I tripped over a suitcase she rolled in my way, and I fell down the stairs. She and Sophie took me down to the basement somehow. I can't really remember much from that night. I was barely conscious.'

'Oh my God.' Ava covered her mouth. She'd known Emily was desperate to be in her life, but she'd never have believed she'd go to such lengths.

'And then I reckon Emily must have been putting something in the water she was giving me, because it pretty much knocked me out. Somewhere along the way, you came home, and I guess she decided to move me to the Bhandaris'. I don't know how she had the key.'

'Wow.' Ava let out a breath, anger mingling with disbelief. How could Emily do all of this? She'd invited Emily into their home, and while she may not have wanted to be friends any longer, she'd been nothing but accommodating. And yet Emily had trapped and drugged Dan, then shut her and Lexi in the basement. Who *was* this person? How could Ava not have seen that side of her?

'I didn't know what would happen to me,' Dan said. 'How long she'd keep me down there for.' His face twisted. 'When I was there – when I was actually able to think – I realised that I haven't been a good husband. Maybe not even a good father.' He looked down, and she could see how hard it was for him to say those words. But he didn't need to. She was the one who'd damaged their relationship.

'I'm sorry,' she said once more. 'I never should have asked you to keep quiet about Alfie. I—'

'I shouldn't have agreed.' Dan cut her off. 'I didn't have to agree. Or I should have talked to you about what I was feeling, but I didn't try. It was easier to pull away. Easier until I couldn't keep doing it, anyway.' He took her hands. 'We've been through something terrible, the worst thing that can ever happen to parents. But it doesn't have to destroy us. I don't want it to. I want to celebrate what we still have... to live and do things together, not hunker down at home like we're in some kind of prison. For Alfie. And for us.'

'Me too.' Tears filled her eyes, and she squeezed his hands. 'I've already started talking to Lexi about Alfie. And I want us all to sit down and go through his things together. I do want to keep him alive for her, like you said we would all those years ago.' She wiped her cheeks, surprised they were wet. 'I never stopped loving you. I just... I couldn't let myself reach to it. All I could think about was making up for what happened by focusing on Lexi. It was the only way I could deal with the pain, but it wasn't right.' She let out a breath. 'And I want to make things right now. For us, like you said.'

Silence fell between them, but it wasn't the cold distance of the past few years. Instead, it was rapidly filling with happiness, expanding every second. Happiness – and hope.

Dan drew away, and she looked up in surprise. 'I have something for you.'

She covered her mouth as he slid out her rings – the rings she'd thought had been gone forever. 'Where on earth did you get those from?' She couldn't imagine Emily parting with them.

'Sophie gave them to me,' Dan said. 'She didn't know they were yours, of course. But she'd taken them from Emily's stash, along with some other things. She'd sold them to a pawn shop, but she felt guilty, so she managed to get them back. She told me she didn't want to be like her mum, and she gave them to me to give to the police. I couldn't believe my eyes when I saw them.'

Ava shook her head. She couldn't believe how this had all turned out. She looked up at the house again, thinking how she'd built a life and worked so hard to keep her loved ones safe, but no one had been happy.

The guilt of that night would always be within her, but she wasn't going to stay trapped inside it. She was going to step out of it, along with her family – including Alfie. She slid the ring onto her finger and met Dan's eyes, an emotion growing between them that she hadn't had in ages: love. It would take time and effort to overcome the distance between them, but she wasn't afraid to feel any longer.

For the first time since her son had died, she wasn't afraid to live.

THIRTY-FIVE
LEXI

I sit in the warm patch of sun in the back garden, watching my parents talk. It hits me that I've rarely seen them sit down and chat – they've just orbited around each other, barely stopping to see the other. But people need to talk. *I* need to talk, and I haven't been doing that either. Sure, I've spoken with Dad when he's been at home, but mostly I'd be up in my room watching YouTube as if strangers yammering at me through my tablet could make up for the silence and emptiness I felt inside.

But it's different now. I don't need to run off to escape what I don't understand, and I don't need to put walls between us. For the first time, I want to be with my family. I get up and plunk down beside Mum and Dad.

'Will Sophie be OK?' I ask, biting my lip. I can't imagine what she's been through these past few days, and what might lie ahead for her. Whatever happened between us, I can't be angry with her anymore. Without her, Dad might still be locked in the Bhandaris' basement – or worse.

'Yes, she will,' Dad says. 'She's going to go live with her grandparents in Norwich.' He shakes his head. 'She's a very brave girl to come and let me out like that... and to tell the police what her mother did. I was so surprised when she unlocked the door and took me to the police. She said that she didn't want her mum to go to jail, but that she was worried that Emily might have really hurt me. The police will want to talk to me again at some point.' He looks at me. 'And maybe you and your mum, too, if Emily told you anything.'

I nod, thinking of Mum asking her about Mr Bhandari and the stolen watches. Then I gasp. Maybe it wasn't Sophie who'd taken my money. Maybe it was Emily.

'Let's go inside,' Dad says. 'I need a shower. And then... well, I might need to sleep for a day or two to recover!'

We all get to our feet and go inside the coolness of the house. The sink is full of dishes from the party and the bin is overflowing, but for once, Mum doesn't manically try to restore order. Instead, she sits down on the sofa, puts up her feet, and closes her eyes. I stare, thinking I've never seen her so *calm*.

While she's resting, I edge down the stairs to the basement. I don't need to hide anymore, I know, but it still feels weird to be down here. I open the storage room, trying not to look at the dark patch of dried blood on the ground. Now that I know for sure what it is – and where it came from – it's more horrifying, and I want to hold Dad close and make sure I never forget how lucky I am to have him.

I pause as it strikes me that this must be how Mum feels about me. That she wants to keep me close. That she can't bear losing me. Understanding why she held me so tightly – that it wasn't about a lack of trust, belief or even *love* for me – makes me feel stronger.

Slowly, I take down the box with all of Alfie's things and draw out the photo of him and me, all wrapped up in the usual blue and pink colour scheme and nestled together in a circle of blankets that look like a nest. I stare at his little scrunched-up red face, wondering what he'd be like right now. Would we get along, finishing each other's sentences, like you always read about in books? Or would we bicker and fight, like my classmates do with their siblings? Would he resemble me, with sandy brown hair and blue eyes, or would he be completely different? A pang goes through me that I'll never find out, but at least I know about him now. At least I know he existed, and who he was, although he never had a chance to grow up. He's a part of this family, wherever we go. He's a part of me, and with Mum's help, he'll come alive.

I take the picture from the box and leave the dark basement, heading up into the light. Mum opens her eyes and looks over at me. 'Everything all right?' she asks.

I sit down beside her. 'Mum...' I touch her arm. 'I don't want you to think that it's your fault. Whatever happened, it can't be. I know you love me. I know you love *us*.' I angle the picture towards her. 'Is it OK if we keep this up here?'

She stares at the photo, and my heart pangs as tears come to her eyes. I don't want to upset her, but I know she feels the same. 'Of course it's OK.' She takes the photo and puts in in front of us on the coffee table, and I lay my head on her shoulder as we both sit there, gazing at it.

And even though Alfie's gone, somehow it feels as if he's right here too.

With us, like he should be.

THIRTY-SIX
EMILY

Emily sat on a bench by the water and closed her eyes. She took a deep breath of the river-scented air, the smell of wet stone and algae meeting her nostrils. For the first time in years, she had nowhere to go; nowhere to be. No job, no child, no place to call home... nothing.

For so long, she'd desired. She'd schemed. She'd done all she could to get the life she'd dreamed of, away from the cramped three-bed semi and the emptiness inside. All she'd wanted was to feel worthy, the equal of that beautiful woman she'd seen from the school bus so long ago. That need had overtaken her like a virus, replicating until any hint of the original girl had been almost wiped out.

Then she'd met Ava, and she'd realised again what it was to be seen and to feel important. The virus had slowed, and she'd basked in the warm glow of recognition. She'd clutched onto that for all she was worth, and when Ava pulled away, instead of turning towards Sophie – the one person who would love her unconditionally – that virus had burned brighter, desperately trying to banish the darkness by reaching towards both Ava and more money, more status. She'd done awful things to try to grasp onto them. The hotel guests she'd stolen from, Mr Bhandari, Dan and Ava, Sophie, and…

She screwed her eyes shut, Alfie's face flashing into her mind. She'd pushed the memory aside for so long, telling herself she'd had nothing to do with his death. He'd died of SIDS, like the coroner had ruled. She'd been so relieved when Ava had told her.

But Emily knew that wasn't true. She knew she'd hurt him. She hadn't meant to, of course, but the outcome had been the same whether she'd meant to or not. It was funny how what she'd done to keep Ava close had been the thing that had driven her away.

She got to her feet and walked along the river, the memory of the night so long ago rolling into her mind like a wave. She'd given birth to Sophie a few weeks earlier, all alone in the hospital. Ava had said she would be with her if she could, but that night she'd been suffering with mastitis and hadn't been able to get out of bed. She'd felt so alone as she'd lain in the hot stuffy ward for hours, waiting for her baby to finally be born.

It would all be worth it, she'd told herself, gritting her teeth through the endless contractions and swearing under her breath at the midwife who'd ignored her pleas for an epidural until it was too late to have one. She wouldn't just be Emily any longer. She'd be a mother. She'd have immediate recognition and an automatic entry into the parenthood club, plus a bigger bond with Ava. She couldn't wait.

Her idyllic notions hadn't exactly panned out, though. No one seemed to treat her any differently now that she had a baby in tow, except to give her foul looks if Sophie started crying. Her flat seemed smaller than ever, and she hadn't a clue what to do with a baby. She was more broke and more bored than ever before.

Except when she was with Ava. With Ava, she didn't mind if Sophie started crying or if she needed her nappy changed for the millionth time. They were together, going through this journey. At Ava's house, by her side, being a mother was almost manageable. Living the life she had was almost manageable. She started coming over late at night, with Sophie sleeping soundly in her buggy, to chat and relax with a cuppa.

And then she'd ruined everything. It had been an awful day, with Sophie on a rare crying streak and Emily wondering if this was some kind of curse – some kind of payback – for what she'd done when she was young. Her head had been ringing with her baby's cries, and the mum next door with five kids of her own had pounded on the wall and told her to 'shut that baby up'.

Emily had shoved Sophie in the buggy and slammed out of the flat, not sure where she was going. She'd hurried through the night, the voices of the couple next door having a domestic following her as she crossed the dark car park and walked down the street, the low brick semis giving way to the larger, tidy houses.

Her feet followed a path to Ava's as if they knew they belonged there. Finally, she was standing in front of Ava's house. No lights were on except a soft glow from the nursery, and everything was quiet on the street but for the sound of the television coming from the Bhandaris'. It was so loud that Emily could practically make out every word. She glanced down at her baby, worried she'd be awoken. Thankfully, Sophie was sleeping soundly now.

She stood outside the house on the pavement, an intense longing sweeping over her. It was late and Dan was probably asleep, but the nursery light was on. Ava might still be awake. She didn't need to stay long. She needed to see her friendly face, and to know she wasn't alone. She stared up at the camera and the door clicked open. Quickly, she slipped inside the house. The silence wrapped around her, and she breathed it in. It was so different to her block of flats, where nothing was quiet.

Praying Ava was still up, she left Sophie sleeping in the

buggy and crept up the stairs to the nursery, easing inside the room. Her heart sank when she noticed Ava wasn't there – she must be asleep in the bedroom, although she'd told Emily she usually stayed in here. The soft glow illuminated the pearly white of the matching cots where the twins were sleeping quietly, their little chests rising and falling under the pink and blue cashmere blankets.

She should go, she told herself. She shouldn't be here – she shouldn't have come inside in the first place without letting Ava know. She'd wanted to trade a smile and some chat with her friend, but if Dan or Ava woke up now to find her inside, they might not understand, and she couldn't risk that.

But as she turned to leave, Alfie started stirring, making noises that were gradually building up to a cry. She knew them well; her heart always sank when she heard those sounds from Sophie. Frantically, she looked around the room as if an escape hatch would open and let her out. Sophie was downstairs, though. She couldn't leave her here. As her mind spun, Alfie started crying in earnest.

Oh *shit*. She crossed the room to the cot. Alfie was lying on his back stretching his little hands open and closed, his face slowly turning red as he built up to wail louder.

'Shut up,' she hissed, panic rising inside. She had to get out of here before Ava come. 'Shut *up*.'

But Alfie stared up at her with those big blue eyes so like Ava's, still moving and squirming, his volume increasing. Emily knew it wouldn't be long until Ava came to settle him. She'd told Emily she could never let the babies cry, not like some books suggested – not like Emily herself would do. Ava had said it was like someone was taking a cheese grater to her insides, and she simply couldn't bear it. Emily had nodded and pretended she'd felt the same, although when Sophie cried, the only thing she felt was annoyed.

'Please be quiet,' she whispered now, staring down at the

baby and trying to adopt that same calm tone Ava used. But the baby gazed up at her and opened his mouth wider as if to spite her, and her panic morphed into anger. He couldn't ruin this for her. She wouldn't let him. She held him close to her to muffle the sound, rocking back and forth like crazy until he was finally quiet and still. Maybe... maybe too quiet and still? He was OK, she told herself. He'd simply gone to sleep – finally. He'd been tired, that was all, and she helped him calm down. His chest was still moving. He was still breathing. Wasn't he?

She quickly put him in the cot with Lexi. Ava often said that helped them sleep better, and it would ensure he stayed quiet until she left. Ava probably wouldn't remember – she said she was so tired these days, she rarely remembered her name – and if she thought she'd put them down separately, she'd hardly suspect someone coming in like this and moving the babies.

Emily had left the room and crept down the stairs, then wheeled Sophie out of the house and back to her own flat. Sophie was still sound asleep. Emily let out a sigh of relief that she hadn't been discovered, then crawled exhausted into bed.

It hadn't been until noon the next day that she'd heard the terrible news about Alfie. It had been awful, but Emily had told herself once more that he'd been fine when she'd left him – sleeping soundly, ready at last to relax. Sudden infant death was the killer everyone feared, not her. She'd had nothing to do with it.

Or so she'd told herself, though she knew deep down that wasn't the case. She'd done the worst thing possible to the person she'd cared about most: she'd taken away her child. Even if she hadn't meant to, it was unfathomable.

How could she have done that? She tried to make sense of it, but the virus that had driven her forward had died, without hope or ambition to feed on, and all she could feel was that emptiness inside. People passed by, not looking at her. Was she even still here?

She gripped onto the bench, trying to anchor herself. There was nothing left to latch onto: not her mother, not money, not Ava or Sophie. She couldn't rely on anything or anyone now to make her feel worthy. All she had was herself, and there was no more she could do. No more that could make this right. No more that could make *her* right.

Was there?

An idea crept into her head, and she bit her lip. Perhaps there was something she could do. It wouldn't change the past, and it could never make up for it. But by lifting the burden Ava was carrying, she might be able to finally feel that she'd done something important. That maybe there was something good – something of worth – inside her. Something that did make her solid and real.

Maybe she didn't need anyone else to feel important. Maybe she only needed to believe it herself.

She grabbed her phone and started typing. Then, when the message was sent, she gazed at the water in front of her, its silvery fingers reaching out to her. Soon, the police would find her. Soon, she would have the life she'd deserved for what she'd done.

But for the first time, she felt a flicker of hope.

Maybe everything wasn't lost, after all.

Maybe *she* wasn't lost.

THIRTY-SEVEN
AVA
TWO MONTHS LATER

Ava sat back, pushing her hair away from her face. A few more boxes to pack, and then they would be ready to go. After all that had happened in this house – how she had hunkered down, protecting herself from the pain and guilt she'd locked away so tightly, afraid to face anything that could let it escape – she was ready to step into the world. To be a family, with Dan by her side as an equal partner in marriage and life. Easing the distance between them wasn't always simple, but with every day that passed, they were finding their way towards each other once more.

She looked at the photo on the coffee table of Lexi and Alfie, the one that her daughter had brought up from the basement. She'd kept it there as she'd emptied the house, filling her eyes with his face, allowing herself for the first time to remember not only the grief and the pain, but the love and the wonder he had brought to her. And now that she knew his death hadn't been her fault, there was more room for that love and wonder than ever.

She closed her eyes, her mind flashing back to the moment she'd got the text from Emily. She'd scanned it, her mouth dropping open. At first, it had seemed impossible to believe. Emily had crept in the house that night and suffocated Alfie? *She'd* put him in the cot with Lexi? No. She couldn't have. She might have done awful things, but something like this... it was too much. It was unfathomable. Maybe this was her way of getting back at Ava – of tormenting her for shutting her out of her life.

She'd shown the message to Dan, who'd turned white, then gone to the police. They'd had Emily in custody after finding her by the river the day of the party, and after questioning, she confirmed what she'd told them, explaining in great detail what she'd done that night. She would be locked away for a very long time, the officer said, shaking his head.

Ava had stared, trying to process what she'd heard. She hadn't caused her child's death. It had been Emily. It had been Emily all this time, and she'd never had any idea.

Her stomach had heaved, and she'd rushed to the toilet and thrown up, questions battering her mind. What was Emily doing there that night? *How* could she do such a terrible thing? Ava was sick again and again, shaking with rage as she thought of the years after: how Emily had tried to soothe her, comfort her... how she'd stayed so close, even if they hadn't been friends after Ava had pulled away. How she'd been here in Ava's own home and tried to hurt Ava's husband. And for what? For *what?* A friendship built solely on the fact they'd been pregnant at the same time? A friendship that probably wouldn't have lasted, anyway? What had Emily wanted so much that she'd taken away the life of her son? Even if she hadn't meant to, the cruelty of saying nothing was staggering.

For a while, she'd debated asking Emily first-hand, but knowing the answer would not change what had happened, and Ava didn't want to focus on the darkness of that night. She could blame herself for letting Emily into their lives; for not seeing who she really was. She could relive those details over and over, using anger to get her through the day, but she chose not to. Dan had been right: it wasn't her fault. Her actions hadn't led to Alfie's death, and she'd no way of knowing what Emily had been capable of. She couldn't huddle under a protective cover, suspecting everything and everyone. Not anymore.

'Mum?' Lexi came down the stairs. 'Do you need help with anything?'

Ava smiled, thinking that things between her and her daughter were better than ever. They actually talked, and Lexi had started coming downstairs and hanging out in front of the TV with her at night, instead of holing up in her room. It was a small step, but it meant a lot.

'I'm OK, thanks. I think we have everything.' She took her daughter's hand, and together they gazed at the picture of Lexi and Alfie on the coffee table in front of them.

'He'll always be with us,' she said, squeezing Lexi's hand. 'He's a part of me, and a part of you. Nothing can take that away.'

She took the photo from the table and wrapped it in newspaper, then carefully laid it in the box. But this time, she wasn't packing it away to protect herself from pain. She would open the box in a new home, a new life.

She would be free.

A LETTER FROM LEAH MERCER

Dear reader,

I want to say a huge thank you for choosing to read *What's Mine Is Yours*. If you enjoyed it, and you want to keep up to date with all my latest releases, just sign up at the following link. Your email address will never be shared, and you can unsubscribe at any time.

www.bookouture.com/leah-mercer

I hope you loved *What's Mine Is Yours*. If you did, I would be very grateful if you could write a review. I'd love to hear what you think. It makes such a difference helping new readers to discover one of my books for the first time.

I really enjoy hearing from my readers – you can get in touch on social media or my website.

Thanks,

Leah

www.leahmercer.com

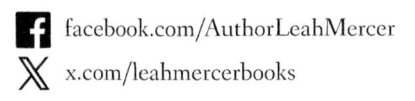

facebook.com/AuthorLeahMercer
x.com/leahmercerbooks

ACKNOWLEDGMENTS

As always, a massive thanks to all the readers and reviewers who continue to pick up my books and support me. A huge thank you to Hannah Todd for her ongoing encouragement along the way. Thanks, too, to Helen Jenner and the talented Bookouture team for all they do to get my book out to the world! And finally, thank you to my husband and my son for listening to me ramble on about fictional characters and plotlines.

PUBLISHING TEAM

Turning a manuscript into a book requires the efforts of many people. The publishing team at Bookouture would like to acknowledge everyone who contributed to this publication.

Audio
Alba Proko
Sinead O'Connor
Melissa Tran

Commercial
Lauren Morrissette
Hannah Richmond
Imogen Allport

Contracts
Peta Nightingale

Cover design
The Brewster Project

Data and analysis
Mark Alder
Mohamed Bussuri

Editorial
Helen Jenner
Ria Clare

Copyeditor
Anne O'Brien

Proofreader
Catherine Lenderi

Marketing
Alex Crow
Melanie Price
Occy Carr
Cíara Rosney
Martyna Młynarska

Operations and distribution
Marina Valles
Stephanie Straub
Joe Morris

Production
Hannah Snetsinger
Mandy Kullar
Ria Clare
Nadia Michael

Publicity
Kim Nash
Noelle Holten
Jess Readett
Sarah Hardy

Printed in Great Britain
by Amazon